TORTURED SKYE

A HAWKE FAMILY NOVEL

BILLIONAIRES OF NEW ORLEANS: THE HAWKE FAMILY
BOOK 2

GWYN MCNAMEE

TORTURED SKYE
by
Gwyn McNamee © 2017

Editing: Barbara Hoover and Kathleen Payne
Cover Design: Michelle Johnson at Blue Sky Designs
Cover Model: Sam Wiles
Photographer: Christopher Correia at CJC Photography
Interior Design: Swish Design and Editing

 Created with Vellum

To anyone who ever struggles to make it through the day...don't let the storms of your past cloud your future.

ACKNOWLEDGMENTS

I have to start with the most important people in my life—my husband and my daughter. Trying to write *Tortured Skye* while caring for an infant would have been impossible without my husband's support and amazing daddy skills.

Once again, I owe a tremendous debt of gratitude to my beta readers—Dawn, Kim P., Jennifer W., Janice, Renee S., Diane E., Audra F., and my super-betas, Star and Christy. You have all helped me more than you could ever know. Writing Gabe and Skye's story wasn't easy, but you ensured it was told properly.

Christy, I'm sorry I made you such a bitch in high school. I could never hope to accurately portray what a badass bitch you truly are. Thank you for listening to me when I have meltdowns and telling me like it is when something sucks balls and needs to be revised. I fucking love you!

Audra, try to keep it in your pants next time. No one likes a slutbag...except me...I love your face! Thanks for all your priceless advice in this series.

Star, I'm sorry your namesake doesn't have the same drinking skills you do. But to be fair, I did name these characters before I even knew you, or the fact you also had a sibling named Sky. So, cut me some slack. I will never forget your epic alcohol tolerance in real life.

I also want to thank Ryan D., my source for all things Army Ranger. He went above and beyond to provide me the information I needed to make sure Gabe was portrayed as accurately as possible.

I love you all!

1

GABE

*W*aking up with a beautiful woman's mouth wrapped around your hard cock shouldn't be a bad thing. In fact, most men dream about just this.

Fuck, what the hell is wrong with me?

Her blonde head bobs up and down on my dick. She swirls her tongue around my piercing, sending a zing of electricity straight to my balls. I grab her hair and jerk her off me with an audible pop. Wide, confused, bloodshot brown eyes meet mine, and she scowls. "What the hell, Gabe?"

She knows my name. That's a positive sign; we must have at least talked last night. I almost wish I could remember hers, but it doesn't matter at this point. Surveilling my room, the pile of empty condom wrappers on the nightstand and the half-empty glasses of whiskey assure me she had a good time.

Excellent. That makes kicking her out a lot easier. At least I know she's leaving satisfied.

I release her hair and extricate myself from under her before sliding out of bed and walking naked to the bathroom. The door slams shut behind me, and I flip the lock. Two seconds later, the knob jiggles, and an angry growl sounds from the other side of the door.

"Seriously, Gabe? You're just going to lock yourself in the bathroom without a word?"

Yeah, actually, that would be fucking awesome.

But I'm too much of a gentleman to do that. I unlock the door and crack it open, keeping my foot behind it so she can't push her way in.

"Look, I'm sorry. I have to be somewhere early this morning. Thanks for last night. You can let yourself out."

Fury turns blondie's pale skin red, and she stomps over to the bed, searching the floor for her clothes—bare ass and tits shaking and bouncing with every movement. My cock throbs, reminding me of the impending blue-balls situation.

Shit.

I close the door and lock it again without an ounce of regret. She knew exactly what this was. No matter how drunk I get, I'm *always* up front with the girls I end up with. They know it's a one-time thing, except with a few regulars I know I can trust not to get attached.

Blondie may have been a miscalculation last night, but I can't even remember where I met her, so it might have been an off night for me too. The evidence of the evening's escapades glare at me from the mirror—scratches down my back, a giant hickey on my collarbone, and faint bite marks around my nipple ring.

Fucking fabulous.

I turn on the shower jets and crank the temperature to scald-my-skin hot. A cold shower would probably be more appropriate for my current predicament, but the need to burn off whatever happened last night is one I can't shake.

A door slams. Thank God she didn't put up any more of a fuss. I really can't handle that today.

This is the only day in almost a month I don't have any work obligations. That should make me happier than a pig in shit, but I have to go to the barbeque today, and I'm not fucking prepared to deal with that right now.

I step into the hot spray, wincing when the water hits the torn skin on my back and then my hard cock when I turn around.

I'm going to have to do something about that. If I don't, today is going to be even more unbearable than it already promises to be. Sometimes, I really miss shooting those shit-heads in the desert; it seemed easier than life here most days.

The water beating down on my chest soothes some of my distress. I drop my head under the spray and take my dick in my hand. I can't even remember the last time I had to mastur-bate. That was the whole point of last night, to get this need out of my system.

Yeah, well, that was a miserable failure.

Sliding my palm up and down my length, I close my eyes and picture blondie and what she must have looked like riding me last night, or bent over with my dick jammed inside her. My cock pulses in my hand, and I increase the pace, needing to get this done.

A flash from last night returns, of the blonde towering above me, bouncing up and down on my cock with her perfectly round, silicone breasts bobbing with every move.

I groan and jerk faster, gliding my palm over the head and against my piercing with every stroke, urging my body to give me the release I need.

Her pussy clenches around my cock, and the orgasm I've been chasing finally starts at the base of my spine.

But then, her blonde hair morphs into jet black, and her brown eyes become a familiar blue.

No! Fuck!

It's too late to stop now.

With two final tugs, I come, shooting my load against the tiles of the shower and down my hand. Each pulsing spurt should be blissfully mind-numbing, but even as my body shakes and my head spins wildly into the ecstasy of release, I know it won't last.

I pant under the scalding water, waiting for the post-orgasmic haze to clear and the inevitable regret and anger to take over. It will come. It always does right after I do.

Godfuckingdamnit!

Why the fuck can't I get Skye Hawke out of my fucking head?

Months of endless nights with brunettes, blondes, and red-heads, and I still only come harder than a freight train with *her* image in my head.

Standing under the water, I've never felt so dirty—not even when I killed people for a living.

That was war. This is my life.

I have to find a way to fix this, to cure myself of the unhealthy obsession. If I don't, it just may be the end of what little sanity I have left.

The thought of ending up back in Doc Cochran's chair makes me shiver despite the heat of the water. I've managed to keep my shit together, mostly, for the last six months without paying her to listen to me spill my guts. I'd like to keep my sanity *and* my money, if at all possible.

It's probably my own fault things have gotten this bad. I didn't tell Doc everything the last time we had a session.

But, how the fuck was I supposed to know I'd still be thinking about *her* seven months later?

I went back to Doc to deal with the fallout from killing Abello's men. For months afterward, I drowned in a gluttonous pool of booze, smokes, and women. I got up to a bottle, a pack, and a half-dozen a day, respectively. The tipping point was the same reason I'm dreading the barbeque today and hating myself for jerking off—Skye.

After what happened with her at the wedding, I realized I needed to do something to get my head on straight. I would never have allowed it to occur if I were in my right mind...at least, that's what I told myself.

But I didn't mention anything about Skye to Doc when I resumed my sessions. It's not like she could have done anything about that anyway. She treats mental health issues, not I-want-to-fuck-my-best-friend's-little-sister issues.

She wasn't surprised to see me back in her chair, and I didn't know if I should be pissed about that or not. I couldn't tell her everything, because that would not only have been a violation of our agreement with Abello and my father; it would also have put her life in danger if they ever came after us again just by virtue of her knowing the truth about what happened. Even without all the details, she withheld judgment when I told her I had killed three people, and she reminded me I am not a cold-blooded killer and never have been.

Every life I took, I did so with honor and without another choice. I remind myself of that every day and try not to let the memories take over my life.

I live every day hoping my symptoms don't return, and that I can keep my shit together.

But with the passage of time, I only fall further down the rabbit hole of my fixation with Skye, and it's taking a toll on my miserable ass.

∼

SKYE

The mid-summer sun seeps into my skin and, combined with my third margarita, it warms me and helps me momentarily forget the clusterfuck my life has become.

Lounging next to the pool in Mom's backyard, my earbuds blaring angsty alt-rock, I begin drifting off into the space between wake and sleep when a shadow falls over me, blocking out the rays and disintegrating any bliss I was so close to achieving.

Fucking thanks.

I reluctantly open my eyes and find my mother looming above me. Her lips are moving, and logic tells me she's speaking to me, but I have zero interest in whatever it is she's trying to say. She should know by now not to interrupt my sunbathing.

Just as I'm about to close my eyes and ignore her, she reaches down and yanks the buds out of my ears.

"Hey, what the fuck?" I prop myself up on one elbow, glaring at her even though I know she can't see through my shades.

She scowls. "Skye, language..." Her eyes flit toward the pool where Angelina is swimming with Ben to ensure her young ears haven't been subjected to my foul mouth.

Like she hasn't heard it a thousand times at home.

"What do you want?"

"I was asking if you knew when Savage and Danika are supposed to get here. You spoke with him earlier, didn't you?"

I sigh, dropping back down and grabbing my half-full third margarita. I take a sip before returning my attention to her. "Yes, I spoke with him. He said she wasn't feeling well. But they're still going to try to be here before noon."

She smiles and nods. "See, was that so hard?"

"Yes."

Her scowl returns, and she eyes my glass. "How many drinks have you had today, Skye?"

"Not enough, apparently." I drain the last drops of the delicious tequila concoction and set my empty on the small table to the side of my chair. Sometimes, I wonder how I would survive this family without alcohol. There's always some sort of drama.

I'm the only sane one left. Although, if you ask them, I'm the worst of them all...well, except maybe Stone.

Mom ignores my comment and plows ahead with her agenda. "What about Gabe? Do you know if he's coming with them?"

Hopefully not.

Leave it to my mother to bring up the one person I don't want to think about, let alone discuss. How she's so oblivious to the tension between us blows my mind. She must be denser than she appears.

"I don't know, I didn't talk to him, and Savage didn't mention him at all."

She lets out an exasperated sigh. "Fine. I'm going to finish getting the burgers ready. Why don't you try switching to water for a while."

"Thanks for the unsolicited advice, *Madre*."

She retreats to the house without glancing back.

I don't mean to be a bitch to her, but she grates on every last nerve I have. The only person who ever seemed to understand the dynamic with her was Star. Since the accident, things have only gone downhill, and the tension between me and the woman who gave me life has quadrupled. I know she means well, but we're like oil and water, never going to mix.

I pop my buds back in, close my eyes, and try to relax again.

Deep, calming breaths, Skye. Enjoy the boozy bliss.

A second loss of rays wakes me, and I shoot up, ready to tear my mother's head off with my bare teeth if I have to. "Jesus, what do you want this time?"

The words are out of my mouth before I have time to register who I'm looking at.

"Shit, I'm sorry." Dani holds her hands up in surrender and eyes me like I'm a rabid dog ready to attack—which isn't far from the truth.

"No, no, no, I'm sorry. I thought you were my mother again." She gives me a sympathetic smile and slowly lowers herself down onto the chaise next to me. Her normally bouncy and happy demeanor is gone, and she's as pale as I've ever seen her. "Damn girl, you look like shit. How are you feeling?"

She sighs, resting her hands on her protruding belly. "Okay. Better than this morning. I swear to God, this morning sickness bullshit was supposed to end when I hit the second trimester. I'm already twenty-six weeks along, and I still feel like shit. I guess I lucked out by not really feeling it until into my third month, but on top of the occasional queasiness, I'm also just exhausted all the time."

Yet another reason I never want to have kids.

"Did your doctor prescribe you Zofran?"

"Yeah, it helps with the nausea, but it knocks me out. I'm so tired when I take it, I'm completely useless."

"How's Savage doing?" I peer over her shoulder at my brother talking with Storm under the back awning. He waves, but his eyes never leave Danika. He watches her like a hawk, ready to swoop in should something happen. I can only imagine what it's like living with him hovering around 24/7.

No fucking thanks. I don't need a babysitter.

She glances over her shoulder and waves before turning back to me. "He is...well, he's Savage. It drives him crazy not being able to control this."

"I don't doubt it." I know my brother, and I understand his need to be master and commander in every situation. Watching his wife suffer must be hell for him.

As if summoned by the mere mention of his name, he appears next to us. "Hello, ladies."

I lean over and give him a half-hug, ruffling his perfectly

combed hair in my usual attempt to push his buttons. "Hey bro, how are you?"

Running his hand back through his hair in an unsuccessful attempt to return it to its rightful place, he smirks at me, fully aware I did it intentionally. "I'm fine. How are you?"

I shrug. "Oh, you know, the usual."

Tired. Annoyed. Not drunk enough to do this today.

He nods and reaches out to take Danika's hand in his. "You feeling okay?"

She nods and smiles at him. "I'm fine, I think I'll go help your mom and Storm in the kitchen."

"Okay." He pulls her hand to his mouth and kisses the back.

Ugh. They are so disgustingly adorable and in love.

I can practically feel the love they have for each other radiating from where they sit a foot away from me. I should be happy for them, especially after everything they've been through. We still don't know all the details of what went down last year. Everyone has been keeping their mouths shut about the shooting of Uncle Dom's men, but we know Dani, Savage, and Gabe were there. No matter how many times Storm, Stone, or I ask Savage, he just won't talk, and Mom doesn't even bother to ask. We all know Dom's involved in some questionable stuff, but he's good to us, and she would rather live in blissful ignorance than have to admit he may not be squeaky clean.

Whatever happened, it was bad. We know that much. Three people died and the media basically swept it under the rug saying it was a police operation against organized crime. But no details were released—all very hush-hush and super sketchy. No explanation whatsoever as to why Gabe, Savage, or Dani would have been there.

The wedding was a new beginning for Savage and Dani, and the beginning of the weirdness between me and Gabe that threatens to make today utterly unbearable.

Danika stands and immediately wobbles, grabbing her

head in one hand and trying to steady herself on Savage's shoulder with the other.

"Dani? You okay? What's wrong?" Savage's voice is laced with panic. I jump up and wrap my arm around her to help her balance, taking her wrist so I can check her pulse.

"I'm okay. I just stood up too fast, and I haven't eaten today. Maybe a drink of water or juice or something would be a good idea."

Storm appears behind Savage. "Everything all right?"

Dani's pulse is normal, and I release her when she seems stable on her feet. "Yes, she just got a little dizzy. She hasn't eaten today. Why don't you take her into the kitchen and get her something to eat?" Storm nods her agreement and takes Dani's hand, leading her back to the house with Savage close on their heels.

I drop back onto the chaise and am about to return to my less-than-blissful relaxation, when the hair on my arms stands on end and tingles ripple along my skin. Turning toward the house, I find Gabe stepping from the backdoor. Even with his sunglasses on, I can feel his eyes boring into me, stripping me bare even though I'm already practically naked in my itty-bitty string bikini.

My skin heats instantly, and I look away quickly, reaching for my drink as both a distraction and to hopefully help numb my fraying nerves knowing he's here.

Empty. Shit.

I recline on the chaise, rest my arm across my forehead, and try to regain my composure as my blood pressure rises. At least he isn't half-naked like he usually is when we're hanging out by the pool. If I had to watch him walk around in nothing but board shorts all afternoon—all muscles and tats and that fucking nipple ring—I would spontaneously combust.

Even though I tried to avert my gaze as fast as possible, I couldn't help but notice his long-sleeve, button-down shirt with the sleeves rolled up to just below his elbows and the collar flipped up. Definitely a strange choice with his khaki cargo shorts on a ninety-five degree day; he must be sweltering.

At least he's suffering as much as I am.

Angelina squeals and races past me, squirting me with her water gun. I shriek when the cold water hits my hot skin, and I whip off my sunglasses and glower at her. She pauses a few feet from me, gun raised and pointed in my direction, ready for another attack or to run if need be.

Game on, little girl!

I grin at her, and she giggles.

"You little brat, I am so going to get you." I rise and step toward her slowly, and she squeals again before she takes off running around the pool toward the deep end where Ben watches her, laughing at my expense.

"Angel, no running." She stops immediately at her father's warning and glances back at me as I close the distance between us rapidly. With another giggle, she leaps into the pool, splashing Ben before her floaty arms cause her to pop to the surface with a laugh.

I can't suppress my smile no matter how foul my mood. That kid is fucking adorable. The result of yet another blissfully happy relationship. Although, Storm and Ben aren't nearly as obvious as Savage and Danika. I think the newness wore off about the time Angelina was born, but the love is still very much there; I can see it every time they look at each other.

I need another drink.

At least if Star were here, I'd have someone to be miserable and alone with. Although, I never felt alone when she was alive.

Ben pulls Angelina from the water and towels her off. Gabe and Savage man the grill on the corner of the patio and seem oblivious to the vicious assault that just occurred.

A swim sounds like the second-best option since Mom is

acting like the alcohol police today. I wander over to edge of the pool and take a deep breath before diving into the cool, crisp water, praying it will wash away the annoyance, awkwardness, loneliness, jealousy, and anger currently consuming me.

2

***

GABE

Skye dives into the water, barely causing a splash when she disappears from view and takes my breath with her. She steals it every single time we're in the same space. I'd have given anything to have been able to bow out of this barbeque today, but I can't disappoint the woman who is basically my mother, and I can't avoid Skye the rest of my life. After all, she is family, in a way.

And therein lies the problem.

I've been trying to put my finger on the exact moment things changed between us. The easy answer would be the wedding. I knew she was struggling—seeing Savage and Danika so happy, the first big family event without Star here—everything had to be slow, agonizing torture for Skye.

The moment the ceremony ended, she disappeared, only to return for the photos a half-hour later smelling like whiskey with glassy, red, puffy eyes. I prayed the photographer would be able to retouch the pictures so Savage and Dani weren't faced with Skye's misery every time they remembered their big day.

Frankly, I don't know how she made it through the reception—probably with the help of the free-flowing champagne, or something stronger. When I finally noticed she was gone, I went on a search and finally found her sobbing alone on the patio. By then, she was lost and there was no bringing her back. Picking her up from the floor and carrying her to my room seemed like a good idea at the time since she was incoherent, and I had no fucking clue where her room key was.

She curled into me the moment I touched her, burying her face against my neck. Her tears trickled down my skin. When I entered my room and laid her on the bed, I thought she was gone to the world. But she resisted my attempt to pull my arms from around her and clung to me, wrapping her arms around my neck, as if her life depended on it.

"Skye, you're okay, try to get some sleep."

I grasped her wrists, trying to remove her hands from my neck, but she tugged me closer, her swollen, red-rimmed eyes boring into mine. "Gabe..." Her voice was nothing more than a whisper, but she said my name like a benediction.

"Skye...don't..." I tried again to free myself from her physically, but the pain written across her face wouldn't let me pull away.

She shook her head and inclined closer to me. "You've always been my rescuer. You've always been here for me, even when you were thousands of miles away. I need you now, more than ever." She leaned in slowly, giving me every chance to pull away.

But, I didn't.

Instead, I let her press her lips to mine and did nothing to stop her from deepening the kiss until her hands were buried in my hair, holding me in place with a strength I didn't know she possessed.

Somehow, despite the fog enveloping my brain, reality slammed into me. I jerked away, pulling out of her grasp and stepping back from the bed—her wide, confused eyes following my retreat.

"I...I'm sorry...I..." Words failed me as I stared at her—no longer a little girl, no longer just Savage's little sister. She was all woman, and she was hurting in a way I could never understand. I shook my head, turned, and fled the room without glancing back.

Maybe I made the wrong choice. God knows I've second-guessed my decision to leave her every day since then. Especially when I realized I'd never be able to look at her the same way again.

A flash of my solo session in the shower this morning has me cringing inwardly.

Aww, hell...

If I'm being honest, things changed between us long before that night, when she started writing me during my deployments. The whole Hawke family wrote me. It's not like I was getting anything from dear ol' Dad, and that's the way I wanted it.

Their letters kept me up-to-date with the people who had become my family and the world around them. They kept me connected. But, as the girls grew, their letters to me changed. Star was always so cerebral. She asked me the tough questions, and I was always able to tell her anything. Star was my confessor, but Skye, she was my escape from everything going on around me. She talked about her life, school, and asked advice on boys and dating. Things she should have been talking to Savage about, but she had never felt comfortable going to him with her problems, and I can't really say I blamed her. Even at that age, Savage was a control freak and would have undoubtedly tried to interfere where he wasn't wanted or needed. She kept my mind off the things that would have driven me mad and, in the process, made me feel like I wasn't so alone.

I never felt closer to her than when I was thousands of miles away.

Why? Who the hell knows?

Mrs. Hawke always treated me like a member of the family, but I never thought of any of the Hawke girls as sisters, not really. I would die for them, or kill, and they know that, but I was also able to appreciate the beautiful women they eventually became. And I knew she was no longer the fifteen-year-old girl she had been when I left for boot camp after high school graduation.

I just never thought I would have this kind of a reaction to one of my best friend's little sisters.

The crystal blue water of the pool returns to smooth, glassy perfection.

Skye hasn't surfaced yet.

"Gabe!" Storm's voice draws my attention away from the water, and I turn to her.

"What?"

She steps from the sliding glass door of the house and approaches me, pointing to the grill. "You going to flip those burgers?"

I follow her eyes to the grill and scramble to flip them all before we end up eating some very well-done meat. "Sorry, got it."

How long did I space out for?

As soon as the meat is safe, I return my attention to the water. Still no Skye. I'm not worried, not really. Skye was an all-state swimmer in high school and is as at home in the water as she is on dry land. But, still, she has been down there a while...

Setting the tongs on the side of the grill, I glance over at Storm, who's busy setting the table with plates and silverware. "Hey, can you watch the burgers? I'm going to let Skye know it's almost time to eat." She nods in agreement and heads toward the grill as I set off toward the pool.

Good excuse, Gabe. Real smooth.

I groan inwardly and run my hands back through my hair. It's longer than I normally keep it. I'm so used to having it high and tight, I usually never let it get like this, but I've been insanely busy, not to mention distracted, since the wedding.

When I reach the edge of the pool, I see her lying on the bottom. Her black curls spreads around her like a dark halo, and her cornflower blue eyes stare into the sunny sky.

Fuck...she's not moving.

She blinks and shifts up onto her feet before pushing off the bottom and swimming toward the shallow end of the pool where I'm waiting.

I don't know if she saw me through the water, but as she emerges, she seems oblivious to my presence—her head dropped back, eyes closed, face turned to the sun. Water flows off her body, trickling down the flat expanse of her stomach and long, lean legs. She shakes her head and slides her hands back through her hair, wringing it out as she walks toward the stairs.

Her eyes open and immediately find me. She assesses me, and her mouth turns down slightly.

SKYE

As if it isn't bad enough I can't escape him in my dreams, now I'm stuck here with him in all his glorious flesh all afternoon.

I've been avoiding Gabe like the plague ever since the wedding. Unfortunately, Sunday family dinners, or barbeques, are not optional. The agony of his rejection stabs at me over and over again just being in his proximity, at least once a week.

Joy of fucking joys.

The cool water of the pool is doing nothing to temper the flame on my skin. When I opened my eyes on the bottom of the pool and found him watching me—his image wavering through the water—I would have given anything to be able to stay down there eternally.

But eventually, someone would have jumped in to save me —with my fucking luck, it would have been Gabe. And then, I would have had to feel his smooth skin and tight as fuck muscles pressed against my body as he swam up with me, and God knows I can't survive that.

I slowly step toward him, unable to tear my eyes away even though all I want to do is swim back to the bottom and wait until my lungs burn again. He appraises me through his sunglasses and then reaches up and nudges them down his nose so I can finally see his eyes.

The sea green storm staring back at me surprises me, and I momentarily halt my approach.

Why does he look so pissed? Or is it annoyed? Or confused?

His intense gaze holds mine for a moment before he pushes his glasses back up and clears his throat, shoving his hands into the pockets of his shorts. "Uh, food's almost ready."

"Thanks." I mumble my response and ascend the stairs, brushing past him without making eye contact again.

I swear, that man's eyes have hypnotic powers.

My towel is draped over the back of the chaise I've been lounging on, and I beeline for it, desperate to put as much distance between myself and that beautiful, frustrating hunk of man meat as possible.

I grab it and quickly dry off, bending down to reach my legs. A strange groaning noise floats across the water to me, and I whip around, searching for the source. Gabe has returned to the grill, and he's focused on piling the burgers on a plate. No one else is looking in my direction.

Must have imagined it.

I wrap the towel around my waist, pop my sunglasses back on, grab my phone, and make my way to the covered patio. It's inevitable. I just can't avoid him, or the awkwardness, anymore.

There's an open seat at the table between Savage and Storm. I rush to it before anyone else can take it, forcing me to sit closer to the source of my daily torture.

Gabe arrives with a platter of burgers and reaches to the center of the table to set it down. I find myself unable to stop ogling the flexing muscles of his forearms and the twinge in my core makes me clench my teeth.

Every fucking time I see him.

He sits across from me, between Mom and Ben, and everyone starts passing the dishes and chatting.

I avoid any of the conversations. I don't want to hear about Savage and Dani's baby or Storm and Ben's new house any more today—I just can't deal.

How could you leave me here alone with these people?

Things were so much easier when Star was around. I never had to force myself to converse with anyone, and no one bothered to try to make me because Star was always there, ready to jump in and engage everyone. She knew I needed my space, and since she died, things have only grown more unbearable.

My family practically smothers me with love and attention. I know they mean well—they're just concerned about me. But sometimes, it feels like I'm drowning—that same burning in my lungs and foggy head I get when I stay at the bottom of the pool too long. If only I hadn't blown off the ski trip for that dumbass, Aaron. I would have been in that car...

"Skye, did you hear me?"

I hear my name but completely missed whatever came before that. "Huh? Oh, sorry, no. What?"

Mom eyes me judgmentally for a moment before she continues, "I was just telling everyone that Stone called a few minutes ago and said he is coming for a visit next weekend. Apparently, he has some business to take care of with Dom."

Gabe, Savage, and Dani all stiffen, and a look passes between them that tells me they are less than pleased with the news Stone is going to be meeting with Dom. I, on the other hand, am thrilled he's coming.

Thank God!

He is the only one left in this family who actually gets me and doesn't push me to be someone I'm not.

"Oh, that's awesome. I'll call him later and find out his plans." I'm definitely going to need some serious one-on-one time with him so I can vent. Why does he have to live in fucking California? We need lawyers in Louisiana, too.

The awkward glances between Savage, Dani, and Gabe continue, but I know I'll never get any information out of them, especially in front of Mom, so I concentrate on my lunch and take a bite of my burger.

Gabe leans forward and reaches across the table to grab the potato salad. The collar of his shirt shifts toward one side, exposing the now-obvious reason for his odd apparel today—a giant hickey on his collarbone.

My body temperature skyrockets in a second, and the bite of the burger I just took sits like lead in my throat. I swallow it down and grit my teeth together.

I wonder what whore gave him that...

"...I swear he was on something..."

"What? No, he was just tired and overworked and letting loose a little."

The conversation between Mom and Storm makes its way through the green wall of jealousy, and I know they are talking about Stone and the wedding.

Of course he was on something.

But it's not like either of us were out of control. Stone was in-check and so was I...well, until I had my breakdown and threw myself at Gabe.

"Stone is fine, guys. He was fine at the wedding, and he's fine now." I don't know why I feel the need to defend him. Stone is perfectly capable of defending himself, but he's not here, and the family ganging up on him behind his back just feels so familiar and wrong.

Everyone stares at me, and I realize that may have come out a bit more intensely than I had intended.

"Skye, calm down, we're just worried about him, that's all." Leave it to Savage to try to be the peacemaker, but all his calm voice does is push my frayed nerves even further toward the breaking point. He's always treating me like a petulant child who doesn't get her way, and I'm fucking sick of it. I'm twenty-eight years old, for Christ's sake.

I grab my phone, shove away from the table without another word, and storm into the kitchen through the slider. I'm getting out of here.

Fuck them. If they want to sit there and bash Stone when he's not here to defend himself, I want no part of it.

3

GABE

I can practically see Skye's blood boiling. Why the rest of the family can't understand they're about to set her off, I'll never know. I can always see it from a mile away.

She slams the slider closed behind her and disappears into the house. Storm moves to get up and go after her.

"No, don't, I'll go." I don't know what possesses me to volunteer, apparently my lack of sanity is directly tied to how little clothing Skye is wearing.

When she bent over to dry off after climbing out of the pool, I couldn't even choke back my groan of appreciation. She's so fucking beautiful and such a pain in my ass. I didn't know it was possible to want to fuck someone so much and yet still want to strangle the life out of them. God knows, I want to do both to Skye most of the time.

The silence of the house is odd. It's usually so busy and loud, but I can hear my own breath and it's a little unsettling. I search for her, making my way through the familiar rooms and halls. I finally find the locked bathroom door down the back hallway.

Here goes nothing...

I knock. No response. I knock again. "Skye, it's me, open up."

Something slams. "Fuck, why can't you people just leave me alone?"

I ask myself the same question every damn fucking day.

Her nasty comment may have dissuaded the rest of the family, but not me. I've never been afraid of Skye or her attitude. Maybe that's a huge mistake on my part.

"Knock it off and open up, Skye."

A resigned growl slips from under the door and the lock clicks. I push it open and enter just as she sits on top of the toilet. She pulls her knees up to her chest. Anger radiates off her in waves.

I pull myself up onto the counter next to her and wait for her to say something.

She doesn't speak, or even acknowledge my presence.

Well, this is going to be fun. I might as well just dive right in.

"So, what's your problem?"

"I don't have a problem." Her reply is cool, and she keeps her eyes locked on the tile floor.

Her dark hair is still damp from the pool and a strand clings to the side of her face. I have to consciously force myself not to reach out and brush it off.

Concentrate on why you're sitting in a fucking bathroom.

"You're going to kill your mother going off on her like that. You should ease up a bit."

Her hard eyes snap up to meet mine with an icy glare. "Mind your own fucking business, Gabe."

I refuse to look away despite the fact that my eyes naturally want to slip down to her exposed cleavage. The towel she has wrapped around her doesn't conceal much of anything. "It is my business, Skye. I love your mother, and sometimes the way you act around her is just...well, childish. It upsets her, and I don't like seeing her upset."

Her eyes narrow on me and a sneer overtakes her perfect lips—lips that have been on mine, lips that taste like fucking vanilla and everything I shouldn't have.

"Maybe she was upset because she saw that damn hickey on your neck. Maybe she's sick of you being a total manwhore, and just doesn't have it in her to tell you how much she hates the way you go through women, the way normal people go through underwear."

Well...Shit.

She saw it.

It terrifies me how much I hate that she's viewed the evidence of last night's fuckfest. The feeling in the pit of my stomach is new to me—it burns and twists and stabs at me from the inside. I think it might be guilt, and that's something I certainly have no reason to be feeling in this particular situation. There are a lot of things I've done in my life I should and do feel guilty about, but sleeping with that completely willing woman is not one of them. And I certainly shouldn't feel guilty about Skye being upset by it. I'm nothing to her. Not really.

Before I can even contemplate a response to her outburst, she jumps up from the toilet and stomps out of the bathroom, slamming the door shut behind her, and effectively, in my face.

That went well.

I slide off the counter and turn on the tap, waiting for a minute until the water gets ice cold before splashing it on my face. The freezing spray cools and feels incredible on my heated skin.

Getting called out like that by Skye, my best friend's little sister, would be bad enough under normal circumstances, but knowing it's making me actually feel guilty is a whole new fucking ballgame.

Talk about fucked.

I dry my face with my sleeve and pull my collar down, exposing the offending mark.

Jesus, what adult gives someone a hickey like this?

Quick flashes of stumbling into my condo with blondie last night come back to me, and I cringe. I actually fucking *cringe* remembering a hot night of sex.

Fuck.

The door to the bathroom opens, and Storm stares at me with a slight smirk on her face. "Given the way Skye flew out of here, I imagine it didn't go well."

I drop my collar back into place, praying Storm didn't see the evidence of last night. The last thing I need is judgment from her too. "Yeah, not exactly."

She leans against the jamb. "Why does that not surprise me?"

"Where is she, back outside?" Storm pushes away from the door, and I follow her down the hallway toward the back patio.

"No, she's gone. She was supposed to catch a ride home with us since we picked her up, but some guy pulled up out front in a brown Jeep, and she left with him. Of course, she didn't bother to say goodbye to anyone. I only know this because I saw her leave when I heard a car door slam and looked out the front window."

Some guy?

My stomach roils at the thought of who that "some guy" might be and what they might be on their way to do. I wish I could say it was some altruistic, brotherly, protective feeling, but I'd be lying. I'm jealous, and fuck if that doesn't make me want to break something.

Storm heads outside, but I stop in the kitchen to grab another much-needed beer from the fridge. I gulp it down in three swallows, praying the cold brew will help calm my heated temper. This isn't right. I can't be jealous of Skye's boyfriend, or whoever he is, because she's nothing to me—nothing more than my best friend's little sister.

Placing my hands on the counter, I drop my head down and close my eyes, trying to picture her as that little girl with dark pigtails instead of the voluptuous woman she is today.

Total. Miserable. Failure.

All I can see is the pain in her eyes when she kissed me and the way her lips glistened and called out for me to take them with mine. I don't know what would have happened if I hadn't stopped that kiss—probably something we would have both regretted in the morning and every single day after that.

So why the hell can't I forget it, and her?

~

SKYE

"You okay?"

I glance over at Lucas and offer a half-hearted smile. "Yeah, I'm fine. Just family stuff, ya know?"

He grins before returning his eyes to the road. "Do you want to talk about it?"

Fuck no.

Lucas is funny, sweet, and pretty damn good in bed, but the last thing I want is to go down the "feelings" road with him. It's the one thing that has made this work for the last couple months—he never pushes me to talk. I tell him what I need, and he gives it to me without getting bogged down in the *whys.*

He's certainly not what I anticipated when he invited himself to sit at my table in the hospital cafeteria. I was ready to tell him to buzz off when he introduced himself, but instead, I found myself laughing within minutes and easily falling into conversation with him. Despite the fact he worked in human resources, he wasn't a total nerd, and his background as an

EMT before he went into HR, and mine as a nurse practitioner, gave us a lot to talk about. It helped me avoid discussing anything too personal.

He doesn't know about Star. He doesn't know what agony it's been without her the last four years. He doesn't know that I go to her grave once a week to talk to her like a fucking crazy person. He doesn't know I should have been there—in that car with Savage and Star. He doesn't know how that guilt eats away at me every fucking hour of every damned day, and I don't plan on telling him. Lucas is easy, and I want it to stay that way.

"Well, I'm glad you called. I didn't think I'd see you today." His hand slides across the center console and finds my thigh. He rubs it gently, and it reminds me of how good he is at releasing my tension.

"Me too."

Thank God he was in the area and able to pick me up from Mom's. A good fuck should help me forget about the family drama, and Gabe, and that goddamn hickey. My hands curl into fists just thinking about it.

What adult walks around with a fucking hickey on their neck?

We pull up and park on the street in front of my apartment building.

Lucas turns to me. "Are you working tomorrow morning?"

"Yeah, I'm seven to seven tomorrow."

He grins and turns off the ignition. "Excellent. I go in at seven thirty." His door opens, and he climbs out then pops the back door and grabs a bag. I watch him over my shoulder, unease overtaking the anticipation of awesome sex tonight.

Before I can open my door, he comes to my side and does it for me, holding it like a true gentleman.

What exactly is going on here?

First, he's asking me if I want to talk about my family drama, and now, he has an overnight bag and is opening doors for me?

It's not like we haven't spent the night together before, but those were usually sloppy drunk nights when we came back and fucked and passed out. This is different. This is something he apparently thought out and planned for.

His hand settles on the small of my back, and he guides me up the walkway to the outer door. "We can ride to work together tomorrow."

I stiffen at his words, freezing with my keys midway to the lock. He leans forward and searches my face. "Is that a problem?"

Hell yes, it's a problem.

We aren't exactly public about our relationship at work, and there's a good reason for that. Even though I work in one of the private family practice groups affiliated with the hospital, and am technically not a hospital employee, the last thing I want or need is all the gossipy nurses discussing my love life and questioning me incessantly about it every time I go in.

If I say it's a problem, I have a feeling it will start a fight I'm not ready for and will also mean I'm not getting laid tonight. I don't want or need either of those things to happen.

"No, Lucas, it's fine. I'll just catch a ride home when I'm done." He almost always leaves before five—one of the perks of an office job instead of direct patient contact. I play off my momentary concern for being worried about getting back here after my shift. He grins and seems to buy my quick lie.

The moment I close my apartment door behind me, Lucas tosses his bag onto the couch and pulls me against him. His lips find mine, and the heady rush of anticipation for sex momentarily makes me forget the drama of the day.

He's pretty good at that and, on a day like today, I can really appreciate it. With a nudge, he urges me to walk backward toward my bedroom.

Guess we aren't wasting any time. Thank God.

Time means talking; talking means thinking; thinking

means examining the weirdness that's going on with him today, and I just don't have the fucking time or energy for that.

We fall on the bed. He sits back long enough to pull his shirt up over his head, exposing his great body—tanned skin, hard, cut muscles—and I let myself drink it in. I grin at him, and he smirks.

"What?"

"Nothing, just enjoying the view."

He drops back down to me and slides a hand over my bare stomach. "I think I like you in nothing but a bathing suit and a towel."

"I'm sure you do."

"Makes for easy access." His fingers slip under my bikini top and find my right nipple.

I groan, and he catches the sound in his mouth. He twists my sensitive flesh, and I drop my head back with a gasp.

Yes!

Forget about Gabe, Skye. Enjoy yourself.

4

SKYE

*M*orning light hits my eyelids and warmth envelops me.

Hot, hard flesh presses against my back, and a large, warm hand squeezes my left breast.

I moan and arch back. A satisfied groan answers me and fingers tug at my nipple playfully before sliding down my stomach. They find my clit and rub slow, rhythmic circles, working me up at a torturous pace while lips explore the back of my neck.

Fuck yes!

My clit pulses under his ministrations and a finger slips into me. I'm so fucking wet already. A finger just isn't going to cut it this morning.

I need him, inside of me, now.

A whimper slips from my lips when the finger slides in and out faster, brushing up against my clit with every movement.

"Shit." I bite my bottom lip and roll my hips back. My ass is greeted by a hard cock pressed between us.

Why are you not in me?

I want to scream it, but the only thing that comes out of my mouth is a gasp when another finger joins the party and my body starts trembling. I'm so close to coming already, but I need to come around cock, not fingers.

Nothing but cock is going to cut it.

With as much will power as I can muster, I fight off my impending orgasm to reach behind me and grasp his dick.

He growls in my ear and kisses my neck while I stroke him. His fingers fill and stretch me, and he increases his pace.

My head spins and any ability to think clearly fogs.

There's no fighting it anymore. I come, crying out and bucking against his hand. My fingers tighten around the thick shaft, and he gasps in my ear.

"You're fucking beautiful when you come."

I barely hear him—it's nothing but a hazy whisper in the periphery of my world while my body spins off into nirvana. My pussy clenches around his fingers, and I tug on his cock, urging him to replace his hand with what I really want.

His chest vibrates against my back with his chuckle. "Patience..."

"No...please..."

My orgasm wanes and in the afterglow, my only concern is getting him inside me as quickly as is humanly possible.

Now!

The wall of his body heat disappears, and his cock slips from my hand as he rolls to the other side of the bed. I start to protest, but the sound of ripping foil assures me I won't have to wait long.

He sidles up behind me and kisses my neck while he pulls my hips back to get into a better position. The head of his cock slips inside me, and he stills.

What the fuck?

The pause is only momentary before he pushes into me in one hard thrust. I gasp and squeeze my eyes shut. His cock stretches me, and fuck, does it feel incredible. He pulls my leg up over his thigh, spreading me open and giving him better access.

He withdraws slowly before shoving into me again—deep and hard. We move in unison, establishing a fast, driving rhythm. His hand grasps my breast and tugs at my nipple.

It won't take long for me to come again. Being fucked like this—hard and fast—right after coming is a surefire way to set me off again.

Our gasps and groans mingle, and I squeeze him with my inner muscles.

A moan in my ear meets my cry as I come.

"Oh, fuck! Gabe!"

His body tenses, and he stills behind me. "Who the fuck is Gabe?"

My eyes fly open and the bliss from my orgasm vanishes instantly when I realize what happened.

Holy shit! Lucas!

This is bad. This is so, so bad.

He pulls out of me quickly, and I turn my head toward him. He props himself up on his elbow, watching and waiting for an explanation, although it's pretty clear nothing I say is going to remove that look of betrayal from his eyes.

"No one. It's no one."

His eyebrow shoots up, and his lips press into a hard, thin line. "No one, huh?"

I shake my head and roll over toward him. He shifts back, away from me and toward the edge of the bed. Somehow, I know that reaching out to him would be a bad idea right now, so I lie completely still, waiting for him to erupt.

It's not like I don't deserve it.

Fuck. What's wrong with me?

Lucas takes a deep breath and stands. He doesn't even look back at me before he disappears into the bathroom, closes the door, and starts the shower.

"Fuck!" I scrub my face with my hands and try to figure out where the hell it all went so wrong.

When you said the wrong man's name, dumbass.

Gabe is fucking up my sanity and my life.

Shit, what am I supposed to say to Lucas?

I reach over to the nightstand and grab my phone. Last night is a bit of a blur. I remember Lucas picking me up and the sex when we got back here. But after that, a potent mix of little food and lots of alcohol the rest of the night has left things a bit fuzzy.

Before I have time to review my text messages from last night, the shower shuts off. I need to come up with a plausible explanation for my slip of the tongue, and fast.

When the door opens, I expect him to be shooting daggers at me and ignoring my presence or ranting and raving like a madman. Instead, he calmly bends down and digs into his bag for his clothes, letting his towel drop when he changes.

The silence is deafening and makes me feel about a thousand percent guiltier than if he had just come out raging. When he's dressed, he turns to me and raises his eyebrows. "Are you getting out of bed? We have to be at work in half an hour."

We have to be at work?

He can't seriously still want to drive into work together after what just happened? Can he?

His dark eyes search mine, waiting for my response.

"Uh, yeah, I just need a quick shower, and then I'll be ready to go. Give me five." I climb from bed and brush past him on my way to the bathroom.

Well, this is hella awkward.

And I thought things with Gabe were uncomfortable. This gives "uncomfortable" a whole new definition.

GABE

It feels like I got hit by an RPG again. The ringing in my ears, ache in every damn joint in my body, and the hammering pain in my head only compare to the time the caravan I was in was attacked in Iraq, and I was thrown from the turret when the Stryker flipped.

I clench my eyes closed against the offending morning light and groan.

My throat is on fire, and the tell-tale taste of nicotine in my mouth and smell of smoke clinging to my hair and skin alert me that I fell off the wagon again. Another six months smokes-free out the fucking window.

Fuck. What happened last night?

After leaving the Hawkes', I went to one of my favorite clubs to try to find someone to help me forget the Skye drama. I vividly remember the images of Skye in that bathing suit flitting through my head on the ride to the club in the cab.

There's a foggy memory of a bottle of Maker's Mark, but after that, *nada*. I'm afraid to even check the bed for who's next to me. Did I come home with someone last night?

I take a deep breath and a quick glance to my left assures me I'm safe.

The space next to me is empty, and the sheets are cold when I reach out and lay my hand on them.

Thank God.

I can't deal with another incident like yesterday morning—not when I feel like this.

A terrible squawking beep comes from my nightstand, and

I scramble for my phone. It's only 6:00 a.m. Savage and I usually don't go to the gym until seven on Mondays.

Why the hell did I set an early alarm?

I turn it off and open my texts, searching for answers about last night. The last message is from Savage telling me he wants to get started early today.

Asshole. That explains the alarm.

My eyes move down to the next text conversation, and my breath stalls in my chest.

Shit.

Skye's name is there in black and white. I don't read what I can see of the message. I don't even want to open it. Who the fuck knows what I may have said in the state I was in last night. If I don't open it, I can ignore it. That's the adult thing to do— ignore it, and it's like it never happened.

A shower sounds like a much better idea than dealing with whatever reality lies in those messages. My pores seem to be seeping a nauseating stale booze smell to mix with the smoke, and there's no way I'm going to be able to concentrate on my workout smelling like this.

I set my phone on the nightstand, and it vibrates.

Fuck. It's Savage.

> Meet me in the hall in five. <

No shower. Fabulous.

I stare at the screen.

Just get it over with.

Skye's name practically burns under my fingertip as I click on our exchange.

It's worse than I thought.

I sent the first message, initiating whatever clusterfuck this surely was.

< Can't stop thinking about you >

Seriously, fuck me!

Why the hell did I think it was a good idea to text her and

tell her that? I must have been a full bottle in. A vague, hazy memory of a dark-haired, blue-eyed girl at the club hovers in the corner my mind. I push my free hand back through my hair and groan. I probably saw her and it sent me down the road to Idioticbehaviorville.

Skye's response breaks my fucking heart and makes me feel like even more of an asshole than I already do.

> That's not fair. <

She's right; it's not fair. I have no business telling her I'm thinking about her, or texting her in the middle of the night, or doing anything to her.

At least it doesn't appear I elaborated and explained how I think about her with my cock in my hand. How I did exactly that right before I saw her yesterday.

And it's all because of that fucking night. If I hadn't let her kiss me, I could have remained blissfully ignorant of how sweet she tastes, and how soft her lips are...

I should have asked Storm to help me with Skye that night. We never would have been in that situation. I never would have been tempted. I wouldn't be thinking about her practically every waking moment. And I wouldn't be doing asshole, unfair shit like this to her.

All she did was point out the truth of what I'm doing to her and, rather than apologize, I only reiterated my position.

< It's true. >

Safe enough response, I suppose.

Given the situation, and my apparent level of intoxication last night, it could have been much worse.

Her final text burns my eyes and brings back that unfamiliar pang I felt yesterday, knowing she left with another man. That feeling I have absolutely no business having.

< You rejected me, left me alone when I needed you, but I'm not alone pining for you anymore. >

As if her words weren't enough...

This fucking picture. Shoot me in the fucking heart why don't you...

Her...

In bed...

With someone else...

His sleeping silhouette...

Her smirking face...

And her middle finger.

It's not like I don't deserve it, but that doesn't make the sting any more bearable.

Climbing out of bed is agonizing, and I clamp my eyes shut to prevent my stomach from ejecting what's left of the booze.

Did I even eat, or did I just enjoy a liquid diet last night?

When I make it to the bathroom, I have my answer staring back at me in the mirror.

Fuck. I look like death warmed over.

Another scan of my phone reminds me I don't have time to shower before Savage will be waiting in the hall. A quick brushing of my teeth and change into workout clothes is all I manage before I open the door and find him already there.

"Jesus, Gabe, you look like fucking hell. What happened last night?"

I sent a text to your baby sister basically telling her I want to bone her.

"Uh, nothing. The usual."

He doesn't appear convinced, but he doesn't push it, either. A year ago, he never would have let this slide. He would have been down my throat and up my ass about drinking enough to be this big of a mess. Not to mention he would whoop my ass for giving in and smoking again, which I'm sure he can smell all over me and hear in my voice.

But he also knows that after everything we went through last year, he needs to back off me. He has no idea how much killing Abello's men affected me, but he suspects it, and has gratefully been focusing all his attentions and worry on Dani instead of me.

I'm thankful for the reprieve, although I do feel for Dani... having to be the focus of all Savage's worry and dominance. Thankfully, she's one fucking tough woman and probably the only person on this planet who can truly handle him.

"Well, are you still good to go, or are you going to puss out on me?"

God, I wish I could puss out, but what I really need, and deserve right now, is an ass-kicking.

5

SKYE

I never stood a chance of getting into work with Lucas without being seen.

What was I thinking, agreeing to ride in with him, especially after this morning?

That was the most awkward car ride I've had in my entire life.

Silence.

The entire fucking drive was made in utter, complete silence. The only sound breaking it was the droning of the local radio news anchor.

Our walk to the elevator that would take us up into the building from the underground employee parking structure was the same...silence.

When we reached the elevator bay and waited for the doors to open...silence.

Now, standing in the elevator on the way to our respective floors, surrounded by curious coworkers...silence.

The tension in the elevator car is only rivaled by the tension in the air outside.

August is always like this in New Orleans. The atmosphere is heavy with the continual threat of rain and thunderstorms. We're going to get wet today.

The weatherman on the radio this morning also said a tropical depression had formed near Puerto Rico overnight. After Katrina, the constant danger from developing weather systems in the Atlantic keeps everyone on alert. No one wants a repeat, and we'd rather be over prepared.

This one better dissipate before it gets anywhere near us, I don't have the energy to deal with a hurricane right now.

The ding sounds, alerting us we've reached the main floor, which is also Lucas' stop.

I don't know whether to say something to him or not, especially because there are other people in the car.

Shit, I might just make it worse.

A brief glance over at him tells me nothing. He's still wearing a mask of indifference. The doors slide open and several people exit. Lucas steps forward and follows them out without a look back or a word.

Fuck, fuck, fuck!

Way to royally fuck up a good thing, Skye.

The doors slide closed, and I ride up to the second floor where I step off and make my way over the skywalk to the building that houses the physician offices in the hospital complex. I use my keycard to slip in the back door to the practice offices. Sometimes, I miss working in the main hospital. It was always more exciting to be in the center of the action when I worked in the ER, but working in a family medicine private practice gives me a much better schedule and more flexibility.

The employee break room is deserted this early. I'm almost always the first one in. Dumping my bag and jacket in my locker, I almost forget to grab my cell from my purse. I haven't even had time to check my messages. That car ride was uncomfortable enough without me blatantly ignoring him by burying my face in my phone. Instead, I stared out the window at the city passing us by and wondered what was going on in his head.

How did I let things get so messed up? Star would know what to do, what to say, how to fix this. If it even can be fixed. How the hell will Lucas ever forgive me for what I did? How the hell do I get Gabe out of my heart and fucking head?

I really need you right now, Star. Tell me what to do.

As always, the fact that she isn't here hits me like a bolt of lightning, and I have to drop down into a chair when the stabbing pain invades my heart. If I let the tears start, they won't stop, and I'll be utterly useless during my shift.

So, instead of dwelling on my missing other half, I open my messages...and my day goes from bad to worse.

The picture sends a pretty direct message even if I hadn't typed the words right above it.

What the hell was I thinking?

I sent that to him?

Fuck, fuck, fuck!

Why?

After months and months, why would I suddenly send him something like that?

I scroll up to his messages and get the answer.

Motherfucker!

Where does Gabe get off sending me a message saying he can't stop thinking about me?

He crushes my soul, avoids me for months, lectures me about my relationship with my mother, and then sends me this?

Is he just fucking with me? Or is it true?

I guess it explains why I said his name at such a disastrous time. He got in my head last night with this bullshit. The fiasco with Lucas is all his fault.

Jamming my phone into my pocket, I head out to the reception area and check the patient schedule for today. It's not too bad. Between me and the two doctors I work for, we can see a significant amount of patients every day, but the receptionists know not to put too many on. One thing you don't want to deal with is a cranky, overworked doctor.

Or a cranky, overworked me.

Cranky, overworked, and pissed the hell off.

Gabe didn't respond to the picture. Maybe he didn't see it?

Yeah, right, Skye, and maybe pigs will fly out of your ass.

None of this would have happened if Star had been at the wedding. I never would have been falling into the abyss. It never would have caused me to act on my feelings for Gabe. I knew it would only fuck things up. Throwing myself at him like that...

God!

He's Savage's best friend and practically grew up as my brother. How fucked up is that?

I jump when someone claps me on the shoulder. "Shit, Mackenzie, I didn't hear you come in."

She chuckles and brushes past me to take her seat at the reception desk. "Sorry, I didn't mean to scare you."

"You may need a defibrillator to get my heart going again."

"Handy we have one of those, then." She grins before turning to her computer. "Things look relatively light today."

I sigh. "Thank God for that." Usually, Mondays are a pain in the fucking ass.

"Are you all right? You look a little upset."

Upset doesn't even begin to describe it.

Forcing a smile I don't feel, I stand and make my way around her. "I'm fine, just tired and not looking forward to the shift."

She purses her lips, and I doubt my acting abilities were Oscar-worthy, but she lets it slide. I slip away before she can question me any further. Maybe reviewing patient charts will take my mind off the clusterfuck I've created.

Then again, maybe not.

By the time lunch rolls around, I've managed to only review the conversation with Gabe twice. And I only cursed my own stupidity twenty times, so it feels like a win.

I grab a salad from the buffet line, lustfully eyeing the French fries and grilled cheese I really want.

Fucking diet.

Who would have thought losing Star would actually make me gain weight? I'm apparently one of those people who drown their sorrows in booze and food, because I've gained at least fifteen pounds since the accident.

I drop my tray on the nearest open table and dig in to my less-than-satisfactory lunch.

My skin prickles when he walks in, almost as if I can feel the disdain in his glare. I peek up and briefly make eye contact before Lucas beelines for the food line, not bothering to glance back in my direction.

Shit. I really fucked this up.

The decision of whether or not to try to talk to him is removed from my control when he turns toward me, locks eyes with me, and proceeds to walk straight past me to a table against the back wall.

I guess that answers that *question.*

I didn't realize we were in middle school and were playing the "you can't sit with me" game.

My salad has become even less appetizing than it was before. I dump it in the trash and leave the cafeteria as fast as my legs can carry me.

There's no way this is going to end well.

Gabe's name slipping from my lips may well have been the deathblow to me and Lucas. I'm going to need a drink, or ten, after work tonight.

On my walk back to the office, I pull out my phone and call the first person who comes to mind.

"Hey, what's up?"

"Hey Storm, any chance you can pick your baby sister up from work around 7:00 and take her for a drink tonight?"

She lets out a sigh and then laughs. "I should be annoyed at having to drive all the way over there to get you, but I really need a drink, too. I'll tell Ben to pick up Angelina from daycare and I'll come get you. We need to go to the club though, I need Savage and Gabe to sign off on some plans and can kill two birds with one stone."

Fuck.

The *last* place I want to go right now is the club. Especially if Gabe is going to be there. But if I decline, Storm will ask why, and there's no way she needs to know about my morning slip or the ongoing saga of my unrequited love for Savage's best friend.

"All right, sounds good. I'll see you around seven."

Maybe I can avoid him at the club tonight. If I'm lucky, he'll be up in his office and won't even come down to the bar area.

Yeah, right, who am I kidding? I've never been lucky.

GABE

Renee—stage name Scarlett—bends over in front of a patron in one of the chairs lining the stage and smiles at him from between her legs. He leans forward and slips a twenty into her G-string before she snaps up and makes her way back to the pole. "Cherry Pie" blasts over the speakers as Scarlett swirls around the pole in time with the music.

Beautiful, mostly-naked women surround me all day long, but none of them do a single thing for me. The only one who does is the one I can't have. All I have is a long line of mindless fucks who drain my dick but not my desire for her.

Fuck my life. For real.

I lean back against the counter that runs along the wall behind the bar and watch Scarlett finish her dance to rousing applause from the crowd. There are quite a few people here for 7:30.

Normally, I would be out of here on a night like this—Mondays generally don't get too busy, and I doubt the crowd will grow much—but Storm called and asked Savage and me to stay to review some final plans for yet another of our expansion projects.

I'm really starting to regret our decision to push development of multiple new locations all at once. We opened the second club and a restaurant less than a year ago, and now we are already neck-deep in development of a third club location and another restaurant. Not only do we need to supervise the construction of two separate buildings, but we have to hire staff and find suppliers for each location. We were lucky to find great managers for the second club and the restaurant, but the more locations we open and people we hire, the less control we have. Plus, Savage is pushing for a fourth club on Bourbon Street, which is utterly insane.

Yes, there's a shitload of money to be made from the tourists down there, but it would be impossible to maintain any semblance of control or decorum in a club located in the French Quarter. If he wants to maintain the strict policies and image we have in place for the brand, there's no way we can do it there. We've been butting heads on this for over a year—going back and forth about the pros and cons—and now a great location is available, so I'm sure it will be coming up again during our meeting with Storm.

The last thing I need right now is the complication of my

feelings for Skye. Then again, maybe if I'm busy enough, I won't have time to fantasize about her.

Yeah, right.

I turn and pour myself a shot of Jameson, downing it quickly and savoring the burn.

Byron walks by and swats me on the arm. "I know that look, man. Girl trouble, am I right?"

I scoff and turn to him. "What would you possibly know about girl trouble?"

His hand pauses midway to the bottle of Maker's Mark he was reaching for before it drops to his side. He closes his eyes and takes a deep breath before facing me.

Shit, Gabe. Way to stick your foot in your mouth.

"Byron, shit, I'm sorry. I didn't mean that."

His eyes open, and he watches me speculatively. I know exactly what's running through his mind. He's wondering if he's going to be fired, or if I'm going to start making some crude jokes or smartass comments.

"Look, man, Savage and I have known for a while. Actually, I knew before we even hired you. Background checks and all..."

I trail off, and he nods, pressing his lips into a thin line and clenching his hands into fists at his sides.

"We don't give a fuck who you fuck, okay? It's completely irrelevant to you doing your job."

He nods again. His shoulders relax slightly, but he still doesn't say anything. I take a tentative step toward him and place my hand on his shoulder, giving it a reassuring squeeze.

"Just don't expect to be let backstage when we finally add a Ladies' Night."

That finally cracks him, and he laughs and claps me on the shoulder with a grin. "Duly noted, man."

Whew.

Alienating Byron, or even worse, losing him, would have been devastating for the business. He runs this place so well,

Savage and I couldn't operate without him. Who gives a fuck if he's gay? He could be a Brony for all I care, as long as he does his job well.

"But, as I was saying, if it's girl troubles, which both you and I know it is, then my advice is just to apologize."

Apologize. Yeah, right.

"I did the right thing. I don't have anything to apologize for."

Byron pours us both another shot of Jameson. He raises his and grins. "Do it anyway."

I grunt at him in acknowledgement of the suggestion, though I have no plans on taking his advice. We clink our shot glasses before I down mine in one quick swallow.

The problem with apologizing to Skye is having to admit, out loud and to her face, not only that the kiss had actually happened, but also that I'd kissed her back.

One stupid moment. A snapshot in time. One kiss that ruined everything.

I went from an easy brotherly relationship with her to thinking about her 24/7, in a most decidedly non-brotherly way.

Avoiding her doesn't help. Ignoring her doesn't help. Fucking other beautiful women doesn't help.

But tonight, once I'm done with Storm, I'm going to give that last one another shot.

Byron turns his attention to one of the waitresses, and I return mine to the stage. The opening riff of "Kashmir" begins, and I chuckle to myself. Nora is about to strut out from backstage. Only she would pick Led Zeppelin for her signature dance and Cashmere for a stage name. The girl is smart and has a crazy sharp sense of humor.

I bet some of the younger men in here don't even get the play on the word when her stage name is announced with the song. The lack of classic rock appreciation in this generation kills me.

"And now, welcome Cashmere!" The announcement is met with applause, and Nora enters the stage to whoops and hollers. Byron waves to someone who just entered the club, and I glance over, expecting to see one of the regulars.

Aww, you've got to be fucking kidding me...

Those same damn blue eyes that haunt my dreams and every waking moment of every day drill into me as Skye approaches the bar with Storm.

Storm smiles, waves to me and Byron, and proceeds toward us. Skye just sidles up to the far end of the bar and motions for Clarissa, the other bartender, to come over to her.

The low, black tank-top she's sporting barely contains the swell of her breasts when she leans forward across the bar top to talk to Clarissa.

My jeans are suddenly four sizes too small, and I bite back a groan as the zipper presses against my cock.

Sweet Lord, this woman is trying to kill me.

6

GABE

Clarissa pours Skye a drink while I try to keep my dick from escaping the ever-tightening confines of my pants. It strains against the denim and zipper, and I have to move up against the front of the bar to block my reaction to her.

These constant hard-ons whenever I see her are really starting to get inconvenient. At the house yesterday, the only thing keeping me from sporting wood was the fact that the entire family was there; it was like being watched by God.

"Gabe? Did you hear me?"

I turn my attention to Storm, who's regarding me expectantly.

Get your shit together, Anderson.

"What? Sorry, no." Hopefully she thinks I didn't hear her because of the music, not because I was imagining throwing her little sister on the bar top and ravaging her. Having her sprawled across it with her legs wrapped around my neck and my tongue in her pussy sounds like fucking heaven.

Storm releases an annoyed sigh. "I said, I need a drink first, but then let's head upstairs to review the plans with Savage."

Work.

Yeah.

Work would be good.

"Oh, yeah, sounds like a plan."

Byron pulls vermouth, vodka, and olive juice and makes Storm a martini while I watch Nora on stage.

Keep your eyes forward. Don't look at Skye.

"Kashmir" continues to flow through the speakers, and I can't help myself, I turn my head slightly so I can see Skye in my peripheral vision.

Her eyes are glued to the stage, and she nods along as Nora gyrates to the sultry tones of Robert Plant.

God, she's fucking beautiful.

The black, swirling mass of her hair is pulled back in a messy bun that shakes slightly with her movement. My eyes slowly descend down her long, elegant neck until I find her nipples pebbled against the tight tank-top.

Holy shit.

I jerk my gaze back up to her face and watch as she pulls her bottom lip between her teeth and her eyelids lower slightly.

Well, fuck me.

Skye is getting turned on watching Nora dance. I thought my pants were tight before, but now, it feels like my cock is in a vise.

Pushing my hair back off my forehead, I take a deep breath and try to control the swelling by thinking of anything else. I need to get out of here and away from her before I blow a load in my pants like a twelve-year-old schoolboy.

Shit, I can't even remember the last time I came anywhere but in a girl's mouth, pussy, or my hand. As good as coming would feel right now, doing it in my pants while at the bar is less than ideal, and that's definitely where this is heading.

Getting out of here is feeling more and more like a necessity.

I glance to my left and watch Storm sip her martini. "Hey, Storm, do you really need me to go over the plans? Can't Savage do it?"

Storm rolls her eyes and tosses back what remains in her glass. "Do you really want him making all the decisions? Besides, I need you to help me back him down when he goes all dictator on me."

Fair point. I can't abandon Storm to wrangle Savage alone. She hasn't done anything to deserve that. He's practically unbearable unless Dani or I are there to act as mediator and control-freak wrangler.

"Fine, but let's go get this done fast. I'm getting a headache." More like a cockache, but whatever.

I adjust my dick as discreetly as possible and round the bar on the opposite end from Skye, trying to keep as much distance between us as possible. Work was the one place I rarely saw her, and having to be on-guard here really fucking sucks.

Storm joins me. We pass Skye on the way to the elevator, and she glances down at my crotch and back up, arching an eyebrow at me and giving me that damn sexy little half-smirk of hers.

Well, shit. So much for discretion.

She saw it. There's no hiding it completely, and she wouldn't look so damn smug if she hadn't.

The elevator ride up to the second floor is awkward as fuck, not because Storm saw anything, but because she's rambling on about something, and I can't stop thinking about having Skye's smirking lips wrapped around my hard cock.

I don't even remember being this horny when I was in the sandbox for months at a time.

Ding.

"Seriously, Gabe, what the hell is up with you today?"

What? Shit, busted again.

"Sorry, Storm, I'm just not feeling well. Let's get this taken care of so I can get out of here."

With one quick knock to Savage's office door, I push it open and walk in. I have no doubt he's been watching on the security cameras and knows we were on our way up.

As expected, he's behind his huge wooden desk, eyes glued to his computer, watching over his empire. He glances up when we enter and nods toward the chairs facing his desk before returning his attention to the computer screen.

The leather creaks when I drop into the chair, and Savage flinches. I smirk because I know exactly why. Doc Cochran's chair is annoying as fuck, and after his first session with her last year, he came home in a rage complaining about it. It doesn't bother me nearly as much as it does him, but his reaction always amuses me.

"You ready to look this over?" Storm spreads the blueprints for the restaurant on the desk, right over the piles of various paperwork, and Savage shoots daggers at her.

He crosses his arms over his chest. "Well, I guess I am now."

Storm swats at him across the desk. "Oh, stop it. You're never around anymore, I need to get you when I can."

I nod, in complete agreement with Storm. "Well, she's kind of right, Savage. You've been spending more and more time at home with Dani, and I totally get it, but we do need to make these decisions."

The blue of his eyes turns icy, and he narrows them at me. "Fine. But don't either of you start giving me crap about spending more time with my pregnant wife."

"Whoa!" I lean forward and hold my hands up. "We weren't. It was just an observation. Right, Storm?"

She gives me a what-the-fuck-crawled-up-his-ass look and turns back to Savage. "Exactly. Seriously, Savage, do you really think I, of all people, would give you shit about something like that?"

Storm is a workaholic like Savage, and she has had to take conscious steps to ensure she arrives home at a reasonable hour and gets to spend quality time with Ben and Angelina. If she had her way, and didn't give a shit about her family, she would probably sleep in her office just so she could get a jump on work early the next day.

"No. I'm sorry. I'm just stressed out trying to get everything done here in less time than before. And I'm worried about Dani all the time. Let's do this." Savage leans over the plans, and I stand and join Storm on this side of the desk. "What's this?" He points to an area on the second floor section of the diagram.

Storm pulls it to the center of the desk and points to it again. "That's the private party dining room you wanted. It's the only major change since we looked at these last month."

Savage studies it for a moment.

Jesus, man, hurry the fuck up so I can get out of here and take care of my cock situation.

While the blood has, thankfully, mostly returned to the other appendages of my body, the ache has not abated. I know it won't until I've either rubbed one out or found a wet hole for it tonight.

With an exhausted sounding sigh, Savage shoves the plans back toward Storm. "This looks good. Did we decide what time we are meeting Ben at the build site tomorrow?"

I return to my seat, not at all wanting to think about our early morning plans. "Eight-thirty. We'll have to head straight there after the gym. And then we are meeting him Wednesday morning at the new club site."

"In that case, I'm heading home to Danika. Are you both heading out?"

Thank God he didn't bring up Bourbon Street again. This meeting is already taking longer than I have patience for. Storm rolls the plans up and tucks them under her arm. "Yeah, I'm just going to grab Skye and another drink, and then I'm taking off. Talk to you later."

I nod. "I'm leaving too."

After I spend a couple minutes finding some fucking relief.

SKYE

I don't know whether to be pissed or ecstatic when I see the very prominent bulge in the front of Gabe's jeans after I caught him staring at me.

Part of me wanted to crawl across the bar and jump on that thing while another part wanted to crawl across the bar and smack him for being such an ass. Those texts he sent me were way the fuck out of line. He can't reject me and then send me stuff like that; it's just fucking cruel.

If I hadn't seen him checking me out, I would have thought he was getting turned on watching "Cashmere" on the pole.

Not going to lie...Nora is fucking smoking hot on stage.

There's nothing sexier than a woman who's confident enough to shake her shit on stage and who's also smart enough to be a doctor. I still don't know why she dropped out of the pre-med program at Tulane. She's always a bit cagey when I ask her about it and brushes it off saying she wasn't smart enough. Which is bullshit. She's smarter than most of the doctors I know, and I've told her that. Maybe, someday, she'll believe it too and get out of here. I know Savage and Gabe treat her well, but she isn't meant for this. Even if she is damn amazing on that pole.

So. Fucking. Sexy.

She makes me second-guess my love for dick.

And Gabe.

Finishing my third drink, I survey the club and wish I wasn't stuck here waiting for Storm. I could always take a cab home, but then I'll have to deal with her bitching about why I didn't wait for her. Sometimes, she can really be a pain in my ass.

If I'd known she was coming to the club, I would have called a cab or tried to find another ride. I needed a ride and a drink, but what I definitely didn't need was to be in this close proximity to Gabe.

At this point, the booze coupled with the emotional and physical exhaustion of working, and what happened with Lucas, has left me dead on my feet. And knowing Savage, their meeting could take hours.

I yawn and motion for Byron to come over.

His eyes narrow on my empty glass, and there's obvious judgment there.

Yes, Byron, I like to drink. So fucking sue me.

"Hey, another?"

"No, just wanted to let you know, I'm going to head upstairs to find somewhere to lay down for a couple minutes while I wait for Storm. If she comes down, let her know where to find me."

"Gotcha. They should be in Savage's office, so you can probably use the couch in Gabe's."

Gee, wonderful.

I climb the stairs and duck into Gabe's office, not bothering to flip on the lights. The overwhelming need to just crash is dragging me straight to the couch on the far side of the room, perpendicular to his desk.

The soft leather cradles me, and I sink into it, dropping my head on the armrest. I close my eyes and take a deep breath.

Bad idea.

That familiar scent assaults my senses—Gabe. His unique

mix of musk and clean linen lingers in the air in here. It's like being surrounded by him.

This is the last fucking thing I want to deal with. I need to just close my eyes, even if it's only for ten minutes, before I can head home and crawl into my very lonely bed tonight.

I don't know how long I've been asleep when the door creaking open wakes me. Gabe's office is still dark, but his form is silhouetted in the light spilling in from the hallway.

He steps into the room and closes the door behind him before making his way over to his desk. The darkness swallows him until he opens the blinds on the windows behind him, letting in the faint glow of moonlight.

With an exhausted-sounding sigh, he lowers himself into his large leather chair, drops his head back, and closes his eyes. His profile is lit, and I watch him take a deep breath and run his hands back through his hair.

"Fuck..."

I freeze.

Shit.

Did he see me? Does he know I'm here?

My heart races, and I hold my breath. I don't know why I don't just announce my presence, but something tells me to keep quiet.

He growls and reaches down to his lap, which is trapped in the shadows. The familiar sound of a zipper going down breaks the silence of the room.

Oh, holy motherfucking shit.

He isn't...

He *is*.

A contented sigh slips from his lips followed by a muffled groan. I can just make out the rise and fall of his shoulder as he moves his arm.

Gabe Anderson is jerking off fifteen feet away from me, and he doesn't even know it.

Holy shit.

Warmth spreads through my core envisioning what's going on in those shadows, and I have to press my thighs together to ease the throb in my clit.

How the hell am I supposed to lie here silent when one of my biggest fantasies is happening right across the room?

Life is so unfair.

I want nothing more than to cross the room and drop to my knees in front of him. His hard cock would be fucking heaven in my mouth.

Damn.

There's no way I can remain still. The rush of blood to my clit needs to be answered.

Please, don't let the fucking leather creak.

I slip my hand down into my leggings and underwear. I drag my middle finger through the wetness pooling there and up around my clit, biting my lip to muffle the moan that threatens to make its way out.

Gabe groans and the leather of his chair makes the very noise I'm dreading will reveal me.

Stupid leather furniture.

Moving as quietly as I can, I swirl my finger around my wet clit while keeping my eyes locked on Gabe. His head is still tossed back, and my mouth waters imagining biting into the straining cords of his neck.

That man is my kryptonite.

His breathing picks up, his chest rising and falling rapidly. I increase my pace, pushing myself toward orgasm, not bothering to worry about what will happen once we both come.

"Oh, shit...Skye..."

My name falling from his lips is my undoing, and I come, biting the inside of my lip hard enough to draw blood to keep from crying out with my release. Pleasure courses through my body, and I struggle not to move on the couch.

The room is still and quiet as I come down, and my mind finally wraps around what just happened even as my heart continues to race and blood still rushes in my ears.

Holy shit. Gabe just jerked off and said my name as he came.

He grunts and reaches for something on his desk. I freeze. How am I going to get out of here without him seeing me?

His chair creaks as he stands with his back to me. The zipper of his pants breaks the silence of the room before he tosses something in the trash next to his desk. He turns to face the desktop. If he looks up right now, he will be staring directly at me. But he doesn't. With his palms pressed flat against the desk, he drops his head and releases a low growl.

The sound rolls through me like thunder. I can practically feel the frustration emanating off him in waves; it invades the still air in the room.

I know how he feels. I just don't understand what any of this means.

After a few moments of holding my breath and praying he doesn't flip on the lights, he lifts his head and pulls his hands from the desk. He shoves them back through his hair as he makes his way to the door.

It shuts behind him with a gentle click, leaving me even more confused by the mind fuck of a situation.

___

7

GABE

*W*hat's been happening between me and Skye— avoiding and dancing around each other, the lingering heated and dirty looks, not to mention what I did in the office last night—just cannot continue.

I actually jerked off at fucking work thinking about her. Who the fuck does that?

A desperate man.

That's what I've become. I'm so desperate to get her out of my head; I'm willing to do just about anything at this point. Even if it means finally admitting what happened and talking to her face to face about it.

It's better than doing nothing because sitting here across from Savage while remembering what I did last night just down the hall is hella unfuckingcomfortable. I can't even look my best friend in the eye.

"Everything looked good today, don't you think?"

I return my attention to Savage and nod. "Definitely. We

should be breaking ground on the restaurant right around the time the club location is finished." From one project to the next. Expansion of the Hawke brand is great for both of us, but the time it's taking to build multiple new locations at once is exhausting.

"We're still meeting with Ben at the new club tomorrow morning, aren't we?"

I nod. "Yeah, as far as I know. I'll text him to confirm." At least with Ben there, I'll have a buffer.

Savage leans back in his chair and tucks his hands behind his head. "What about Bourbon Street?"

"What about it?" I know what he's asking, but I don't really want to discuss it further. It's not going to change my mind.

His eyes narrow at me. "Why are you fighting this so hard? This could be an incredible opportunity for us. Prime locations like this don't come up every day."

"You're right, they don't. But it isn't the right move for us, not if you want to maintain the level of control we have here now."

Savage scoffs and drops his hands back to his lap. "That's bullshit. We can handle anything."

"You remember that fight that broke out here last year? Shit like that will be more commonplace in the French Quarter. We'll have more and more patrons coming in off the street who are wasted or on something and out of control. I don't want to deal with that, do you?"

His shoulders fall slightly, and he leans forward, placing his elbows on his desk. "Is there a potential for some complications there? Yes, I admit that, but don't you think it's worth the risk?"

"Savage, you know I love you, man. But, I've taken enough risks in my life, I really don't want to take one in business right now. I'm worn out just trying to handle what we already have going on. We have a *good* thing going. Let's revisit this once the other locations are up and running and we have a minute to breathe."

He eyes me, and I can almost see the wheels turning in his head, trying to process what I said and hold back his initial knee-jerk reaction. After a moment, he leans back again. "You're right. This probably isn't a good time. The baby will be here before I know it, and I'm not going to want to put in as much time here."

Thank fuck he saw the light. "Exactly. And I don't want to spend more time here than I already do."

"I get that. I also see what you're saying about the loss of control we might have down there. Maybe it's for the best if we avoid the French Quarter altogether. Now, if you don't mind, I'm going to head home for the night. Dani is feeling better, but she's still exhausted."

I climb from my chair and make my way toward the door. "Go."

Seeing Savage happy makes up for all the extra work and hours I end up spending here. Four years ago, I don't think either of us ever thought he'd be where he is now—happily married and expecting a baby.

I don't want that, never have, but knowing he did and now has it, makes me happy as shit for him. He deserves it after all he's been through. We all deserve to be happy, but he most of all. He and Skye. They lost the most. And while I know all of us struggle with Star's death, it weighs heavily on them in a way that's unfathomable.

Skye never would have kissed me if Star had been alive. I'm confident of that. But there's no point in considering what-ifs.

It happened. Now, we can't avoid dealing with the fallout anymore. We're practically family. We can't continue to hate each other.

Oh, come the fuck on...

My office smells like sex.

How is that even possible when I've never fucked anyone in here? The sticky evidence of last night's self-love was in a tissue at the bottom of my trashcan, but the trash was emptied this morning. So why does every breath I take in here bring to mind images of hot, sweaty, raunchy sex with Skye?

Because I am well and truly fucked.

It doesn't just smell like sex. Her vanilla and honey scent invades my lungs too, and my cock springs to attention.

This has to end.

Tonight's the night. I have to take action to end this or things will spiral out of control.

The nicotine demon is already back. Any more stress and I know what will happen—the nightmares will return with a vengeance, and I'll be right back in Doc's chair. I never want to need her or that again. Things are good—*were* good. I need to get them back there.

A knock on my door almost makes me jump. "Come in."

Dawn strolls in—all five foot three of her, plus another five inches of Lucite. She drops down into the chair opposite me, tugging the flowing satin nightgown tighter around her waist.

"I need to talk to you." She pulls her bottom lip between her teeth. "I think Renee is still in trouble."

My blood simmers, and I lean toward her, clenching my fists on the desk. "What makes you think that?"

Ever since her baby daddy showed up last week and caused a scene during her shift, I've been vigilant in making sure she's protected. She doesn't deserve to live in fear of that dickhead. And while I made it crystal clear for him not to come back, they always fucking do. They just can't seem to stay away.

"Because I'm pretty sure I saw his truck outside on my way in today."

Fucking idiot.

"Did Renee say anything to you?"

She shakes her head. "No, but I don't know if she even saw him. He was parked down the road a bit, probably because he knew if he drove into the parking lot, he would show up on the security cameras."

"How long ago did you see him?" If that fucker is stupid enough to come back, maybe he's stupid enough to sit out there waiting for me to come kick his ass.

With a shrug, she gets to her feet and makes her way to the door. "I don't know, maybe twenty minutes? Look, don't tell Renee I said anything. I just thought you should know."

I push away from my desk and stand. "You did the right thing, Dawn. I'll take care of it."

SKYE

I never thought I'd become my mother, but here I am, baking cookies at midnight because I'm stressed the fuck out and can't sleep. De-stressing in the kitchen was always her thing.

When I got off my shift tonight, the only thing I wanted was to crash and sleep for days, but reliving the look on Gabe's face, and my name coming from his mouth last night has kept me wide awake all night. Wide awake and horny as hell.

So, cookies.

And loud, pumping music. My neighbors probably hate me right now, but dancing around my kitchen helps me work off some of this tension and anger.

Fucking Gabe.

First, he kisses me, or at least, kisses me back. Then, he pushes me away and pretends nothing happened and there's nothing there between us. Then, he sends that message. And now, he fucking jerks off thinking about me. I mean...what the ever-loving fuck is that?

These are the nights I would give anything to have Star back. I need my sounding board, the one person who understands me without me having to say a word. Instead, I have angry rock music and chocolate chip cookie dough—half of which I've already eaten before anything is even baked yet.

I scoop the last remaining bit onto the cookie sheet and slide it into the oven.

The song ends and pounding on the door makes me jump. I never would have heard it if it weren't for the change in music.

It's 11:50 on a Tuesday night, who the hell would be here now?

Nobody good at midnight.

Two days ago, I would expect it to be Lucas, and I would welcome the opportunity for a couple orgasms and an escape from my own head. But I fucked that up royally, so there's no way it's him.

I grab my gun from the nightstand and make my way to the door. One glimpse through the peephole, and my heart actually stops.

Gabe.

What the hell is he doing here?

"Hold on a second." I take my gun back to its proper place before returning to the door. No sense tempting myself by having it available around the man who drives me insane. Then again, as long as there were enough women on that jury, I could probably be acquitted because it's clearly justifiable homicide at this point.

His sharp green eyes pierce me the moment I open the door. "We need to talk, Skye."

I lean against the door and pretend to be ambivalent. "At midnight?"

He scowls and steps closer to me. "Are you going to let me in, or what?"

My hesitance only lasts a moment before I remember what happened last night and decide it's worth hearing him out.

I hold the door open and usher him in, breathing in deeply as he passes.

Fuck...he smells amazing.

That familiar mingling of clean linen and deep musk fills my nostrils. I resist sighing.

The music is still blasting in the kitchen so I move past him to shut it off. When I turn around, he's leaning against the archway into the kitchen, appearing lost and, frankly, a little terrified. I've never seen Gabe scared before—not in the almost twenty years I've known him. The fact that he is now tightens my gut.

He glances down at his right hand and runs his left thumb over the split knuckles there.

"What happened to you?"

His head jerks up, and he drops his hands, almost as if he's embarrassed by my noticing. "Oh, nothing. Just had to take care of some business for one of the girls." He glances around the kitchen. "So, you're baking?"

Brilliant observation.

The flour all over the counter and the smell of baking cookies are a dead giveaway.

"Yeah, so what?" I lean back against the counter and grip the edge, trying for nonchalance when, in reality, my heart is racing and my hands shake. Having Gabe alone in my domain, knowing how much tension has been building between us since the wedding, has me as terrified as he looks.

"Well, it's midnight..."

I shrug. "No shit, Sherlock. Now, why are *you* here at midnight?"

He runs a hand back through his hair and averts his eyes momentarily before returning them to me. "Because we need to talk, Skye. We can't keep doing what we've been doing."

What, jerking off to each other?

I probably shouldn't mention that to him. If he knew I was in his office, things could get even weirder between us.

Instead of confessing what I witnessed last night, I bite my tongue and wait. He watches me. I don't know what he thinks I'm going to say. He's the one who showed up here; no way I'm saying anything until he spills whatever it is he came here to say.

I let the silence linger between us until it's uncomfortable. When his eyes narrow on me, I quirk an eyebrow and wait.

Ball is in your court, big guy.

His penetrating gaze rakes over me, from my face down my body. Everywhere he explores, my skin warms as if he were caressing it with his hand and not those expressive eyes. The way he strips me bare with just a look is unlike anything I've experienced before. And now, I'm just waiting for the bomb to drop that will surely destroy me.

8

GABE

*J*esus.

She must be trying to kill me wearing that. The tiny cotton shorts and loose tank leave nothing to the imagination. It's not like I haven't seen it before, and seen even more skin when she prances around in her bikinis, but something about seeing her casually dressed and comfortable like this gives me the chills and awakens my cock at the same time.

She's so fucking beautiful.

Tendrils of her dark hair have fallen out of her messy bun to frame her face, which has a white splotch of flour on the cheek. All I can think about is tugging that band out of her hair and burying my hands in it while I lick her face clean.

Skye quirks her eyebrow at me and crosses her arms over her chest, pushing her breasts up and out toward me.

Fuck me sideways.

I take a deep, cleansing breath and carefully consider my

words. It's too damn hard to think straight when she's looking at me like that, when *she* fucking looks like that. She's every man's wet dream, and I can't have her.

And isn't that a fucking bitch.

"Well?" She taps her bare foot impatiently, and the dark red paint on her nails is just another nail in my coffin. Absolutely everything about her is sexy, and my willpower is waning.

Where do I even start? I guess at the beginning.

"I did the right thing, Skye. We would have regretted it." The words leave my mouth, but I know they're a lie the moment I speak them. We might have hated the fallout from our actions, but us, together, could never be something to regret. I know that deep down, no matter how much I've been fighting it.

Her eyes spark with anger, and she shifts her weight to her other foot. "I wouldn't have regretted it."

"You were drunk, and on something, don't tell me you weren't."

She sighs and narrows her eyes at me. "I took a Xanax. It's not a big deal. I have a prescription, and I fucking needed it."

"I know that day was awful for you, being there without Star. We all felt it, but you were not in your right mind when you kissed me, Skye. I did the right thing by leaving."

The more I talk, the more I know I'm trying to convince myself more than her.

"I may have been drunk, but I knew *exactly* what I was doing, Gabe. And you know that."

Do I?

I try to think back to before the wedding, to how things were between us before the kiss that started all the shit. It's a haze, so many years of interactions blurring together but one thing stands out in striking contrast.

Well, one person. Savage.

My best friend.

My business partner.

My brother in every way but blood.

Which makes Skye my sister.

Remember that, Gabe.

"No, you didn't, Skye. What do you think would happen if we hooked up? What would Savage say? What would your mother say?"

Her cheeks flame, and she clenches her fists. "It's none of their fucking business what we do, Gabe. We are both adults. We have the right to be happy and, as much as you may try to deny it, we can make each other happy."

Happy is something I haven't been or even considered for so long, I can't even remember what it felt like. I left a huge part of me in the desert, a piece of my soul disappeared with every life I took, no matter how justified it may have been. And the shit with Abello last year only intensified my guilt. It was the right thing to do. I know that. His goons would have killed Dani without a second thought, and where would that have left Savage? Sacrificing my sanity for Dani's life and their happiness was well worth it. But no amount of sex or therapy has brought *me* happiness; it's beyond my reach. Skye should know that.

"What makes you so sure of that?"

Her eyes drop to the colorful linoleum, and she shifts as if she's uncomfortable under my stare. When she brings her gaze back up to meet mine, the stormy blue there breaks my heart. Skye has been tortured since Star's death—that much has been obvious—but now, knowing she thinks *I* am the way for her to find happiness and knowing I can't give her that, it shatters me.

"Because it's what I've wanted since I was sixteen. Because we know each other better than anyone. Because I've seen the way you look at me, and I know you want this too."

Shit. She isn't wrong.

I've always known she felt something for me, something

more, but hearing her say it, lay it all out there like she just did, is something else completely. Skye always plays it close to the vest when it comes to her feelings for people. She keeps everyone at arm's length and pushes away anyone who tries to get close with her singular brand of attitude and snark. When Star died, Skye essentially closed herself off. But she's not closed off now. She's wide fucking open to me, and I don't have it in me to lie to her. If nothing else, she deserves the truth.

"I won't lie to you, Skye. I haven't been able to stop thinking about you since the wedding, and it's been killing me to fight it."

A spark ignites in the depths of her hungry gaze, and she drops her arms to her sides. "Then don't. Don't stop thinking about me. Don't fight it anymore. I'm right here, and you know what I want."

"But what about—"

"No!" She takes a step toward me and holds up her palm, effectively silencing my protest. Challenge dances in her eyes. "None of that matters. What matters is you and me, right here, right now."

∽

SKYE

I watch him struggle—with the situation, with himself—and I wonder if I pushed too hard.

Christ, Skye, why can't you just take things slow instead of trying to force his hand.

Easing him in to the idea of an "us" would probably have been the better course of action. Because right now, he looks like he's ready to turn tail and run. If he does, I don't know what the fuck I'm going to do, because I can't go on seeing him and pretending there's nothing between us.

I may have to move.

Biting my bottom lip, I contemplate potential places to relocate.

I think Portland is supposed to be nice, and about as far from New Orleans as I can get.

Just when I'm about to abandon all hope, the look in his eyes flips in a second, from wary to something darker, more primal. He steps toward me, and I instinctively move back until my ass hits the counter.

Hunger.

That's what it is—hunger. He's the predator, and I'm his helpless prey.

His hands tunnel into my hair, and his lips are against mine before I can even say another word. He plunders my mouth— our tongues thrashing and ragged breaths mixing. This is Gabe unhinged, and boy, it is fucking beautiful.

My head spins with a thousand questions, but my body won't let me ask them. If I voice them, this will end, I know it will.

And I need this. I want this more than my next breath right now.

He presses me into the counter, and his hard cock meets my lower abdomen.

Damn this height difference.

With a frustrated groan, he drops his hands from my head to down under my ass and lifts me up onto the counter, aligning his cock in just the right place to rub exactly where I want him. I grind against him and bury my hands in his thick, blond hair, holding him in the perfect position for me to devour his mouth.

"Fuck..." he mumbles against my lips.

I chuckle and tug his bottom lip between my teeth playfully before pulling away to grin. "That's exactly what I was thinking."

It's like he's reading my mind.

His left hand slides up under my tank to grasp my breast. He pinches the nipple between his thumb and forefinger, sending a zing of pleasure straight to my clit. I gasp into his mouth and press my core against his dick, making it abundantly clear what I want.

"You sure?" The question comes out rough and on a ragged breath. He's hanging on to any restraint he has left by a thread, just like I am.

"Please don't make me beg, Gabe, not now."

When his lips find mine again, it's with a barely-contained hunger. My body hums in anticipation, and he slips his free hand up my shorts. I'm always wet when I think about him, but having him here, about to get what I've wanted for over a decade, has me absolutely drenching his fingers.

He pushes two into me.

Fuck yes!

I squeeze down around him, and he breaks away from our kiss and leans forward to groan into my ear. "Christ, you're so fucking wet."

He has no idea how many nights I've spent dreaming of this moment and imagining all the things he would do to me. I've made myself come more times than I can count thinking of his face, his touch, and his cock.

Fantasy be damned, the real thing is so much better.

His thumb slides up and presses against my clit, causing my hips to buck up of their own volition and pushing his fingers deeper inside of me.

"Jesus, Gabe..."

A slow, torturous swirl around my clit has me grinding my teeth together and biting back another curse. He tugs at my nipple and thrusts his tongue into my mouth all in time with his fingers. I'm spinning into orbit, and I haven't even gotten my hands on him yet.

I need to touch him.

All I can think about is that goddamn nipple ring and how much I want to tug and bite it. My hands tingle, and my mouth waters just thinking about it. And now, I can actually act on the desire I've built up for years.

With a brush of my hand, I lift his shirt, and my palm finds the warm expanse of his abs. He shivers and flexes under my touch. The rippling of the tight muscles there is testament to how hard he works to stay in shape, and it leaves no doubt in my mind that he will work just as hard at sex.

Shifting my hand up, I search for the object of my exploration. When my fingers find the metal ring in his left nipple, I can't suppress my grin and have to break away from our kiss. I tug on it and revel in the widening of his eyes and the gasp that escapes him.

A sly smirk spreads across his lips, and he growls—actually fucking growls—before taking my mouth again.

I can't wait any longer. His hot skin under my touch and his ministrations are just too much.

Cock. Now.

I reach down and unbutton his jeans before lowering the zipper. His hot mouth on my neck as he kisses his way up to my ear makes my breath stutter. He bites and tugs at my lobe, and when my hand finally grasps the base of his cock, he groans in my ear and a litany of curses fall from his lips.

"Jesus fucking Christ, Skye. Just...fuck..."

I revel in his hard flesh in my hand and tug on it to liberate it from his jeans completely. His cock springs free and a heavenly chorus of angels sings the hallelujah chorus. But when my palm finally contacts the head of his dick, I freeze.

9

GABE

*S*he stills with her hand around my cock, and I jerk my head back from exploring that spot behind her ear to search her face for an explanation.

Maybe she changed her mind and came to her senses.

Wide eyes meet mine, and her jaw drops open. "You have your fucking cock pierced?"

I hadn't considered her reaction to my apadravya piercing. I'm used to women commenting on it, but I figured Skye would have heard about it by now, considering how many women have seen and experienced it. She has to have crossed paths with at least one of them over the years.

They all assume I did it for some altruistic reason—so sex would be more pleasurable for them—or even so it would be more pleasurable for me. But, they couldn't be more wrong.

I did it for the same reason I'm inked on half my body—the pain. Pain is the only way I know to quiet my mind. I'm forced to focus on my body instead of always being in my head, surrounded by the guilt and second-guessing. When I ache is the only time my brain shuts off and everything becomes peaceful. I figured there couldn't be much more painful than having a metal rod shoved through the head of my cock, and I was right. It hurt like a motherfucker for a while, but that faded all too quickly. The fact that it feels fucking incredible now when I'm inside a woman—for both of us—is just a happy side-effect.

A grin is the only response I can muster because there's no way in hell I'm telling her the real reason it's there. That's a conversation I've only ever had with Doc Cochran, and that shit stays in her office.

Where I'm probably going to end up again if I go through with this.

Skye swirls her palm around the head of my cock, shifting the piercing through the hard flesh and it twitches in response.

It feels like I've waited forever for this moment with her. I should be doing this somewhere else—a bed, a couch, a fucking chair—anywhere but her goddamn kitchen counter with the smell of baking cookies lingering in the air. But I can't wait any longer.

She doesn't let me second-guess myself long. She leans back and releases my cock so she can pull her tank-top off over her head. Her breasts bounce free, directly in front of my face, and I'm hypnotized by their perfection.

Jesus H. Christ.

I lean forward and catch one pale pink nipple in my mouth. Moaning, she tugs at my arm. My fingers are still buried inside her, and I realize she wants me to take them out.

The moment my hand is free of her body, she shoves at the waistband of her shorts. I struggle to retain suction on her nipple as she slips them off and lets them drop to the floor.

She grasps my head, tugging on my hair to move me away from her chest.

I start to step back so I can get out of my jeans, but she wraps her legs around my waist and tugs me in closer, regaining her hold on my cock.

Her small hand barely wraps around me.

Shit, what if I hurt her?

She uses her feet to push my jeans down until they're at my ankles and the tails of my button-down shirt dangle around my cock and her arm. I don't even have time to think about taking it off before she's rubbing the head of my dick through her wetness.

Sweet mother of...

Crap, condom.

"Skye...condom..."

Her head jerks up, and she watches me, waiting for me to act.

Jesus, the one fucking time I don't have one in my wallet. "I don't have one, I didn't come here expecting this."

She searches the kitchen frantically and points to her purse on the counter several feet over from where we are twined together.

I reach over and grab it, dumping the contents next to us.

No time to be gentle about it.

The familiar gold package sits in the middle of the pile.

Don't think about why she has it, Gabe, just be thankful.

I tear at the foil and slide it on in record time. My hands return to her, grasping her hips and jerking her to the edge of the counter.

My cock throbs harder than I imagined possible. I lock eyes with her and gently push just the head into her.

She whimpers and bites her lip, then shifts forward, fully impaling herself on me in one swift motion.

"Fuck, you're so fucking tight." I grit my teeth when my body screams for me to pull back and pound into her. "Don't want to hurt you."

She flexes her pussy around me. "You won't."

No further urging is needed. On a slow glide, I pull out until just the tip is inside her and then I push forward, bottoming out deep in her core.

Skye cries out, and I slant my mouth over hers and kiss her, sliding my tongue along hers in time with the thrusting of my hips. Her hot, wet, tight channel clasps my cock, and I clench my eyes shut to concentrate on not coming.

Her hips slam against mine, and her bare feet dig into my lower back, urging me forward with more force on each stroke.

A thud has me opening my eyes. I find her with her head dropped back against the cabinet, her mouth hanging open, and her breath is nothing more than heavy panting.

The angle has the head of my cock pushing straight against the hot wall of her pussy and the tug on my piercing along her inner walls has me gritting my teeth again.

"Oh, fuck, Gabe..."

I zero in on where our bodies connect.

Fuck...bad idea.

Watching my cock disappear inside of her with every thrust does nothing to help my struggle to hold back my orgasm. But I refuse to come before she does.

I've waited for this for too long to be a douche canoe who only cares about himself.

I slide my hand over to where we meet and rub my thumb over her clit. She bucks on my cock, and her head falls forward.

Her glazed eyes meet mine, and though I'm sure I'm going to hell for this, at least I'll go happy.

A high-pitched buzzing tears her eyes from me and over to the corner of the kitchen.

∾

SKYE

"Shit...the cookies." I can't believe I forgot they're in the oven.

Gabe growls and uses his free hand to turn my face back to him. "Fuck the cookies." His eyes darken and bore into mine, and he thrusts up into me so hard, my head slams back against the cabinets.

There's no question about what's going to happen here. His cock inside me outweighs the potential for any lost sweets.

"Yes...fuck...the...cookies."

And just keep fucking me.

He resumes the punishing tempo, and I bite my lip to keep from releasing a scream I know would make the neighbors come running.

His hand expertly works my clit while his cock stretches me, that damn piercing pulling, tugging, pressing in all the right places.

I always knew it would be good with Gabe, but I never expected it to be this earth-shattering, and I haven't even come yet.

My legs quiver, and I dig my heels into his back, urging him to come closer, push deeper. He yanks my head down so he can kiss me again, and I bury my hands in his hair, wanting to keep him tied to me in every way possible.

The unmistakable smell of something burning hits my nose, but I can't manage to care when my entire body is vibrating and heat is spreading out from my core.

"Jesus, Gabe, I'm gonna come." I grunt out the words against his lips, and he somehow manages to increase the tempo with his cock and his thumb against my clit.

The fingers on his left hand dig into my hip, and I drive against him harder, faster, racing toward the orgasm I can feel just on the horizon.

He pulls my bottom lip between his teeth and groans, biting down when I clench myself around his dick even tighter.

My head spins. The room swirls around us.

With one last deep thrust and a tug on my clit, I come, releasing twelve years of pent-up need and desire for the man with his cock buried deeply inside me. Gabe grunts, and his rhythm falters before he follows me over the edge, screaming my name into my mouth.

Our sweat-slicked foreheads press together and our panting breaths mingle. Stillness surrounds us, but the blaring sound of the smoke detector breaks me from the reverie.

"Shit, shit, shit!" I pull my face away from his reluctantly and lick my swollen lips. The familiar metallic tang of blood surprises me. I hadn't even realized he bit me that hard.

All I felt was bliss.

His eyes twinkle with amusement, and he playfully squeezes my still-quivering thighs and tosses his head toward the oven. "You should probably take care of that, huh?"

I nod and grin at him. "I'll get the cookies, you get the smoke detector."

We both groan when he pulls out of me. I instantly miss his cock filling me and his heat warming me.

He holds out a hand, and I take it, letting him assist me off the counter. When my feet hit the floor, I wobble and cling to him to keep from falling over.

Amusement sparks in his eyes again, and he gives me a second to right myself.

Turning my back on him to attend to the cookies is difficult. There's a good chance he will bolt once he reaches the smoke detector near the front door; it's the perfect escape route.

Don't disappear on me, Gabe.

My heart can't take it.

I don my oven mitts and open the oven, letting thick, black smoke pour out.

"Shit." I frantically wave my arms, trying to disperse the smoke. Out of the corner of my eye, I see Gabe toss the used condom in the trash and disappear around the corner toward the front hall.

The cookies are nothing more than charred, black blobs on the baking sheets.

It was worth it.

The screaming siren of the smoke detector cuts off sharply, and I pause with the last sheet in my hands and focus on the door to the kitchen.

Please come back. Please come back. Please come...

When he reappears around the corner with a battery in his hand and a wicked smile, my heart soars.

His pants hang low off his hips, the zipper still down and button unhooked. He follows my eyes and chuckles, reaching for his crotch.

I drop the sheet tray onto the counter with a bang, and his head snaps up.

"No. Don't bother. You'll be losing those in a minute."

10

SKYE

*T*hat bitch named morning comes all too fast, and my alarm blares on my nightstand. I reach over without opening my eyes and slam my palm down on the snooze button before burying my face further into my pillow for another moment of peace.

The covers are nowhere to be found, making my plan to ignore life and go back to bed less enjoyable. I roll onto my side and open my eyes to an empty, cold bed.

He fucking left.

My heart sinks, and I almost curse him before the closed bathroom door and tell-tale sound of the shower running hits me. I inspect the room and see his jeans and shirt tossed haphazardly on the floor where he dropped them before we climbed into bed for rounds two, three, and four last night and this morning.

The dull ache between my thighs and my nakedness

remind me of just how fucking amazing he is before a twinge of jealousy hits thinking about *how* he got that good.

Buzzing on my nightstand pulls me away from becoming the green-eyed monster, and I reach behind me to grab my phone.

I roll onto my back and close my eyes, bringing the phone to my ear. "Hello?"

"Skye? Why are you answering Gabe's phone?"

My eyes fly open just as the bathroom door does.

Gabe appears in the doorway—water dripping down his tattooed, muscled torso and over that damn V thing that turns women to mush, to the tiny towel wrapped around his waist, barely hiding what I know is underneath.

He grins at me, and his eyes roam my body appreciatively. "Good morning. I hope I didn't—"

I cover the phone and hiss, then mouth "Savage" to him.

His eyebrows shoot up, and he approaches the bed.

"Oh, hi, Savage. I'm not sure how I ended up with Gabe's phone. I must have accidently grabbed it at the club last night when I stopped for a drink."

All the color drains from Gabe's face, and his body goes rigid. He stands by the side of the bed looking like his mom just caught him jerking off.

I climb up onto my knees and crawl across the bed to him.

"When did you come to the club? I left early, but I didn't think Gabe was going to stay late."

Shit.

"Uh, it was later, I don't remember what time."

"It's unfortunate you grabbed the wrong phone because I need to speak with him..."

I'm only half-listening to Savage; it's hard to pay attention to anything when Gabe's glistening body is on display right in front of me.

A drop of water trickles from his shoulder down over his

left pec, and I lean forward, catching it with my tongue and following the path up to suck on his shoulder blade. Having to see the fading hickey some other woman left on him isn't exactly pleasant, but I can't be too pissed about it, considering I haven't exactly been a nun.

It's time for me to stake my claim and leave my own marks on him.

Gabe shudders, and his body tenses. Warm, strong hands grab my shoulders and unsuccessfully try to push me away.

Oh, no you don't.

I've fantasized for years about mapping his tattoos and body with my tongue, and we didn't pause long enough last time for me to indulge.

"...he was supposed to meet me half an hour ago."

"Hmm..." I hum against Gabe's pec, slowly licking and nipping my way closer to his nipple. "You could try to call him on my phone. Hopefully he grabbed it thinking it was his."

I glance up through my lashes and find Gabe eyeing me warily, not looking amused in the least by my explorations.

He needs to chill and have a sense of humor about this.

"Good idea, Skye, I'll try that. Thanks." The line goes dead, and I wrap my tongue around Gabe's nipple ring and tug it between my teeth. He gasps and digs his fingers into my hair.

"Seriously, Skye...while you're on the phone with your brother?"

I chuckle against his skin and tug his nipple sharply. A hiss escapes his lips, and he yanks my head back, attempting to dislodge me from his sensitive skin.

The tiny towel wrapped around his hips can't hide his body's response to me, and I grin in victory.

As much fun as I'm having, I relent when I hear the buzzing of another phone. I turn toward the sound and realize my phone must have fallen between the bed and nightstand last night.

With an awkward lunge across the bed, I reach down and grab it and toss it to Gabe.

"Hello?" He turns his muscular, tattooed back to me when he answers, and I can't contain my chuckle.

I can't believe he's so worried. This is hilarious. Gabe needs to lighten up, and I know just what to do.

Try to ignore this.

"Yeah, we must have switched phones, I'll be there in like, half an hour."

I relax back against the pillows and spread my legs open, angling myself toward where Gabe stands.

The soreness I still feel from last night's aerobics doesn't deter me from my mission. I need to lick every single drop of remaining water off that man, and then, I am getting fucked this morning, and Gabe is going to forget about his concerns over Savage.

～

GABE

Savage is pissed, and I don't blame him. I not only blew off the gym, I also completely forgot about our meeting this morning at the build site.

Fucking shit.

As if it's not bad enough I fucked his little sister last night, I also blew him off this morning. "All right, Savage. Yeah, okay, like I said, I can be there in a half hour..."

I turn to search for my jeans and freeze. My already-hard cock jumps and strains against the loose confines of the towel.

Skye is spread eagle across the bed with her fingers buried inside her glistening pussy.

Oh, sweet fuck...

How the hell am I supposed to leave when she's doing that?

"Uh, Savage? Make that more like an hour. I'm going to drop by Skye's to grab my phone so I don't have to deal with her friends texting me chick shit every five minutes."

I end the call before he can respond and set the phone on the nightstand. Skye gives me a sultry, knowing look and pulls her fingers from inside her to rub them around her clit.

Premature ejaculation hasn't been this close to reality since I was fourteen. Placing my knee on the bed, I shake my head and scowl at Skye. "You are fucking evil, woman."

She shakes her head and sits up, shifting to her knees until she's face to face with me. Her hand tugs on the towel lightly, and it falls, letting my erection spring free between us.

The look of satisfaction in her eyes sends a flurry of emotions through me—anger, fear, regret, pride, contentment, lust...and something else I can't quite put my finger on.

Her tongue hits my skin again and, *sweet fuck*, she licks off each remaining drop of water—one at a time—roaming over my body with precise movements designed to drive me fucking insane.

I grasp her shoulders and try to bring her away from my body, but just like before, she resists me and works her way lower, toward my throbbing cock.

Last night was hard, fast, and hot as fuck, all three...no, four times. We didn't take the time to breathe let alone for foreplay. The mere thought of where her mouth might be headed has my knees practically buckling.

She glances up at me when she reaches the appendage in question, and I watch, rapt, as she slides her tongue along the entire length, from root to tip, in one long, slow lick.

*Sweet mother of all that's holy...*I shift my hands into her hair and try to keep from guiding her mouth over the head of my cock and jamming it down her throat like I so desperately want to.

Let her do it.

Her pink tongue flicks out, lapping up the bead of precum that's been hovering there since she put her mouth on me.

Without further preamble, she slides the head through her plump lips and sucks me down.

Animalistic sounds wrench from deep in my throat, and my fingers tighten in her hair.

The heat of her mouth suctioned around my cock is indescribable. I won't last long, and there's no way I'm coming before her.

No fucking way.

I tug on her hair until I jerk her off my cock. She assesses me with confusion and lust clouding the blue of her eyes.

"What's wrong?" Her tongue slides out across her wet lips, and I can't help myself, I lunge at her, knocking her back on the bed.

She laughs and grabs my waist, but I kiss her quickly and then pull back off her.

"What are you doing? You can't leave like that!"

I glance down at my straining cock and back at her with a grin. "I wasn't planning on it, but you do *not* get to have all the fun."

Her eyes widen, and I grasp her ankles and jerk her to the edge of the bed. I drop down to my knees and bury my face between her legs, not bothering with any of the torturous teasing she put me through.

I'm not that mean.

My first taste of her is everything I've dreamt it would be and more. My tongue searches her body, seeking the exact spot that will drive her insane right away. She bucks against me, grinding her pussy against my face. I slip two fingers inside her easily—she's already dripping wet—and curl them upward into her flesh.

"Gabe, please..."

She begs and squirms and pants as I probe and search until

I finally settle over her clit, sucking it between my lips with a growl.

Her thighs tense around my head, and I know her release is imminent. I increase the pressure, flicking my tongue over the tiny nub until she screams my name and arches toward the heavens.

I've never seen anything so beautiful.

Fucking perfect.

When she finally collapses back onto the bed, I pull away and sit back on my haunches. A moment later, her eyelids flutter open, and her gaze finds mine.

"Well, fuck."

Her words are absolutely perfect. There's no other way to sum up the situation.

What the fuck do we do now?

My aching cock tells me what needs to happen first, so I climb up on the bed and into her arms.

11

GABE

Savage tosses me the tenth dirty look since I arrived very late this morning. I do my best to ignore it. Instead, I try to concentrate on what Ben is telling us about the status of the construction on the location for the next Hawkeye Club.

But I can feel his eyes on me.

I want a cigarette.

Badly.

My hand automatically moves to my pocket and searches for my lighter even though it hasn't been there for over six months.

Like I don't already feel guilty enough without having Savage give me the stare-down. I swear, it's like he can read people with one look sometimes.

"Gabe?"

"Huh?" I hadn't even realized Ben said anything to me.

"I asked if you want to come in and check out the second floor. The elevator hasn't been installed yet."

He doesn't have to say the rest.

My chest tightens, and my guilt increases three-fold. I know I shouldn't feel bad for him. Savage's rebounded from the accident, and his life is amazing now. He has Danika and soon, the baby. He has everything he's ever wanted. But still, the constant reminders of his very real limitations have to be a slap to the face.

"Yeah, I'll come up." I turn to Savage and make direct eye contact for the first time since I arrived. "I'll take pictures for you to look at."

He nods but doesn't speak, and his blue eyes—eyes that are all too similar to the ones I stared into while I fucked his sister last night, and this morning—tell me we will be having a conversation later whether I like it or not.

Wonderful.

I stall inside for as long as I can, asking Ben every mundane question about the status of the build. This location will be slightly different from the original Hawkeye Club. Instead of housing offices on the second floor, there will be additional smaller stages with multiple champagne rooms so we can accommodate more large parties and special requests. This should help us avoid any of the issues we have at the main club with space availability, and we won't ever have to turn anyone away.

By the time I make it back outside, Savage has already left, and I'm given a brief reprieve.

Thank God.

On the way to the club, against my better judgment and with my conscience screaming at me, I stop and buy a pack of smokes.

I use the back stairs instead of the elevator, so I won't have to walk past Savage's office, and high-tail it to my office, closing and locking the door the moment I step inside.

The lighter is sitting exactly where I left it, tucked behind my stapler and boxes of miscellaneous office supplies. There's less temptation that way.

I pause before I pick it up, the last time I held it running through my mind. It was a couple months after Savage and Danika got married. I had started seeing Doc again—to deal with the swirling mess of shit going on in my head after killing Abello's men and kissing Skye—and one of my goals was to kick the nasty habit...again.

My hands start shaking, and I drop down into my chair and scrub my hands over my face. I knew it would be bad, the internal ramifications for my actions, but I didn't expect for it to go that far. I never expected to need Doc again.

The first time I saw her, after my final deployment, I didn't want to admit I had PTSD. None of us do, but I had reached a point where I saw my life spiraling out of control and knew I had to do something. The nightmares, anxiety, and all-around unease I constantly felt were too much to ignore. And she helped, she really did. Otherwise, I never would have sent Savage to her.

And she helped this last time, too. Sort of. It's hard for me to blame her for my continuing issues when I didn't come completely clean about what had been bothering me. Leaving out the kiss with Skye and my feelings for her was probably a bad move. But at least I managed to be able to sleep at night again, and kick the cigs, until now.

This situation with Skye is out of control, and it's only been twelve hours.

I never should have gone over there last night.

Taking the lighter in my hand, flashes of another beautiful Hawke girl appear and tears well in my eyes. I trace my thumb over the star etched into the lighter case.

She gave it to me before my second deployment, after I had picked up the habit on my first. I still vividly remember what she told me when she placed it in my hand. *"You know you shouldn't be smoking, Gabe. But I know you'll do it anyway, so, here...at least when you look at it and are reminded of me, maybe it will make you think twice before lighting up."*

She was right. I did think twice; I just continued to do it.

Fuck.

If she were here, things would be so different...with Skye, with Savage, with all the Hawkes. I wouldn't be sitting here kicking myself and ready to light up again.

What would she think of me and Skye?

I bark out a laugh and dump a stick from the pack. The lighter flicks to life just like it always has, and as I light up, I can't help but wonder if this is the start of another uncontrolled descent—for both me and Skye.

∾

SKYE

I stare at my phone, willing it to ring, or buzz, just make any fucking noise. Gabe hasn't called, and I refuse to be "that girl" and contact him first.

Stay strong, Skye.

Savage could have busted us this morning, that snafu with the phones was a big one. Maybe Gabe is still at work and can't get away from prying ears. Or maybe he's down on the club level and couldn't hear anyway. Or maybe he's off somewhere with someone else.

No. Stop.

The phone in my office rings, and I groan.

Wrong fucking phone.

With only an hour left on my shift, I have prayed it would remain quiet, and I can get out of here on time.

I'm exhausted from the lack of sleep and extra physical exertion last night...and this morning. I press my thighs together against the tingle brought on by the memories and answer the phone.

"Hey Skye, it's Pam down in the ER. Would you be able to come down for a few minutes? We have one of your patients down here. Minor car accident, nothing major, but he's asking for you."

"Who is it?"

"Maurice Mendenhall."

That poor old man. He's one of my favorite patients. An eighty-year-old widower, he's quick with a joke and sometimes an inappropriate butt squeeze when you walk by. He doesn't have any family, so I'm sure being alone in the ER is difficult for him.

"I'll be right down."

The hallway is quiet, and my shoes squeak on the tile as I make my way across the skywalk. A quick elevator ride down releases me on the first floor, and I head toward the ER.

A hand wraps around my upper arm, and I'm yanked into a supply closet before I can even process what's happening.

"What the hell?"

I whirl around to see who is dumb enough to nab me like that. Lucas presses against my shoulders, backing me up against the door he just pulled me through. He descends on me, slamming his mouth into mine before I can protest.

The kiss is dark and possessive. I press against his chest, and eventually, he backs away with a grin on his face.

"Seriously, what the hell, Lucas?" I smack his upper arm. "Are you fucking insane?"

His brow wrinkles, and his grin disappears as quickly as it appeared.

Jesus, he actually looks confused about why I'm angry.

"Sorry, I just wanted you to know that I forgive you, for what happened, and to tell you I miss you."

I cross my arms over my chest and consider his words. He seems genuine in both his apology for what he just did and in his forgiveness of my major *faux pas*. At least with Lucas, things were always straightforward. I can fuck him without worrying about reprisals from my brother.

Life would be easier with Lucas, and he's willing to forgive me for something that's basically unforgiveable. Gabe can't even bother to call me.

Maybe I owe Lucas another chance?

"Look, Lucas, I just need some time to think."

Not really.

Who the fuck do I think I'm kidding? Gabe will always win. *Always.*

His eyes narrow, and his nostrils flare. "Time to think? What's there to think about?"

"I just have a lot going on right now, that's all. This isn't a good time for me to be trying to split my attentions between my job, my family, and..."

Shit.

What do I call him? He was never my boyfriend. Fuck buddy?

"And what? And me?" He throws his hands up in the air and paces in front of me. "Jesus, Skye, four months. Four fucking months...did you ever feel anything for me at all?"

I don't know, did I?

Of course I care about Lucas. We were good together. Maybe not great, but good. It was calm and easy. And I can't say the sex wasn't great.

But that's all it ever was for me, and I thought we had an understanding about that.

"Lucas, of course I care about you. I've really enjoyed our time together—"

"Care about me? Enjoyed our time together? Are you fucking serious right now? Could you be any more patronizing?"

He moves toward me, making me duck instinctively, but he pushes past me, yanks on the handle, and disappears out the door.

What. The. Fuck. Was. That?

I don't have the energy to worry about Lucas's hurt feelings. I was upfront with him about what we were, and weren't. If he let his feelings run away with him, that's on him, not me.

There's enough stress in my life without having him pining away for me. Hopefully, I made myself clear.

Now, if I can only make sure things with Gabe are clear.

12

GABE

*T*he cold emptiness of my bed feels awful tonight. All I can think about is Skye's warmth wrapped around me in every way possible last night and how incredible it felt.

That damn clock on my nightstand reads 10:30. I can't remember the last time I was in bed this early, but I was utterly useless at everything else I tried to do. Avoiding Savage all day zapped my energy and bed felt like a great idea. After I smoked more cigarettes than I care to admit, I climbed between the sheets hoping the stress of the day, a little booze, and some Nyquil would let me drift off peacefully.

Yeah, not so much.

Skye finally texted me two hours ago, telling me we need to talk.

Talk.

Like talking will solve anything?

We both know we won't end up "talking" if we meet up, and that's the problem. Last night was a mistake. I never should have put myself in that situation or let her tempt me to stray from my purpose. I intended to smooth things over, not dig myself into a deeper hole. I've been breaking out into cold sweats, and my chest has been tight all fucking day.

Dodging Savage's inquisition and my physical break down are proof of how wrong it really was. If it weren't, I wouldn't be so terrified of him finding out and my body wouldn't be screaming at me to get the fuck out of the situation.

When will this fucking Nyquil kick in?

Mixed with the glass of whiskey I had before climbing under the covers, I was sure I would pass out immediately.

I close my eyes and try to think of anything but Skye. The construction...*yeah*...the construction is going well. We should have the new location up and operational in six months, tops. The gym...things are going well there...I've upped my deadlift max to 550 pounds. Killin' it in the gains department...

A door slamming jolts me from my almost-asleep state.

My hand automatically moves to the back of the headboard where I have my 1911 mounted. I tighten my fingers around the grip and slip out of bed silently, my heart beating wildly.

Bam.

Crash.

Someone bumped into something in the living room.

That was probably my bottle of Balvenie hitting the wood floor.

Son of a bitch!

The hallway is pitch black, but the light coming from the floor to ceiling windows in the living room illuminates a figure leaning against the couch and bending down toward the floor.

A very familiar figure—with wavy hair and curves for days.

I lower my gun and flip on the lights, earning a squeal of displeasure from the intruder. "Fuck, that's bright!"

"Are you fucking insane, Skye? I could have killed you!"

She glances up at me from behind a wall of dark hair and

finishes removing her other heel, letting it drop to the hard-wood floor with a thud next to its partner.

"You wouldn't have shot me. You're too controlled for that, and you would never shoot before knowing what or who you were shooting at."

My knuckles whiten around the grip. "Stay here. Don't fucking move."

I retreat to my bedroom, absolutely fuming. I need to calm the fuck down and collect myself. My hand shakes as I return my gun to the back of the headboard.

How can she be so fucking stupid?

My instincts and training make me a walking reaper...an angel of fucking death. And while she's right, I wouldn't shoot without knowing my target...that assumes I'm thinking clearly. I have been thinking anything *but* clearly the last couple days.

If I'd been in the middle of one of my nightmares when she came in, who the hell knows what I could have done.

A shudder rolls through my body. My chest tightens around my racing heart, making it almost impossible to take a deep breath.

I grip the headboard with one hand to steady myself. The last time I had one of the dreams, my own screams woke me, and I was standing in the middle of my living room with my gun in my hand, pointing it at nothing.

That could have been Skye.

A rolling stomach joins my body's revolt. "Fuck..."

Get your shit together.

Everything is fine.

I tell myself that. Over and over and over again, but it does nothing to stop the full-body meltdown.

Breathe.

After another minute, the vise around my chest relaxes, and I'm able to take a few deep breaths. I grab the half-empty bottle of water from my nightstand and down it before gathering myself together to face Skye.

When I return to living room, she's still leaning against the couch, but now, her eyes are focused out the windows toward the water.

"Skye, what the fuck are you doing here?"

Her eyes drift over me, and I'm suddenly very aware I'm wearing nothing but my boxer-briefs. She devours me with her gaze, her eyes lingering over my crotch long enough to make my cock jump to attention.

Shit.

"Seriously, Skye...why are you here?"

"We need to talk." She's been drinking. I can hear it in the slight slurring of her speech and see it in her bloodshot eyes. Although, I guess that could be from lack of sleep last night, too. Mine might be just as bad for all I know. I've avoided looking at myself in the mirror all day.

"Are you drunk?"

Her pink, tempting lips quirk up into an adorable little smirk. "No, just a little tipsy. Had a couple drinks with someone from work."

The twinge of pain in my chest wondering if that someone was a man or a woman makes me take a step back. I can't let myself think like that. She's not mine.

"I'm calling you a cab. You didn't drive here, did you?"

Those expressive eyes sharpen with concern. "Of course not, I'm not that fucking stupid, Gabe. You really think I would drink and drive after what happened to Star and Savage?"

No. She wouldn't. We all lost so much that day.

"And you aren't sending me home. We're going to talk. Now."

Her eyes spark with determination, but I know we won't get anywhere talking tonight. Not when I am so on edge, and she's a couple drinks in. "This really isn't the time, Skye."

She scoffs and takes a step toward me. "There will never be a good time, because you keep running away from what's happening, from what you're feeling. You think it will just go away if you ignore it. Or maybe you thought you could fuck me out of your system?"

SKYE

He recoils at my words, and a slight frown turns his lips down. The defensive posture he took relaxes, and he drops his arms to his sides instead of crossing them over his chest.

Good.

I knew that wasn't what he was doing, but I needed to make sure *he* knew that too.

There's no other way I can think of to make him see what's right in front of him, what's *been* right in front of him for years.

I approach him, and I'm not cautious about it. I don't give him any time to think.

Thinking is bad.

I press my hands to his bare chest—one over his heart and that goddamn nipple ring and one on his other pec. The racing thud of his heartbeat against my palm fills me with hope.

He can't deny what's happening here any more than I can. His hot skin tenses and ripples under my touch.

"Look me in the eye, Gabe, and tell me you don't want this."

His hooded gaze darkens but never leaves mine.

War.

That's what I see there, but below the belt, things are much clearer. His cock presses against me, and I push into him, rubbing my stomach against it to prove my point.

Let's see him say no now.

Rising up on my tiptoes, I run my tongue across his lips. His body vibrates with restrained need.

I whisper against his lips, "Let it go, Gabe."

After a moment of hesitation, he groans and wraps his arms around me, crushing me against him and plunging his tongue into my willing mouth. The warm, spicy tang of the whiskey he must have drunk before I got here mingles with the taste that is all Gabe, making my mouth water. I tangle my tongue with his, craving more, needing to drown in his flavor.

His hands drop to my hips and dig into my flesh. He doesn't even need to say the words for me to know what he wants. I jump up and wrap my legs around his waist, pinning his cock between our bodies. With a small shift, I align him in the perfect position. He groans into my mouth.

God, that's incredible.

He tightens his hold on me, sliding his hands down under my ass as he moves down the hallway toward his bedroom.

Gabe's. Fucking. Bedroom.

I'm headed for the promised land.

Finally. After twelve fucking years.

With every step he takes, his erection grinds into my clit, eliciting moans from me every single time. By the time we reach his room, my pants and his boxers will be soaked. But our progress stops.

I jerk away from his mouth.

"No. Don't stop."

His eyes drop to my lips, and he grins. "I couldn't even if it tried."

He turns and slams my back into the hallway wall. His lips crush to mine, and he grinds his cock against me. I drop my head back against the wall, close my eyes and tighten my grip on him with my legs. He isn't getting away from me.

I don't care if we make it to the bedroom. The promised land can wait. I can't. I need him inside me. I need him to make me forget everything that's fucked up in the world and in my life. I need for there to just be us.

A low rumble in Gabe's chest vibrates against mine, and my already hard nipples ache for his touch. His tongue slides over mine, then slowly retreats, stopping to swipe along my lips.

I open my eyes and find him staring at me—his normally light emerald eyes darkened and hard with passion and need. "What the fuck are you doing to me, Skye?"

"Nothing you don't want." My reply is breathy and barely audible, but I know he hears me because he groans and descends on me again before yanking me from the wall and continuing to his room.

He leans down and deposits me on the bed, breaking the delicious contact with his dick and his mouth. With him leaning over me like this, I almost forget all the bullshit in our lives. He scrutinizes my face—for what, I have no idea—but he seems to find whatever it is he's searching for, because he wraps his arms under me and rolls onto his back, taking me with him.

I straddle his hips, staring down into the eyes of the man I've know most of my life.

Please, God, let us figure this out.

"You have far too many clothes on." His voice is rough with need and, damn, if it isn't the fucking sexiest thing I've ever heard.

I giggle. I fucking *giggle* and climb off him so I can strip out of my jeans and top.

His eyes follow my every move, and his cock strains against the confines of his boxer-briefs. I'm tempted to take him in my mouth again—to force him to finish there unlike this morning —but he reaches over and opens a drawer in his nightstand.

The last piece of my clothing drops to the ground, and his underwear goes flying across the room. In the dim moonlight, I watch him slide the condom on his straining cock. He reaches a hand out to me and urges me back onto his lap.

With my eyes locked on his, I slowly lower myself onto his waiting dick.

Oh, sweet fucking God...

If this is wrong—what's happening between me and Gabe —then, fuck, I never want to be right again.

13

***

GABE

The pop and crack of gunfire jerks me awake. I bolt upright and robotically grab for my gun. A cold sweat covers my body, and my fingers curl around the grip, trigger ready.

I search the area for the threat, and after a moment of confusion, I realize I'm in my bedroom, not back in the fucking desert.

Shit.

My body vibrates, and I drop my right hand, still holding the gun, to the bed. A glance to my left tells me all I need to know—Skye is sleeping peacefully.

She's safe. I'm safe. Everything is fine.

The words do nothing to calm my erratic heart or shattered nerves.

I haven't had a nightmare like that in months. The first time I take Skye in my own bed, they immediately return. Christ, the Doc will have a field day with this one.

The swirling sands and blazing sun beating down on me in that desert won't leave my head. Neither will the blood. This time, it was Mosul, 2007.

I was set up on the roof of a two-story building with Brody, my spotter, providing overwatch for the platoon as they raided an adjacent compound known to house a high value target.

It wasn't the ideal location for me to set up, but I worked with what I could out there. Our guys weren't even in there two minutes before the four enemy combatants started approaching the objective. Two moved up onto the roof across the street while the rest crept around the building.

But instead of taking out the enemy sniper and his spotter like I know I actually did, I watch him drop my guys as they exit the compound. They fall to the ground—one by one. Blood pools under their bodies, turning the light sand dark.

And instead of killing the other two who were firing on me, their bullets tear through me, one after another, knocking me back and bringing Brody down too.

Instead of walking away with the guys unscathed and receiving another medal, I hover above my own body, watching the blood pool under my still form.

Fuckfuckfuckfuck

I can't catch my breath and tremors rock my entire body.

It's still dark in the room, and the clock says it's only 4:12, but I know there's no way I'm falling back asleep.

With shaking hands, I return my gun to its place behind the headboard and slip out of bed, trying not to wake Skye. She doesn't budge, and a sigh of relief slips from my lips.

Thank God...she can't see me like this.

I pull on a pair of boxers and stumble to the bathroom, feeling the true weight of all the fucked up shit running through my brain and going on in my life on my shoulders. A splash of cold water on my face doesn't make me feel any better. I inspect my shaking hands in the light of the bathroom and squeeze them into tight fists, trying to force the involuntary action to stop.

My mind and body tell me one thing.

Cigarette.

Now.

My pack and lighter are still in my jeans on the floor in the bedroom where I dropped them when I went to bed the first time last night. I remove them as quietly as possible, taking a moment to drink in Skye's sleeping form before I escape to the living room.

I shouldn't smoke in here.

Savage will fucking kill me for that alone. I won't be able to hide it from him, either. He'll smell it as soon as he enters my condo, and I'll never hear the end of it. Maybe I can soften the blow about Skye by letting him ream me out about smoking first?

Shit.

I hope he didn't see Skye come in here last night. I won't have my balls for much longer if he did.

I better enjoy what might be my final smoke.

The wall of glass draws me to it, and I settle into the chair next to the windows. Random points of light break up the blanket of darkness that is the city at this time of the morning, and beyond that, the blackness of the water.

Sometimes, I wish I could just hop on a boat and float out to sea, leaving the world and all its fucked up stuff behind me. But, with my luck, instead of landing on some remote, unpopulated island, I'd probably drift to North Korea.

The trees near the water sway violently in the wind.

A storm is coming, and I don't just mean the hurricane brewing in the Atlantic.

Tension and energy permeate the air—inside my condo and outside. Things will come to a head soon. I can't ignore that any more than I can ignore the trembling of my hands.

I flip open my lighter, taking a moment to caress the star engraving before I light up.

The first drag is like a hug from an old friend.

Why did I ever quit this?

I have to keep reminding myself it's a filthy, dirty habit that's just killing me slowly. But for now, I'll pretend that isn't true and just enjoy the buzz of the nicotine and the calming view.

SKYE

I watch him from the hallway. He doesn't see me and guilt creeps in at the way I'm intruding. But there's something going on with him—something more than just worrying about how Savage will react when he finds out about us.

Gabe has always been a rock—for everyone. What he has done for Savage goes above and beyond best friend status. And he's become another son to Mom and an additional brother to the rest of the Hawkes. I understand his concern over how Savage will react, but that shouldn't be breaking him, and right now, he's broken.

The cigarette is a dead giveaway. He hasn't lit up in months.

Kinda creepy that I know that.

His right knee bobs up and down frantically, and he takes another drag, never taking his eyes off the view out the windows.

Pain stabs my chest as my heart breaks, and I don't know why. I'm here...with him. It's all I've ever wanted and yet, I can't fully enjoy it, not with him like this.

He reaches over to the side table next to his chair and snuffs out his cigarette in the bottom of an empty tumbler. It joins the small pile of other butts already there.

How long has he been awake?

I tug the sheet more tightly around me and approach him cautiously. His shoulders stiffen. He knows I'm closing in on him, but he never takes his eyes off the window.

A glint of metal on the side table catches my eye, and I pause beside it. My breath catches.

Oh, my God.

Star.

My knees quiver, and my chest tightens. I reach out and grasp it before I take the final step and drop to my knees in front of Gabe.

He finally turns his head, and his sad, defeated eyes meet mine. I offer him a half-hearted smile and hold up the lighter. "I thought you quit and put this thing away."

A weak grin ticks up the corner of his mouth. "I did."

"What made you bring it out?"

It's just one more reminder of everything we've lost, and I'm surprised he would want to see it every day. This lighter went through five tours with him. I can't even imagine the things he must have seen and done with it in his pocket.

I was with Star when she bought it for him. We wanted to give him something for his nineteenth birthday—his first since enlisting, and the first one he would be spending without our family since he was six years old. I thought it was stupid to give him a lighter and encourage a bad habit, but Star insisted. Instead of giving a joint gift, I opted to get him something I thought was much more practical for his next deployment—a one-year subscription to Hustler's online porn website.

Just thinking about the look on his face when he opened the card and read the note from me makes me smile despite the way my heart is aching holding Star's gift to him in my palm.

It doesn't escape me that he hasn't answered my question about why he has it out again.

His eyes have returned to the view. I don't think I'm going to get an answer. He pushes his left hand back through his hair and sighs. "Fuck, Skye...I don't know what the fuck I am doing."

I set the lighter back on the table before placing my hands on his knees. "None of us do, Gabe."

He shakes his head and returns his eyes to me. "I'm a mess, Skye. I almost shot you last night and this morning..."

This morning?

"What about this morning?"

His whole body goes rigid and he scrubs his hands over his face. "Shit, I didn't think it would be this hard."

The internal war he's waging shows in every movement he makes, but I encourage him to continue, knowing if he doesn't talk about it, he'll just bury himself into a deeper, darker hole. "Just tell me."

He pauses for a moment and takes a deep breath. "I had a nightmare...about being over there..."

I wait for him to continue, but he just bites his lip and shakes his head with his eyes squeezed shut and then drops it in his hands. He was different when he came home after his final deployment four years ago, but I never suspected anything was seriously wrong.

"Gabe—"

"I could have killed you."

"You keep saying that, but I'm right here, and I'm fine."

His head snaps up and the eyes that meet mine are not the warm, deep pools they normally are, they are ice cold. "You won't be fine, Skye. Not if we're together. Savage should be the least of your concerns. I could seriously hurt you."

I can't believe I'm going to ask this, but I know the answer, and he needs to hear himself say it to know it's true.

"Have you ever hurt any other girl who spent the night here?"

He growls at me and fists his hands. "Don't compare your-self to them, Skye, they were nothing, and I never let anyone spend the night when I was still having these dreams. I thought they were done and over with."

I don't need to hear the words to know what he's not saying. The dreams are back because of me. He's so fucking stressed out and worried about what will happen with Savage, he's actually driving himself crazy.

Jesus.

"Gabe, you need to take a step back. Breathe and relax. Everything is fine. You're fine. I'm fine. And Savage will be fine when he finds out about us. He has Dani and the baby to worry about."

He lets out a mirthless laugh. "I wish I could believe that."

It's abundantly clear I'm not getting through to him. There's only one thing I can think of that will rescue him from the dark hole he's fallen down.

I urge his knees apart and lean into him, pressing my lips to his even as he eyes me warily. He doesn't resist me, but he doesn't respond either. At least, not verbally.

His cock is hard to miss, straining against my stomach.

I slip my hand into his boxers and grasp him firmly.

He does nothing to stop me, just watches me with a mix of trepidation and longing. Not exactly what a girl wants to see, but I know he needs this as much as I want to give it to him. He needs to get out of his head, and I can do that for him.

14

GABE

*S*he frees my cock from my boxers. There are no soft, lingering, exploratory touches of her hand or tongue. She immediately takes it in her mouth, engulfing me in a mind-numbing wet heat.

Fucking A...this is Heaven.

I wind my fingers into her sleep-tangled hair and fight my body's urge to thrust up and my conscience screaming at me to stop her.

Wrong. Wrong. Wrong.

This is so wrong.

But fuck, does it feel good...

Closing my eyes, I let my head fall back and try to just savor the blissful suction and attention she's giving me. But, when her free hand slides into my boxers and cups my balls, I can't fight it anymore. I drive up into her mouth, the head of my cock pushing against the back of her throat.

She moans around me and swallows while she swirls my balls in her hand. I almost come on the spot.

White stars explode against my eyelids, and a tingle shoots from my tailbone straight to my cock.

I'm close...so damn close.

I need to be inside her.

Coming down her throat isn't enough for me right now. I need to be surrounded by her, by her clasping pussy. I need to hear her strangled moans while I pound into her.

With a little more force than I intend, I yank her off my dick. Her wide eyes stare at me in confusion.

I don't say anything. There aren't any words to describe why I need to do what I'm about to do. Even if I tried, I doubt she would understand. How could she?

How can she comprehend that my losing myself in her is the only thing besides pain that can clear my head of all the bullshit rattling around in there? If only momentarily.

Hazy pink sunlight filters in the windows, illuminating the right side of her face as she stares up at me.

I need to forget.

I stand and tug her up from the floor. The sheet falls away from her body and before she can say anything, I lift her up and spin her around, pushing her face-first into the chair with her beautiful ass raised in the air. Her glistening pussy calls to me from between her glorious thighs.

"Are we safe?" The question comes out rough and desperate, and I pray to God I'm not scaring her.

She focuses on me over her shoulder and nods, her rumpled hair falling in her eyes.

"Are you okay with—"

With a nod of her head, she silences me. Pushing her ass back against my cock, she lets out a low groan. "For fuck's sake, Gabe, just fuck me."

Fuck, this woman...

I shove my boxers down the rest of the way and align my cock with her wet opening.

There's no way this will be gentle. I can't do gentle right now. I can't do controlled right now.

Her wet heat is molten fire on the head of my cock. I shove into her with one thrust, knocking her forward against the back of the chair.

No, this is Heaven.

Me and her, no barriers, nothing between us.

Just us.

I pull back and drive into her again—deep and hard—and she bucks against the back of the chair.

"Yes!" She cries out and clenches down on me—squeezing my cock and rotating her hips. "Let go, Gabe."

I grit my teeth and dig my fingers into her ample hips while I pull out slowly. My thighs tremble with my effort to contain the beast threatening to break free.

"You sure, love?"

A muffled curse is the only response I'm offered.

She doesn't know what she's asking for.

Her long, dark, satiny strands wrap around my wrist perfectly, and I tug her head back until her eyes are locked with mine as I lean over her. I need to make sure there's no fear or hesitation there. All I find is longing and lust. She stares at me, unblinking. "Go Gabe."

I hammer into her.

Over.

And over.

And over again.

Hard and relentless.

It's brutal, and fuck, does it feel good to let go of everything in my head and only concentrate on the physical connection between us.

SKYE

He's pummeling me.

His cock fills and stretches me. Our bodies slam together, and he holds my head immobile, forcing me to look back and stare into his eyes.

With every retreat, I clamp down on him, savoring the twitch in his tightly clamped jaw and the feral, animalistic gleam in his eyes.

He needs this, and I need him.

Yes, fuck, just let it go.

Every thrust shoves me harder into the chair, and every yank on my hair sends a sting rippling across my scalp. The pleasure borders on pain, but I revel in it. Only *I* can give him this.

The fingers of his right hand dig into my hip. I'll have bruises but fuck if I care.

I feel every single inch of him with crystal clarity with every drive of his hips.

He shifts, pushing me forward until my left cheek is pressed into the leather back of the chair. My breasts crush against the cool material—the slippery surface a sharp contrast to Gabe's hot, slick skin against my thighs, ass, and back.

Warm breath feathers my ear, and I tilt my head to try to see him, but he tightens his hold on my hair, holding me in place and keeping me prone.

Not a word has been spoken since the moment he plunged into me.

The only sounds are our grunts and groans, and our flesh slamming together. Heat engulfs my body, and I know I'm going to come. Hard. That damn piercing rubs me in all the right spots.

His breathing quickens with his increased pace, and he growls in my ear. "Come for me, Skye."

I could never deny Gabe anything. I've loved this man since I was sixteen, and I always will.

My thighs quiver, and I'm so fucking close. Every grind of his hips moves me nearer to the precipice.

I clench his cock, and he moans and rotates his hips slightly, altering the angle of his entry. Four more thrusts and my orgasm slams into me. "Oh, fuck...Gabe!"

The room disappears and blinding white light overtakes my world. I buck against the chair while he continues to plunge into me relentlessly.

A grunt of satisfaction is the only warning I receive before he comes inside me, pushing deep, and then stilling with his body pressed against mine from knee to shoulder.

We both pant, his chest heaving against my back and our breaths mingling where his face is pressed against mine.

That was...

Shit...I literally have no words.

The quiet peacefulness of the moment ends abruptly when he stands, releases my hair, and jerks out of me before backing away slowly.

I push myself up off the back of the chair and turn to examine him.

His wide eyes are on me, but he doesn't see me. His long, lean, muscular limbs tremble, and he runs shaking hands back through his hair before he fists them at his sides.

Oh, shit.

"No, Gabe." I scramble to get off the chair on quivering, unsteady legs and stumble over to him. "Stop."

He shakes his head, his vacant gaze still locked on mine. "Jesus, Skye, what the fuck did I just do?"

"Nothing I didn't want you to."

"But..."

I press my palms against his chest. His heart thrums a rapid tattoo under my touch; it's racing just as much as his mind is. Closing his eyes, he clenches them tightly.

"No buts, Gabe. Look at me."

After a brief moment of hesitation, he opens them. I rise up on my tiptoes and press a kiss to his trembling lips. He jerks away and narrows his eyes at me.

"Thank you."

"What the fuck are you thanking me for?" He takes a step back from me, shaking his head, and I immediately miss his heat. "Jesus, Skye, I just attacked you."

I step into him and wrap my arms behind his neck, locking them and making sure he can't move away from me again. He doesn't wrap his arms around me, but remains stock still.

"No, you just fucked me. You fucked me *hard*. You gave me what I wanted and what you needed."

His body vibrates. He shakes his head and pulls me into an embrace, burying his face in the crook of my neck. His heart continues to race against mine, and his breathing is still ragged in my ear.

Come on, Gabe. Relax.

I slide my hand up the back of his neck and into his hair, holding him against me, and press a kiss to the side of his neck. "Everything is fine."

"How can you say that?" His words are soft and muffled against my skin. "None of this is okay."

I know he's referring to a dozen different things, so his words don't hurt me. Very little can anymore. He needs to accept that this—us—is happening, and I'm not going to let him push me away.

We both have bad shit rolling around in our heads, but he won't scare me off that easily, even if he terrifies himself.

"We'll make it okay, Gabe."

15

GABE

Skye snuck out this morning before the sun had fully risen without giving me the chance to get a handle on what the hell had happened. I stepped into the shower and when I got out, she was gone, having left just a note saying she would call me later.

I don't know what the fuck that was this morning or why Skye didn't run for the hills the minute it was done, but it scared the shit out of me. It's not that I don't know I have violence in me, hell, the Army trained me to kill people. And I got paid to do it.

But what took place with Skye? That was something different. I've never been with a woman like that before—bare skin or bared soul. That's what it felt like to me—my entire fucking soul was being ripped from my body and every bad thing I've ever done was pounded out into her.

She didn't deserve that; no one does.

Yet, she stood there and fucking hugged me and acted like I

had just made love to her instead of pounding her like a crazed, wild animal.

Jesus, I'm fucking losing it.

Before I can second-guess myself or talk myself out of it, I call the number I've managed to avoid for five months but still know by heart.

"Doctor Cochran's office. How may I help you?"

"Hi Janine, it's Gabe. I need to see her."

There's a momentary pause where I'm tempted to hang up. "Oh, Mr. Anderson, hello. Actually, I can get you in Saturday morning at eleven. Does that work?"

Two days. Surely I can make it forty-eight hours without going off the deep end. Hopefully.

"That's perfect. Thank you."

I drop my phone back onto my desk and stare at the stack of applications next to it. Byron does all the hiring, but I do the background checks. My sources are meticulous and very rarely do any of the employees surprise me with anything. I know their dirty little secrets because I have to. If I don't, one could come back to bite me and Savage in the ass. We've worked too hard and been through too much to let that happen.

Yet, here I am, doing something sure to shatter the rock-solid friendship we've had for over two decades.

Why the hell did it have to be Skye?

There were at least fifty single women at that wedding. I could have holed up in a room with any one of them and fucked them and myself senseless all night. But instead, I let Skye kiss me and then spent the rest of the evening drowning myself in a bottle of Macallan alone in one of the empty conference rooms.

That was my second big mistake that night, not doing something—*someone*—else to eliminate the memory of that kiss, the way she smelled, and how fucking blue her eyes were when they were begging me to help her forget how awful she felt being there without Star...

I practically fall out of my chair when my phone rings.

Shit. I'm jumpy as hell.

Blocked caller.

That's never a good sign.

"Hello?"

"Anderson, son, how are you?" The voice is all too familiar, and a rock drops into the pit of my stomach as my blood pressure skyrockets.

"Don't call me son. You haven't been my father for a very long time. What the hell do you want?"

He's got some fucking nerve calling me.

I've managed to avoid speaking with my father since last year's fiasco. I watched his political career crumble on the news and felt a great sense of relief that even though he wouldn't be locked up where he belonged, he at least would no longer be in a position of power.

His resignation as mayor sent shockwaves through New Orleans. He went from shoo-in for Louisiana Governor to announcing his retirement from politics with no explanation overnight. I ignored any and all of his attempts to contact me, but the fucker caught me off-guard this morning.

"Now, Anderson, can't we be civil?"

I clench my fist and bite back a litany of curses that would get me nowhere. "First, stop calling me Anderson. Second, civility? You of all people shouldn't be telling me to be civil. What are you going to do? Have me killed, too?"

He sighs deeply. "I still have no idea where you got all these nasty ideas from. I never—"

"Save it. What do you want?"

Why can't he just disappear off the face of the Earth?

"Son, I was hoping we could discuss my return to politics—"

I bark out a mirthless laugh.

"You've got to be fucking joking." The disdain and disbelief in my voice cannot be misinterpreted by him. He has to know how asinine this conversation is given the circumstances.

"It's been a year—"

I cut him off before he can argue any further, because it would be pointless. "You don't seem to get it. You're done with politics. Done lording power over people and using that power to benefit yourself and vile, evil men like Dom Abello. I would have thought that was made very clear when we made our deal with him."

"But, Ander...er, Gabe, I have to be able to live and have a career. I need to do something." There's a panic in his voice that makes me grin. Now he knows what it feels like to be on the other side.

"Then, go sell used cars for all I care. But if I see your name on one fucking campaign sign, everything that you've done goes public, and you will have to deal not only with the authorities but with Dom too." He knows Dom would kill him before he would let any of the information Dani has be released to the media. Our deal with them works because Dom polices my father better than the actual police could.

Silence lingers on the other end of the line, and I almost hang up.

"I can't believe you would treat your own father this way."

I scoff and let the ice cold I feel in my veins pour out into my words. "You were never my father."

Hanging up on him feels good—really, *really* fucking good. That man has never been anything more to me than a sperm donor, and the last thing I need right now is to worry about him. I pushed him out of my life at eighteen, and I want him to stay out.

Shoving my hands back through my hair, I know there's only one thing that will help me regain my sanity, at least temporarily, until I can meet with Doc and try to find a more permanent solution. I pick up my phone and make another call. I need another type of appointment.

SKYE

I would have much rather spent my day off in bed with Gabe, but he never would have gone for it. Savage would never let him get away with missing work unless he were on his death bed, and then he would have come over to see what was up.

Just imagining the look on his face if he had come in and found me riding Gabe makes me chuckle as I pull into the parking lot of my gym.

A good run is just what I need. Pounding out stress on the pavement always helps me clear my head and explore everything from a different perspective. But the wet streets aren't conducive to an outdoor run, so the track is calling my name. A few years ago, I would have gone straight to Star and dished every single detail about what happened with Gabe. Talking things out with her always helped me find a clear path through any bullshit.

Now that she's gone, I'm left with my running shoes and my own over-crowded head. I can't even bear to swim anymore, other than the cooling dips in Mom's pool. Swimming laps just reminds me of competing with and against Star, and the last thing I need is another reminder of what I lost.

I glance down at my phone before I get out of my car.

Come on, Gabe.

The text that tells me he finally came clean about us to Savage hasn't come yet. I didn't push the issue before I left this morning. In fact, I thought he would probably need a little time alone to process everything, so I slipped out while he was showering.

With everything else going on with him, it's probably best not to stress him out further by putting a deadline on it. But the longer we put it off, the weirder and more taxing it's going to get for Gabe, and stress is the last thing he needs right now.

I'm tempted to shoot him a message to see how he's doing, but that would be desperate and clingy, right?

Shit, Star, I could really use some advice at the moment.

My phone goes in my gym bag before I can do something stupid. A wet blast of air strikes me when I open my door, and I shiver. The darkening sky and whipping winds are just a precursor to the real storm if it makes it here; it's already packed a wallop in the Caribbean and has started in on Florida. We haven't been struck with a hurricane since Isaac in 2012, but it looks like Hera could pack a punch if it hits us directly.

We should know by tomorrow or Saturday where she's headed.

Riding the storm out with Gabe would be ideal—I can think of a hundred ways to pass the time—but I know he would never go for it. Even if he does tell Savage today, chances are he'll want to ease him into the idea of there being an "us" instead of smacking him in the face with it. Besides, I would never leave Mom alone during a storm. As much as we butt heads, and as much as the thought of being stuck alone with her for potentially a couple days makes me shudder, she's still my mother, and no matter what anyone thinks, I love her.

I turn to shut my door and catch a skittering of movement in my peripheral vision. When I look again, it's gone, but the hairs on the back of my neck raise, and the uneasy feeling of being watched rolls through me.

It's probably just some creep hanging out to see girls in yoga pants.

The race into the building to avoid being soaked is quick. I shake the water off my jacket once inside the door and make my way to the locker room.

Just as I'm about to close the door on my locker, my phone rings in my bag.

"Shit."

I rummage around until I find it at the bottom and see it's Stone.

"Hey, baby brother. What's up?"

"Hey sis. I just got off the phone with Mom, letting her know I'm not going to make it out this weekend. With the storm looking like it may hit there, it just doesn't make sense. Chances are my flight would get cancelled anyway, so I'll just save my ticket and use it later."

Damn.

I really need some time with Stone, the only remaining member of the family who doesn't continuously drive me insane.

"Well, that sucks. Don't you have some business or something going on with Dom?"

"Uh, yeah, but it can wait a bit."

I pause, waiting for him to expand. He doesn't, and I know better than to pry into his or Dom's business. "I was really looking forward to seeing you."

He chuckles. "Why? What did you do?"

I drop down onto the bench in the locker room and check out my manicure. "What makes you think I did something?"

"Because I know you. What, did you get fired?"

"Ha, that's a funny question coming from you. Last I heard, you were fucking up on the job and were about to get canned."

A grunt is the only response I get, and I can picture him, reclining in his office chair, feet kicked up on his desk, scowling as if I can actually see him from across the country. "Have no fear, sis, still gainfully employed here."

"Well, that's good to know. Same."

"What about that guy you were seeing? What was his name again?"

I cringe and drop my head back, rolling my neck to work out the kinks. "Lucas. And things are...complicated."

"Complicated? Sounds like there's a story there."

Fuck.

Do I tell him about Gabe? He, of anyone in the family, should understand that sometimes, decisions are made and things happen that are completely unexpected. Stone is the king of unforeseen consequences. He should get it, right?

I have to tell someone.

"Shit, Stone, you can't say anything to *anyone*. I'm serious."

"I'm crossing my heart as we speak. Besides, attorney-client privilege and all that crap."

I bite my lip and contemplate my words carefully. Finally, I decide being direct is probably the best way to go.

"So...shit...um, well, I slept with Gabe."

There's a long pause before his laugh echoes over the line. "Ho. Ly. Shit!" I can practically feel his chest vibrating through the phone. "I have never been so happy to be across the country. I wouldn't want to be within a hundred miles when Savage finds out about this."

16

SKYE

I always feel like a complete psycho carrying two Starbucks venti cups into the cemetery. But I promised Star I would bring her a caramel macchiato every time I came to see her. I guess it's not any crazier than sitting outside the family tomb, talking out loud as if she can hear and answer me.

After my conversation with Stone, I knew I needed to come see her. With the potential storm approaching, this might be my only opportunity to talk with her for a while. At least the rain stopped for a while so I won't get drenched while I'm out here.

I weave my way through rows of tombs, vaults, and copings in the St. Roch Cemetery. The path I take to our family tomb is always the same. Carmen, one of the groundskeepers, waves at me as he walks down a parallel row.

The first time he found me sobbing outside the tomb, mere days after we interred Star, I didn't know how I was going to go on with my life. Carmen had walked over and placed an arm around my shoulders, offering me comfort even though I was a complete stranger. I'm sure he'd seen a thousand people just like me, distraught and hysterical before a grave, but he made me feel as though he understood my pain by simply being there and not even saying a word. He probably thinks the Starbucks thing is insane too, but he keeps his mouth shut about it because I always remove it before I leave.

"Hawke" is emblazoned in the granite on the front of the tomb. My father's name—Samuel—sits below the names of his parents who died before I was even born. I always feel weird coming to talk to Star and not saying anything to Dad, so I give my customary "hi, Dad," before setting the Starbucks on the step in front of the tomb.

Reading Star's name carved into the granite never fails to send shivers up my spine. I don't know if I'll ever be able to accept the fact she's truly gone. Even though I no longer feel the connection we had when Star was alive, I still sense her presence every day and know she'll always be a part of me. Maybe that will never change. I sure hope it doesn't.

My chest aches and tears well up in my eyes. I turn my back to the tomb and wipe them away before taking a seat on the concrete wall across the aisle from where she lies.

"Hey Star, you're never gonna believe what happened. Well, actually, you probably would've expected this. You probably would've seen this coming a mile away if you would have seen the way things have been since the wedding." I take a sip of my sugary coffee and stare at her name on the stone, picturing the way her eyes would widen waiting for me to continue. "I slept with Gabe—multiple times."

Images of our bodies entwined and heaving in ecstasy flit through my head and heat my skin even in the damp air. "I don't even know how it happened, he just showed up at my place and said we needed to talk. He wanted to clear the air about the kiss because things have been fucking awkward and tense between us. But instead of talking, we ended up fucking on the kitchen counter while we let the cookies I was baking burn to a crisp."

I chuckle because Star would be absolutely rolling at that mental picture. "The smoke detector was wailing, and we just kept going at it like two dogs in heat."

Very, very horny dogs.

"And God, Star, it was fucking amazing. Even though it was hard and fast, it was everything I always thought it would be. Shit, Star, I love him. You've always known that. And I should be happy I finally got what I wanted, I finally have him. But…"

I think back to last night and this morning, the haunted look in his eyes and the way he completely disconnected from himself.

"…I'm worried. He pulled out the lighter you gave him. I know he put it away a while ago. It's been six months since he quit the last time. But I smelled it the other night and this morning when I got up, he was smoking in the condo, and he had the lighter sitting next to him. I've never seen him look that lost. There's something going on with him. Something more than just being concerned about how Savage will react when he finds out."

Although, that's definitely something to worry about. Savage isn't exactly known for his calm, even temper.

"Whatever this is, it's been going on for a while. It's something in his eyes. There's something dark there. It reminds me of when he first came back, you know, when things were just a little off. If you were here, you would help me figure it out or you might even already know what's going on. You were always better at reading him than I was. I know he talked to you back then. You were the only person he spoke to about whatever was weighing on him. God, I was so fucking jealous of you for that."

Gabe had always confided in Star. Everyone did. She was

the perfect listener and the perfect advice-giver. "Wise beyond her years," is what Mom always said. And talking to her was like being in a fucking confessional—nothing you told her ever left her lips. The things she knew about and never mentioned to anyone would probably blow my mind.

I did my best to try to pry it out of her, especially things Gabe told her. But, she maintained her vow of secrecy, even when I tried to invoke the twin code. I wonder if she would have kept her silence if Gabe spilled to her now.

"Whatever is happening, it's part of why he's fighting this so hard. It's not just because of Savage. There's something deeper there, something that's eating away at him. He's not talking to me about it. I think part of him still sees me as the immature, irresponsible little girl he used to rescue whenever we would get in trouble. Well, when *I* would get in trouble and drag you along."

I pause to take a couple sips of my drink and scan the cemetery. A group of tourists wanders by a bisecting row, snapping pictures on their way to the chapel.

My eyes burn with renewed unshed tears. "He was always there for us, and I feel so fucking helpless seeing him like this and not being able to do anything. Why won't he confide in me? I know he's having nightmares, and he thinks he's going to hurt me. But he won't tell me what they're about or what I can do to help him besides give him a hole to stick his cock into."

That comes out more bitter than I intended it. "Shit, I know he doesn't think of me like that. And I love that I can give him something to take his mind off whatever is eating away at him, but this morning...it was like he was trying to fuck away his demons. That scares the crap out of me. Not because I think he would ever hurt me, but because I'm worried he's going to hurt himself."

The tears flow now, and I don't bother trying to stop them this time. If anything ever happened to Gabe, I know I wouldn't make it. I thought losing Star was the worst thing that would or could ever happen to me, but the thought of losing Gabe, of never seeing his sexy smirk or bright eyes again, steals my fucking breath.

"God Star, just tell me what to do. Should I just sit down with Savage and tell him everything even though that's not what Gabe wants? Would that help Gabe get through whatever is going on with him by removing the biggest obstacle for us? Or should I follow his lead and hide in the shadows? I don't want to live in the shadows. I've existed in one giant shadow since you died. And I'm just fucking sick of it."

I take another drink of my coffee and stare up at the sky. The dark, ominous clouds send a shudder down my spine. They say that there's only a fifty percent chance of the storm hitting us. But I've heard that before, and I have a bad feeling about this one. We're gonna have to start preparing soon. And hope there aren't any evacuations.

"It looks like the storm is moving in. I'm sure Savage will have a fucking meltdown if the hurricane hits with Dani being this pregnant. I probably shouldn't give them anything else to worry about until at least the storm has passed. But Jesus, everything is so fucked up...I just don't know what to do anymore. I'd give anything to have you here. Please, tell me what to do."

Of course, I get no answer. I'm still alone and adrift without a lifejacket with the storm barreling down on us.

~

GABE

The buzz and whir of the tattoo machine and the constant prick of the needle against my skin lull me into a sort of semicoma. I'm never more relaxed than when sitting in the chair getting inked.

Not even an orgasm can satiate me the way the pain does.

Although, coming inside Skye comes pretty damn close.

Christ, that woman...

But I'm here to try to forget about that, about her, at least for a few more hours.

The fact that I was even able to get in today is a fucking miracle. Jeremy books weeks and sometimes months in advance, but he knows me well enough to know when I call and say I need him right away, it's desperate times. I almost feel bad about the clients he probably cancelled on to squeeze me in. *Almost.*

I was lucky to find him all those years ago. A friend of mine had some great work done and told me to go see him when I was looking to get my virgin skin inked after my first deployment. It took us almost a year to finish what we started that day —a sleeve that runs from the top of my left shoulder all the way down over my forearm to my wrist.

The mock armor starts at my shoulder with a Mandala. Drawing a Mandala during meditation is meant to focus the mind but also acts as a protective space in which the meditator can reside. Focus was essential to my job, and the idea of finding somewhere protected held a deep meaning for me no one could ever understand.

Palden Lhamo dominates my bicep. Despite her frightening appearance, she is a mother protector deity in Tibetan Buddhism. The snarling face represents the ferocity with which humans must resist temptation to stray from being true to themselves and remaining true to their principles. It was so easy to lose myself doing what I did every day. The struggle was constant, and she was a perpetual reminder not to let anything steer me away from what I knew was right.

My forearm bears Chinese Foo Dogs—protectors that reside outside the entrances to homes and palaces. They are a mated pair —the left, male, the right, female. Both foo dogs have orbs under their paws. The male's orb contains geometric designs, which represent the structure itself, his domain of protection. The female has a cub under her paw. The cub represents the people and children within the home, her domain of protection. This portion represents the Hawkes, the only true family I've ever known. They took me into their home and accepted me as one of them when I believed I was alone in this world. Mrs. Hawke has been my constant protector and source of strength. With this permanently inked into my skin, I was always reminded I was not alone, and that they would always be waiting for me when I returned.

Over the years, he's added several other pieces to my body. The koi on my left ribcage was next. The Chinese legend of the Dragon Gate tells of the koi fish swimming upstream, through waterfalls and other obstacles to reach the top of the mountain where the Dragon Gate sat. When the koi finally reached the top, it became a dragon, one of the most auspicious creatures in Chinese culture. Because of this, the koi represents strength, determination, and perseverance in the face of adversity. That's how I always saw Mrs. Hawke. She was left to raise five children alone and still managed to offer love and affection to the little boy from down the street, defending me just as fiercely as she did her own children.

Then, when I became a Ranger, I had *"sua sponte"* inked into my right bicep. The ranger motto means "of their own accord" in Latin, and refers to the Rangers' ability to accomplish tasks with little to no prompting and to recognize that a Ranger volunteers three times: for the U.S. Army, Airborne School, and service in the 75th Ranger Regiment.

And most recently, he completed the massive back piece in honor of my regiment. The 75th regimental scroll extends across my shoulder blades over the unit crest. That took ten sessions to complete. Ten wondrous sessions where I was dead to the world and found safe harbor from the hurricane of unrest in my head.

The needle comes off my skin, and I check Jeremy over my shoulder, smirking at the damn Siracha t-shirt I've seen on him at least a dozen times.

He raises his eyebrow at me from under the newsboy cap he always wears, and I give him a little nod to tell him to keep going. I've been in the chair for six hours already.

This is a tattoo many people would've broken up into two or three sessions. Those people are fucking pussies.

Jeremy works until I can't handle it anymore, and it hasn't happened yet in the twelve years I've been coming to him. There have been times we haven't completed a piece in the first sitting, but that's always been because Jeremy didn't have time or was tired, not because I couldn't tolerate the pain anymore.

Today is the right rib cage.

This is what they mean when they say it hurts so good.

With the thousands of nerve endings in the rib cage, most people agree it's one of the most painful areas to get tattooed—precisely why I chose to do it today.

I concentrate on the sound and the feel of the machine and let myself relax for the first time in what feels like months. This is better than therapy, although I'm not dumb enough to cancel my appointment with Doc. That could lead to a lot worse things than more ink...like another stay in the mental health ward.

It only happened once, shortly after my last deployment. Once was enough to convince me I needed to take better care of myself and that I couldn't ignore my symptoms for what they were—PTSD. It's the last thing I ever wanted to admit, that I wasn't strong enough to handle what I did and saw over there. But being in the VA and witnessing what happened to the people who ignored it and let it get out of control, persuaded me that admitting you needed help was the lesser of two evils.

Doc came to me by way of a recommendation from a guy I served with. He said she was intelligent and compassionate, but also blunt, and assured me she wouldn't let me bullshit her. I figured those were probably all good qualities for a psychiatrist.

I wasn't wrong.

Her straight-forward, no-nonsense approach to therapy really helped me see what I was doing to myself and how fucking stupid I was for trying to ignore or brush off the nightmares and panic attacks. And while she doesn't exactly support ink therapy, she understands why I do it.

"You sure you want to keep going, man?" Jeremy pulls the machine off my skin and glances up at me again.

"Why? You getting tired, old man?" I love giving him shit when he wants to stop. He's only ten years older than me, but making him feel old makes me feel young.

He grins at me and shakes his head. "No, I'm just asking 'cause we are hitting the eight hour mark now. I don't think anyone has ever sat this long for me before."

Eight hours?

Where did the last two hours go?

I examine the large clock hanging on the wall and confirm the time; it's almost 10:00 p.m. "How much do we have left to go?"

He shrugs and contemplates his work. "Maybe an hour, hour and a half."

"If you don't mind staying, let's just get it done tonight."

"Whatever you want, man." He dips the needle into the black ink and returns it to my skin.

I've been wanting a piece there forever but could never decide what to get. After what happened with Skye at my place this morning, and the phone call with my father, it just came to me.

A lone figure stands with his head tilted up toward the sky where a turbulent storm threatens.

A swirling mass of dark, billowing thunderheads occupies the sky and lightning cracks across the center, striking the ground and illuminating the figure, throwing a ghastly shadow.

Doc is going to really get a kick out of micro-dissecting this one.

It couldn't be a more accurate representation for the way I have felt as of late.

I had let what happened with Abello throw me off my path of recovering my sanity. Things were good before that night. Life was livable. I hadn't seen Doc in months, and I had gotten to the point where I didn't need the meds she'd prescribed to help me sleep and get through the day. The nightmares were few and far between, and it felt like my life was finally back on track.

But killing those men threw me into a tailspin that has only increased now that I finally acted on my feelings for Skye.

And it's only going to get worse.

There is no happily ever after here. There can't be. Not when I know how Savage is going to react. I might as well be shooting him in the fucking heart.

The truth is, I'm getting this tattoo not only as a means of stress relief, but also as punishment. It will be a constant reminder of what fucking up the friendship with the only person who ever truly cared about me feels like. Every time I look at it, I'll know that I put myself there through my own actions. I'll know that the reason I'm alone in the world is because I couldn't keep my fucking dick in my pants.

17

GABE

"Crazy Bitch" bumps through the club speakers while Renee wraps herself around the pole upside down. Her reddish-brown hair dangles down and brushes the stage and her huge, silicone breasts protrude out toward the eager face of one of the front-row patrons.

He's a regular, and I know he won't do something stupid like try to touch her, but I still keep an eye on her.

Her ex won't be back. Even he can't be *that* stupid. Unless he physically can't stay away.

Just like I can't stay away from Skye. Sleeping in my bed alone last night fucking blew. By the time I got back from Jeremy's, it was almost one, and I hadn't heard from Skye. I halfway expected her to just show up again, but she must have known I needed some time alone.

But even my alone time was filled with her—her scent permeating my sheets and her whispered words echoing in my ears.

My cock stirs to life just thinking about it, and I have to shake my head to clear the images of her bent over the chair yesterday morning.

Knock it off, Gabe.

I should be figuring out a way tell Savage. What I absolutely, positively, shouldn't be doing is picturing his baby sister naked.

Shit. Shit! Shit!

It's Friday, I need to get my shit together and pay attention on such a busy night.

"What'd she do?"

Nora's voice behind me makes me jump, and I turn from where I stand leaning against the wall backstage to face her. Danika's sister is something else. The former pre-med student turned stripper stands in her stage uniform—a white thong and a ripped Led Zeppelin t-shirt knotted under her breasts—with one eyebrow cocked up at me, and I already know she sees too much. She always does. It's like she can see straight through people to their cores.

"What'd who do?"

She grins and shifts her weight from one Lucite-heeled foot to the other. "Don't play dumb, Gabe. What happened with Skye?"

"Why do you think something happened with Skye?"

"Because I'm not blind like Savage apparently is. The tension between you two the other night when she came with Storm was palpable. I could feel it from the stage. So, what happened?"

Fuck.

Nora sure has changed since she started working here. She was so quiet and deferential when she started, and Savage and I thought she couldn't be more different than Dani. But the longer she works here, the more outgoing she's become. And maybe it's just because she knows us so much better now, but she doesn't hold back anymore. While she's still respectful, she speaks her mind just like she was a member of the family, which I guess she kind of is since she's Savage's sister-in-law now. Nora has become like a little sister to me, too. A little sister...like how I should be thinking about Skye...

If I spill, the chances of it getting back to Savage through Danika are pretty high, but at the same time, a female perspective from someone who knows all of us may be useful. But that doesn't mean I have to come right out and tell her everything.

"What do you think happened?"

She laughs and leans against the wall while I take a quick glance back at Renee to make sure she's still okay. When I return my attention to Nora, she has a knowing smirk on her face. "I think you two finally banged out all that sexual tension."

"Jesus, Nora...do you have to say it like that?"

Her eyes widen in mock innocence. "Like what?"

I scrub my hands down my face and resign myself to the fact I need Nora's help. "What makes you think we slept together?"

"Because you wouldn't look so guilty if you hadn't."

Shit, am I that obvious?

I always thought I had a good poker face, but apparently, I'm a fucking open book when it comes to my feelings for Skye. "Yes, okay, we...well...you know."

She grins. "I thought so. When are you going to tell Savage?"

Isn't that the million dollar question?

How the hell do you tell your best friend you're boning his little sister without ending up bleeding on the floor? I know he keeps a .45 under his desk, and I definitely don't want that thing used on me.

"I have no fucking clue, Nora. I value my life too much to even consider telling him." He's going to come down on me faster than a hellfire missile when I finally come clean. I probably have a better chance of surviving that explosion than I do whatever Savage rains on me.

"So, you and Skye are just going to sneak around forever?"

"Is that an option?"

She chuckles and shifts onto her feet again as Renee's song winds down. The DJ's voice blasts through the club. "Thank you, Scarlett. Next, please welcome the beautiful Cashmere to the stage."

"Look, if you want my advice, just come clean with Savage. Sooner, rather than later. He has a temper, but you two are too close for this to come between you. I have faith it will work out."

With those parting words, she steps around me and struts out onto the stage as the opening riff of "Kashmir" explodes over the speakers.

Whoever said strippers weren't smart never met any of our girls.

SKYE

> Hey can we talk? <

I read the message from Lucas and chew on my bottom lip. I should probably talk to him. He hasn't done anything wrong. He had every right to get angry over what I did. I owe him a conversation, a real one, not in the supply closet at the hospital. We spent four months together, so just walking away and letting it end like that isn't right. It's time to face the music and come clean about everything with him.

< Yeah. Meet me at Whiskey Bar? >

> I'll be there in five <

Five? Whiskey Bar is just down the street from my apartment, but it's at least fifteen minutes from Lucas' place. He must be in my neighborhood already.

The jeans and tank top I'm wearing will just have to cut it because I don't have time to change or clean up. It's a good thing I showered right after my shift or I would have been meeting him still smelling like sweat and the office.

Threatening clouds greet me when I step outside. Rain falls steadily and is already creating pools in the dips of the sidewalk. I open my umbrella in hopes of keeping even remotely dry on the walk to the bar, but it's a fruitless effort given the increasing winds. Driving would be pointless since I'd never find parking on the street near there.

Over the last several hours, the storm has intensified, the winds already starting to thrash the tree tops. The news says Hera is tracking northwest, and if it remains on its current path, will make landfall probably Tuesday as a category one or two hurricane.

Nowhere near as powerful as Katrina, but still dangerous and destructive.

It almost seems fitting the storm is coming at the same time this shit is happening with Gabe. I have a feeling the fallout from our relationship will have the same results.

The rain pelts my umbrella incessantly, and I race through puddles all the way to the bar. When I finally step into the building, I'm drenched despite my best efforts.

Shit. Drenched and fucking freezing.

I shiver and search the packed room for Lucas. He's sitting at a high-top table in the back corner and grins when he sees me cutting through the crowd toward him.

"Hey." He rises to his feet and pulls me into a hug, burying his face in my wet hair.

That can't be comfortable.

Our embrace lasts just long enough to be awkward. Weird. I've never felt awkward around Lucas before. We always had such an easy rapport and now, it just feels...wrong.

Is it all because of Gabe? Or was it always like this, and I never noticed?

I feel awful about the way things ended with Lucas, and as he releases me from the hug and retakes his seat on the stool, a twinge in my heart reminds me how awful it would have been to be on the receiving end of the wrong name during sex thing.

If Gabe had said someone else's name...*shit*...I would cut a bitch and probably remove his balls and shove them down his throat.

"How have you been?" Lucas' question seems innocent enough, but I know it's not what he really wants to ask. He didn't meet me here to find out how I've been, he wants to know if we're getting back in the sack together.

What do I tell him?

"Uh, busy, you know, working and keeping a watch on the storm."

Not a lie.

His left eyebrow quirks up, and he takes a drink of his beer. "Is that all?"

"Pretty much." I'm not sure what he expects my answer to be. Does he want a play-by-play of every moment of the last two days?

He nods and rubs the condensation off the side of the glass. "Well, I hope the time I gave you to think has helped."

Time to think?

Does he really believe I've changed my mind in forty-eight hours?

"Lucas, that was only two days ago."

His eyes widen. "So, you need more time?"

He seems genuinely surprised. How can he actually expect for something to happen in such a short amount of time? Maybe I'm just really, really bad at reading people and this relationship stuff, but it seems to me that if someone says another name during sex and then tells you they need time to think, it would be obvious, and probably prudent, to give them more than two days.

I don't even know how to respond to his question without sounding like a complete bitch.

His hand snakes over the table and grasps mine.

I scrutinize our hands twined together on the wooden tabletop, and then his warm, brown eyes. There's nothing but affection there, yet his touch is making me uneasy. After having Gabe's hands on me, another man's just feel plain fucking wrong. It's strange, because Lucas' hands have given me count-less hours of pleasure and more orgasms than I can count, but all I want is to have them off me now.

"Skye, I wanted to tell you the other night. I tried to tell you..."

Oh, hell no! I try to tug my hand out of his, but he holds it tightly.

"...that I'm in love with you."

Shit.

My casual dating situation has just turned really compli-cated, really fast. I can't give him any reason to believe there's a chance of anything between us in the future. I was stupid to think I could get away with casual sex with someone for so long without him developing stronger feelings for me. I was clueless to not notice it sooner and end things before they got this out of control.

If I'm not honest now, it'll only hurt him more in the end.

"Lucas, look, I'm really sorry, but I told you I wasn't looking for anything serious—"

He shakes his head and leans forward across the table toward me. "Don't try to tell me you don't feel the same. I know you do."

Being blunt is the only way to go right now. Good thing I

excel at that. "I'm sorry, Lucas, but I don't. I really liked spending time with you, and we had fun, but it was never more than that for me."

His eyes narrow and flash with anger momentarily before he takes a deep breath and relaxes back with a forced smile. "You're just confused."

No. I am most certainly *not* confused, but maybe I did something to make him think there was more going on between us? Mentally cataloguing the last several months, nothing immediately comes to mind. We hung out. We ate. We fucked. We never did anything romantic or coupley that I can recall. And I most certainly never *said* anything that would have made him believe I had stronger feelings for him.

"I never meant to lead you on. I thought I was being clear about what this was."

He shakes his head, that plastic smile still plastered on his face. "Nah, we just need to spend more time together, that's all."

Is he for real?

Does he have some mental deficiency I'm unaware of?

I take a deep breath. How do I handle this?

He just isn't getting it. Maybe it's time to be as direct as possible. Rip the Band-Aid off.

"Lucas. There's someone else."

His hands clench into fists, turning his knuckles white. The brown of his eyes darkens to an almost black, and I can physically see the anger rising.

Aww. Shit.

"I'm sorry, I—"

"Is it Gabe? Whoever the fuck that is. Were you cheating on me with him the whole time?" His booming voice draws the attention of the couple at the table next to us, and I smile at them awkwardly.

Jesus, Lucas, calm the fuck down.

"What? Cheating on you? No, but even if I had been seeing him, you and I weren't exclusive anyway."

He recoils, and the rage in his eyes is replaced by a pain I've never seen there before. "Wow, is that really how it was for you?"

"I thought we were on the same page, Lucas."

The lack of response tells me all I need to know. This conversation isn't going anywhere. He doesn't understand where I'm coming from at all and doesn't want to hear a single word I have to say.

Maybe this is my fault. Maybe I was playing with fire by spending so much time with him and expecting him to remain emotionally detached. Perhaps my ability to emotionally detach myself from people is backfiring.

"All I can say is I'm sorry, Lucas. I really am."

I jump from the stool and beeline for the door, not looking back at the table. I need to get out of here and away from him. I have enough to worry about with the approaching storm.

18

SKYE

*T*wo nights without seeing Gabe and I'm practically crawling out of my skin. After what happened Thursday morning, I thought he could use a little time to decompress and think. So, no matter how hard it was for me, I stayed away.

I anticipated he would call last night, but never heard a peep from him. Now, it's mid-morning Saturday, and I'm tempted to go over to his place unannounced just to make sure he's okay.

But that's probably a really fucking bad idea. He needs a little more time. If he hasn't called by tonight, then I'll make a move.

I usually bitch about having to work on Saturdays, but now, I wish I was bogged down in patients. The doctors I work for know a lot of people can't take off work during the week, so we open the clinic from eight to eight one Saturday a month to accommodate them. The other nurse practitioner and I alternate taking the clinic shift, and this happens to be my month off.

I'm tempted to call her to ask to switch with me so I can work today and take my mind off Gabe. I need to stick to my guns and give him space, but not having anything to distract myself with is making that impossible.

Don't call.

Right?

Fuck.

My phone taunts me from the kitchen counter.

I can't believe I'm making this call, but I need to talk to someone, and my options are severely limited. Star was always it. Storm would be my next choice, but there's no way I can discuss the Gabe thing with her. The same goes with Dani, for obvious reasons.

This is a last resort.

"Hello?"

Shit.

I'm tempted to hang up and forget the whole thing when she answers, but if I don't talk to someone about this, I may go postal.

"Hey...Nora...it's Skye."

"Oh..."

The surprise in her voice is warranted. I don't think I've ever called her for anything but the occasional touching base about who's bringing what to a family gathering. While not technically part of the Hawke clan, she's been known to tag along with Savage and Dani, and I've always enjoyed my conversations with her. I just hope she feels the same way because I need her now.

"I really need to talk to someone about something, and I'm hoping you have some time?"

The momentary pause before she answers has me instantly regretting exposing myself like this. I almost tell her never mind.

"Sure. I'm not working until later today. Do you want to meet for lunch?"

I glance at the clock on the microwave above my stove. It's 10:00 but I still need to shower and get myself presentable. "Yeah, I could meet you at about 11:00, does that work?"

"Perfect. Let's meet at Marley's."

"See you there."

By the time I arrive and make my way to the table where Nora's waiting, my stomach is in knots. What do I say? Do I tell her everything? Some?

Fuck.

Nora smiles as I sit across from her, then eyes me expectantly. "So, what's up?"

I guess we are diving right in.

This was always so easy when Star was my sounding board. I didn't even have to say half the things I was thinking because she just *knew*. The whole "girl talk" thing with someone other than her is so foreign to me, I'm terrified I'll scare Nora off.

"I really appreciate you meeting me. I don't want to put you in an awkward position, but I really need to talk to someone about this. Shit...I don't even know where to begin."

She laughs and takes a sip of her water. "How about we start with you banging Gabe."

What?

How the fuck did she know?

It takes me a minute or so to overcome the shock of her statement and gather my wits. The satisfaction on her face tells me it wasn't a guess. She's got insider information.

"Fucking Gabe...he told you?"

She grins smugly and shakes her head. "He didn't have to. I guessed."

Damn.

"Were we that obvious?"

If she figured it out, maybe we are deluding ourselves thinking no one else knows. Maybe Savage already suspects and just hasn't said anything?

No. No fucking way he would stay quiet if he knew.

With a shrug, she reaches out and snags the menu, focusing her attention on it. "I don't know if anyone else noticed, but the tension between you two the other night at the club was pretty hard to miss. I'm surprised you two didn't do it right then and there."

If she only knew...

Our mutual masturbation session might as well have been us fucking on his desk. What I wouldn't give...something about doing it there, knowing someone could walk in on us going at it is sexy as hell.

"So, what did he say about me?"

Her eyes flicker up from the menu, and she quirks an eyebrow at me. "Really? Are we in fifth grade?"

I kind of want to punch her, but she makes a good point. That question was a little immature. I just really need to know what's going on in his head. Things are tense and only getting worse when I thought they would get better once we were together. He's not talking to me, and apparently, he *is* talking to her, at least, somewhat.

"Sorry. I just—"

She holds up a hand to stop me. "I'm going to give you the same advice I gave him. Just tell Savage. And do it quickly. The longer you let this go on trying to hide it, the worse it will be when he finds out. It may be tense for a while, but Dani can handle him."

There's no denying Savage has mellowed since he and Dani got together. But even she won't be able to tame the beast when he goes into full protective older brother mode. I always felt bad for the boys who showed up at our house when we were growing up. Without Dad around, Savage stepped in and might as well have answered the door with a shotgun. I'm pretty sure that would have been less intimidating than a six-three, two hundred and forty pound Savage greeting you.

"I wish it was that simple, Nora. But Savage won't let this go, no matter how much time we give him to get acclimated to the idea of us together as a couple. Gabe is his best friend, and I'm his baby sister. We will always be those two very separate things, and that's the way he wants it to stay."

Nora drops her menu and reaches out to pat my hand on the table. "Honey, if you really believe that, then you need to decide what's more important to you. Your relationship with Savage or the potential of a future with Gabe."

Right, like that's a choice I could ever make.

GABE

"We haven't had an appointment in a while. How have things been going?"

I narrow my eyes at Dr. Cochran and frown. "Oh, come on, Doc...we both know you aren't surprised to see me."

Let's stop with the clinical formalities bullshit.

The corner of her mouth quirks up, and she nods, her brown bob bouncing around her shoulders with the movement. "Well, the last time you were here, I did recommend you keep coming to see me, did I not?"

Of course she did. What shrink wouldn't tell you to keep coming even when you've finally reached the point of normalcy again? I was finally off all my meds, and I felt good, comparatively speaking. Other than the lingering lust for Skye, I had come to grips with what happened with Abello and my father, and I'd moved on. Continuing to see Doc at that point felt like nothing more than a reminder of the lowest point of my life and my complete failure to handle my shit on my own. I couldn't do it.

Coming here again is like walking back into Mosul without my gun or body armor. But I'll never admit that to Doc.

"You may have encouraged me to keep seeing you."

She narrows her eyes on me this time. "And to continue your meds. I noticed you haven't requested a refill in quite some time. I know you don't need to hear it again, but the medicine isn't like aspirin or Tylenol where you can just take it when you feel you need it. It works by building up in your body, and from the looks of it, you haven't had it for a long time. I imagine some of your symptoms have returned?"

Fucking understatement much?

The leather of her chair creaks when her long legs cross, and she waits for my response. I drop my head against the back of my chair.

"I guess you could say that."

Reliving the nightmares and chest-tightening anxiety are not on the top of my to-do list, but if there's one thing I learned from Doc when I started coming here, it was that not talking only makes things worse. Before Doc, before my PTSD, before the accident, I had Star. She was the greatest therapy I ever had, even when I didn't know that's what it was. Star never let me get too bogged down in the bullshit in my own head. She made me talk and then dished out what advice she had, if any. And the times she didn't have any usually ended up being the ones where I already knew the answer anyway.

I know Doc's not going to press me. That's not her style. She doesn't tolerate bullshit in her office, but also knows that pushing someone like me isn't the wisest move if she wants open and honest dialogue. She likes to wait for me to start before jumping in; it's annoying, sitting in awkward silence, but it works. It always gets me talking.

"The nightmares are back."

"For how long?"

I shrug as if I don't know exactly when they started. "About five days."

She nods and jots something down in her notebook. What I wouldn't give to see those notes. They're probably a great read.

"Did something happen to trigger them?"

Someone happened.

Telling her I'm sleeping with Savage's sister is the last thing I want to do. Savage is a patient. She knows him—the intricate workings of his inner mind. I know what I say to her is confidential, and can't be revealed to him. But it's still awkward and uncomfortable.

"Look, this is weird for me, so I'm just going to come out and say it...I'm sleeping with Skye Hawke."

I'll hand it to Doc, she tries very hard not to react to my confession, but the twitch in her eyebrow and slight quirk of her mouth give her away. The crazy thing is, she doesn't appear surprised. Actually, she looks rather smug.

What the fuck is that about?

"Why the look, Doc?"

She shrugs and leans forward slightly in her chair. "I would be lying if I said this surprises me. When you first starting coming to me and you spoke about the Hawkes, there was always something a little different in your tone when you mentioned Skye."

Huh, I was that obvious?

"And then, when you returned to therapy early this year and you told me about Savage and Danika's wedding, your entire demeanor changed whenever Skye's name came up. I had a feeling something may have occurred with her and that there may be some other feelings there."

"Gee, thanks for telling me that, Doc."

A low chuckle slips from her smiling lips. "That's not my job, Gabe. You know that."

"Still…" It could have saved me some suffering. I could have done more to avoid acting on my feelings had I been more aware of them. Maybe I would have been able to stay away.

"Does Savage know?"

I lean forward and scrub my hands down my face. "Of course not. Do you think I'd be sitting here in one piece if he did?"

She smiles and shakes her head. "Probably not, no. Is that what you think triggered the nightmares? You're concerned about Savage finding out?"

"Concerned? No. Terrified is more accurate. Shit, you know him, Doc. He will not take this well. He's the closest thing I have to a brother, and I betrayed him."

Her slight recoil doesn't go unnoticed. I don't think I've ever seen her react that way to something I've said, and I've told her some very graphic, very messed up stuff over the years. Her lips purse slightly, and she considers me. "Betrayal is a strong word, Gabe. Is that really what you think you did?"

Isn't it?

The Hawkes took me in and gave me the family and love I never had at home. Savage and I have been through so much together. I know what Skye means to him, especially after Star's death. He will protect her with every weapon in his arsenal, even if it's against me.

"I think sleeping with Skye is tantamount to stabbing him in the back, as far as he's concerned. He won't forgive this."

Her eyebrow raises. "Not even if you and Skye develop into something serious? What if things don't end badly?"

I snort and give Doc a pointed look. "When do things ever *not* end badly?"

"That's a pretty negative way to think about things, isn't it?"

Her question makes me scoff. "It's not like a lot of positive things have happened lately."

She jots something in her book and raises her eyes to me

again. "Since I know you haven't been taking your medication, can I assume you've been engaging in...other forms of therapy and self-medication?"

That's her not so subtle way of asking if I got new ink and have been drinking and fucking my way through my nights. I push my hands back through my hair, feeling the burn of my fresh tat as the tight skin stretches across my rib cage with the movement. "I saw Jeremy Thursday night."

The frown on her face is one I've seen many times. "Did it make you feel better?"

I start to answer yes, but then realize that might not be true. I may have felt relief for the ten hours the needle was on my skin, but even that couldn't completely eradicate the inner turmoil over the Skye situation. For the first time ever, the pain wasn't the ultimate relief.

"If I tell you it did, can we just drop it?"

Doc smiles, and it's clear she sees right through me. "If you tell me it did, you would be lying, and therapy only works if you're honest with me and yourself."

"Well, in that case, I guess I am epically fucked, because it didn't work, not the way it always has in the past."

She leans forward and locks eyes with me. "That's because this time it's about more than just your past demons, this is about your future."

My future...

This *is* about my future—with Skye, with Savage, with the entire Hawke family. I could lose everyone and everything, including my own sanity.

19

SKYE

*W*ord spreads fast when something bad happens, especially when that something bad happens to someone very much in the public eye. I got my wish when the office called me in to help with the clinic after I had lunch with Nora.

I was visiting with one of my friends who works in the surgical ICU while I was on my break when she got the call.

Within five minutes of the former mayor being wheeled into the emergency room, the hospital was buzzing, and I was in the elevator on the way down, my phone to my ear trying to reach Gabe.

Come on, Gabe. Pick up.

Straight to voicemail.

Again. And again. And again.

The green marble floor of the emergency room is slippery from the rain but I run anyway. Gunshot wounds to the head usually mean death, and word is, Dunne is barely hanging on to life.

Where are you, Gabe?

Their relationship is not what I would consider warm and fuzzy. As far as I know, he hasn't even spoken to his father since he turned eighteen and enlisted. Even after Dunne mysteriously resigned last year, Gabe didn't mention him or even acknowledge it happened.

He seems perfectly happy to go on living his life as if his father never existed, but this could very well be the end, and he doesn't need something to feel guilty about later. He has enough guilt as it is.

I slide to a stop outside one of the treatment rooms in the ER. It isn't hard to guess which one contains the former mayor; the two uniformed cops and a man in a suit, who is probably a detective, standing outside the room are a dead giveaway.

Dr. Coleman, one of the trauma surgeons, steps from the room and turns to the officers. "He didn't make it."

The officers nod and mention something about evidence collection, but I'm not listening anymore.

Gabe's father is dead.

Fuck. How do I tell him?

Before I can grab Dr. Coleman to try to get more information about what happened, he disappears down the hall toward the waiting room, leaving me standing dumbstruck in front of the door to the treatment room. One of the officers opens the door and sticks his head in. Muffled words are spoken between him and someone remaining in the room. When he's done, he lets the door close and disappears down the hallway with his partner and the other man.

I step forward on shaky legs and push the door open. Two nurses and the respiratory therapist who are still in the room glance up at me but immediately return to their work, unconcerned with my presence.

I've seen plenty of dead bodies, but this, this is so fucking different.

Brian Dunne is laid out on the table. He looks so damn much like Gabe, I have to force myself to take a breath.

I try to separate myself from the fact this is Gabe's father and examine it clinically.

The respiratory therapist removes the circuit from endotracheal tube, leaving the tube protruding from his mouth. She says something to one of the nurses who is recording the inventory on the code cart, then brushes past me and out the door with her equipment.

The IV bag still hangs from the stand but the tubing coils on the floor, having already been disconnected from his body.

They tried to save him with the defibrillator—the pads are still stuck to his bare chest and left flank, the cables running from them to nowhere, having already been pulled from the machine.

The second nurse slides Dunne's hand into a bag and secures it, probably to preserve any gunshot residue evidence at the request of the police officer. She walks around the bed and does the same to the other hand. When she's done, she glances up at me and tilts her head to the side. "Do you need something, sweetie?"

My eyes don't meet hers. They've been drawn to the white sheet under his head where the blood stain is slowly expanding with the fluids still seeping from his body.

Jesus fucking Christ...

What the hell happened to him? How do you go from being mayor to killing yourself in a year? Something pretty major must have happened to precipitate a downward spiral like that.

Things were bad when Star died...really, really bad. I would be lying if I said I wasn't inconsolable and unstable at times. Enough booze to kill a crew of sailors and enough Xanax to knock out a T-rex were consumed over those first few months.

But I never once considered killing myself, even at my lowest point. I screamed, cried, and wished I was dead with her. I begged God to let me go back in time so I could go on the trip with them instead of blowing it off for a stupid guy, but deep down, I would never have harmed myself.

And once Savage returned to the States, he forced me from my hole of despair and made me remember I hadn't lost everything.

For Dunne to take his own life, there must have been something huge going on behind the scenes.

"Honey, are you okay?" I finally tear my eyes away from Dunne and plaster a fake smile on my face.

"Fine. Sorry."

I shove the door open and wander away from the treatment room toward the reception area. Maybe I can find out if anyone showed up for him. I know he never remarried—portraying the lonely widower played too well in his campaigns to change that. But he must have had *someone*. No one who looked like that, and held that much power, was celibate. There must have been somebody at the house, or an emergency notification person listed in his phone.

Turning the last corner toward reception, I debate trying to call Gabe again when a very familiar blond head flickers in my peripheral vision.

Oh, my God...

Gabe...sitting in one of the waiting area's vinyl chairs with his face dropped into his hands.

The love I have for him spills from the break in my heart. I can't imagine what he's going through. It's such a fucked up situation to begin with, but he's obviously upset. How could he not be? No matter what their relationship was, he was still Gabe's father.

With a deep breath, I prepare myself to deal with whatever fallout comes from this and approach him.

Please let me comfort you.

I slip my hand across his shoulder, and his head jerks up, his shadowed eyes looking but barely seeing me. "Skye?"

"I'm so sorry." The words seem hollow and meaningless. They certainly were for me when people said them to me over, and over, and over again after Star's death. "How did you know?"

He presses his lips into a tight, thin line and nods before rolling to his feet. "His housekeeper called me when she found him." He shuffles from side to side and avoids making eye contact with me. "Let's get out of here."

I glance at my watch. "I'm off in an hour. You can wait for me, or I can come meet you at your place."

His eyes flit around the room nervously. "I can't stay here. Come over when you're done." He turns and takes two steps before turning back to me. "Be careful."

...don't let Savage see you.

That's what he didn't say. I know he's under a lot of stress right now, but the patriarchal tone is not appreciated nor is it needed.

∾

GABE

The condo door clicks shut, and I down the last of my third drink and close my eyes even though my condo is dark. She's going to want to talk—about him.

That's the last thing I want to do. Discussing my father will only lead to more anger, and it's already simmering just below the surface, ready to break free and wreak havoc.

I turn my head to follow the sound of her footsteps across the floor. Bright white light blinds me. "Turn it off."

"Why?"

"Just do it, Skye."

She sighs and flips the lights off, then drops down next to me on the couch. The silence hangs between us—heavy with unspoken questions and answers I can't give her.

"Are we going to talk about the fact that your father killed himself?"

Jesus.

"For fuck's sake, Skye…" I rise from the couch and make my way to the bar to pour myself the fourth bourbon since I got home from the hospital. The bottle shakes in my trembling hand. Doc will be lecturing me about drowning my feelings when I see her next time, but fuck it—how often does your father off himself, after all. I turn back to her and lean against the bar.

Even in the dark, I can see her eyebrow quirk up. "Tell me, Gabe. I know this has to be hard for you, regardless of what your relationship with him was."

"You have no fucking idea, Skye."

She jumps from the couch and crowds me back against the bar. "Then *tell* me!"

I shouldn't. What happened last year was never made public. That was the deal we made with my father and Abello. The fewer people who know about what went down and what Dani found, the safer we all are. If I tell her, I'm only going to put her in more danger than she already is just by being associated with Abello through her family.

But Skye is tenacious. She won't let this go. There's no way I can talk about my father without discussing everything that happened; it's impossible. All my feelings about it and him are wrapped up together.

"Fuck, Skye…you better sit down." Her eyes narrow, and she glances next to me at the bar. "Yeah, you'll need one of those too."

She pours herself a bourbon and grabs my hand, pulling

me with her back to the couch. Her palm presses against my chest, and she shoves me down onto the cushion. "Now talk."

It takes several fortifying breaths before I'm able to speak.

"So you know something went down last year, right? With Savage and Danika and me?" She nods and drops down next to me. The news reported the deaths of the three goons I killed and managed to get some video of Savage, Dani, and me at the scene, but I was never charged and the police swept my involvement under the rug at my father's request. It was touted as just another mob hit. "Well, Dani was investigating Dom Abello—"

"Shit!" Her fingers dig into my arm. "Uncle Dom? Why? I mean, I know he's not exactly squeaky clean, but he's not a bad guy..."

I shake her hand from my arm and stand to pace. I can't just sit still when I have this much pent-up anger and fucked up shit in my head. "He's a no-good thug, Skye. Do you have any idea how many people he has had murdered or beaten to advance his own agendas? That's the whole point. Dani discovered a connection between him and my father. Really, really shady shit."

She frowns as if she doesn't believe me and pulls her legs up under her. "Like what?"

"Like killing off his political adversaries to push *his* agendas through and ensure he wouldn't have any real opposition."

Her jaw drops. "You're shitting me..."

Christ. Why did I think this would be easy? Nothing with Skye ever is.

"No, Skye, I'm not shitting you. Dani had a source and had been compiling information on a bunch of different stuff for over four years. Abello somehow found out and lured her to a meeting with her source. She managed to call Savage for help, and we thankfully got there in time."

I watch her processing the information. Her head snaps up, and her eyes widen. "Holy shit, *you* killed those guys?"

A curt nod is the only response I can manage. I don't want to talk about the details. I can't. I already see them dropping to the ground, one after another, every time I think about that day.

"After, we made a deal with Abello. Dani would drop the story if he would stop any action against her or either of us, but especially her. He agreed very reluctantly. Part of the deal was also that he would make it clear to my father that he had to resign as mayor and stay out of politics forever. We knew any threat Abello made would be more effective than what we could do to him."

She sets her drink on the coffee table and runs her hands through her hair, pulling it free from the tie at the back. "So, that's why he resigned?" I nod. "And you haven't spoken with him since?"

"He called me earlier this week and begged me to let him return to politics."

His words ring in my ears. *"I have to be able to live and have a career...I can't believe you would treat your own father this way."*

A shudder rolls through me, and I down the rest of my drink.

"There was something...desperate in his voice."

Skye flies up from the couch and stops my pacing with a hand to my chest. "Oh no you don't. This is *not* your fault."

"I didn't say it was."

She shakes her head. "You didn't have to. I know you, Gabe. It's written all over your face. If what you told me is true about what he was involved in, then he brought any stress or whatever else drove him to this on *himself*. This had nothing to do with you."

She's right, of course.

I know I did what was right. He brought his own misery on himself. The only thing he ever thought about was what benefited him and how he could get what he wanted. He was willing to go to any means, even resorting to getting in bed with the damn mob to advance his agenda. He didn't care who or what he destroyed on his rise to the top.

Skye is the only thing I want, but I know having her will destroy so much. I'm not going to destroy other people's lives the way my father did, the way Abello *still* does.

I can't live with that guilt. I have to let her go.

20

SKYE

*S*omething changes in Gabe's eyes. The wild, angry, guilty man is gone. His gaze now holds need, loneliness, and something else I can't quite place. But the look he gives me tells me our discussion is done.

I understand why no one told me about what happened last year despite my constant probing. With Uncle Dom involved, things are very complicated for the Hawkes. But it's clear Gabe feels guilty about what happened for some reason, and it's been eating at him. His father's death is only going to compound it.

He needs to let things go and let himself be happy. I can make him happy. He just needs to muster up the balls to admit it to himself so he can tell Savage and we can end all this sneaking around.

I'm fucking done with that bullshit.

This needs to end soon, but I won't push it tonight. He's been through enough.

I take the empty tumbler from his hand and set it on the

coffee table. Then I slip my hand up his chest to his neck and pull him toward me. Our lips touch, and I kiss him gently, not the heated, desperate way we usually do. He pulls back and searches my eyes before reaching down and lifting me by my thighs, urging me to wrap my legs around his waist.

Like I would say no.

He works his way back to his bedroom slowly, seemingly in no rush to get us there.

Before this week, seeing the mussed covers of his bed would have caused jealousy on my part, but now I know it was probably from another nightmare and, instead of making me angry, my heart aches for him. Gabe is a selfless, caring man, and he doesn't deserve to have to struggle with any of this. No one does.

He lowers me to the bed, never stopping the languid exploration of my mouth with his along the way. God, can this man kiss...

Every swirl and swipe of his tongue ramps me higher and higher.

My body responds to him—fire scorching across my skin with every touch of his calloused hands. This man does things to me I never thought possible. He makes me believe I can truly be happy again.

But only if he's willing to go all-in with me.

I love him.

No.

I've loved him forever.

I'm *in* love with him—the crazy, head-over-heels, fairytale romance type of love—the forever kind.

There's no denying it. At least, not for me.

The void I've felt since Star died will never fill, but it's no longer the black, bottomless abyss it once was. I can actually see a future I won't just walk through blindly, miserable, and hanging on by a thread. I see one where I have a partner, someone who truly understands me and isn't scared off by the wall of sarcasm and snark I live behind.

I can't let him push me away anymore.

Tonight is the last night we are going to be together in secret.

Gabe tugs on the hem of my shirt, urging me to sit up so he can tug it off. As soon as I'm free, I release the clasp on my bra and pull it from my arms before lying back against the bed. He descends on me, pressing his warm mouth to my neck, and working his way languidly toward my stomach.

When he reaches the waistband of my pants, he pauses and probes along the edge with his hot tongue. My hips buck up against him and my clit pulses.

Fuck, Gabe is so good with that thing.

I need him between my legs more than I need oxygen right now—his mouth, his hand, his cock—I need it all.

Despite the numerous times we've been together over the last several days, it feels like we've never taken the time to truly explore one another. We've always been so hot and heavy, fast and frantic.

He slips his fingers between my skin and the band of my pants and tugs, taking them down my legs slowly, trailing his tongue and lips along behind them. Goose bumps pebble over my legs, and by the time he finally pulls my pants off, I'm practically shaking.

Instead of returning to hovering over me, he slides backward and steps off the bed.

I prop myself up on one elbow. "What are you doing?"

That damn smirk that makes my ovaries explode stretches across his face. He reaches over his shoulder and yanks his shirt off, tossing it into the corner. I take a moment to admire the artwork on his flesh. In the hundred times I've seen it, I've never really taken a moment to examine each of the tattoos or assess their meanings. Tonight, I'm going to explore every inch of ink with my tongue since my last attempt was interrupted with his impatience.

A dark image on his ribcage draws my attention. He didn't have that there two days ago, I definitely would have remembered it. "When did you get that?"

He glances down and shrugs. "Thursday night."

I have a million questions about the image of the man standing alone in a raging storm, but I suppress the desire to ask them. I don't want anything to stop him from losing himself in me and questions tend to do that.

I smile at him. "Lose the pants."

He grins at my order and instead of complying, his hand slides down past his belt, and he cups the giant bulge straining against the fabric of his jeans. "Why? Something you want in here?"

Watching him rub himself is almost enough to make me come on the spot. His tongue darts out to wet his lips, and he unhooks his belt, lowers the zipper, and shoves his jeans and boxers down, kicking them off to the same corner where his shirt landed.

Vivid memories of his cock in his hand at his office the other night only further soak my panties.

"I want to see you stroke your cock."

A brow quirks up. "Do you?"

I nod and shift anxiously under his heated stare.

He grips his dick in his hand and slowly slides it up and down the hard flesh. My legs quiver, and I press my thighs together to ease the throb there.

"Watching you touch yourself has to be the sexiest thing I've ever seen. I swear, I came so hard in your office the other night, I think I actually saw Heaven."

∼

GABE

I freeze. My cock pulses in my hand, but I'm physically incapable of continuing after what she just said. Her eyes widen, and she bites her lip.

Did she just say she was in my office?

Holy fucking shit.

"You were there?"

She nods, unable or unwilling to respond verbally.

I knew something was off that night. Vanilla and honey—the scent that could only be Skye—had lingered there, driving me to the brink of insanity. Now, I know why.

"What were you doing in my office?"

A sly smile spreads across her face. "I went in to take a nap on your couch while I waited for Storm, but then you came in and started jerking off..."

Knowing she watched me make myself come while I was thinking about her is a bit trippy and a lot fucked up. She was *right there.* I could have walked across the room and been inside her instead of coming in my hand.

"And what did you do, Skye, when you saw me stroking my cock?"

Her eyes spark with amusement. "I was wet as fuck and made myself come."

I know what she looks like when she touches herself. That first morning, watching her do it on her bed while I was on the phone with Savage, will be forever seared into my brain matter. And she did it ten fucking feet away from me without me even knowing it.

Fuck.

There's no way I'm staying at the end of this bed any longer. Not after her admission.

The bed creaks as I climb on and work my way over to her. Skye's eyes churn with something I can't place. I can't tell if she's nervous about admitting her voyeurism or smug because she got away with it.

"You never should have admitted that to me."

Payback's a bitch.

She grins and reaches up, wrapping her hand around the back of my neck before dragging me down to her. My mouth stops a mere hairsbreadth from hers. I flick my tongue out and along her lips, savoring the lingering taste of the sweet bourbon mixed with her very own unique vanilla flavor.

It's better than any twenty-five year Scotch I've ever had, and I relish it. But there's something I want to taste more than her mouth.

I should have done it a long time ago—given her the attention she deserves.

I'm such a selfish fucking asshole.

The need to pound into her has been the only thing driving me, and even though I know she walked away satisfied each time, the fact I haven't gone down on her every time we've been together only solidifies what a greedy fucking bastard I really am. I've only tasted her once, that first morning, and it was a race to get her off quickly, not the slow, sensual devouring she should be given.

She deserves so much better, and she'll have it, once I let her go.

Her body undulates under me as I kiss my way down her body to the thin lace thong barely covering her pussy. I brush my finger across the soaked fabric, and she bucks against me.

"You're so fucking wet."

She brings her head up off the pillow and glares at me. "I know, now do something about it."

I tuck my finger into her panties and drag it through her wet heat. She growls at me, and I chuckle, pressing a kiss to the inside of her quivering thigh. "I don't know, you let me go on jerking off when you could have just crossed the room and helped me out. Maybe I should make you do it yourself."

Her fingers twist into my hair, and she tugs my head up until our eyes meet. "Don't you dare."

The words go from her mouth straight to my cock.

This is how it's supposed to be—this give and take, the ability to tease and jab at each other on an equal playing field.

How am I ever supposed to stop wanting this woman?

I won't. I'll just have to be better at hiding it and avoiding her.

But for now, for tonight, I'm going to give her something we've never had before.

Concentrate on now, not tomorrow.

With a grin and a wink, I yank her panties down and off her legs. They end up tossed over my shoulder without care just like the rest of our clothes.

Skye watches me intently as she's sprawled out on display for me. It certainly isn't the first time, but it's the first time I've really taken a moment to appreciate all she's offering me.

She squirms under my exploratory gaze. The glistening moisture between her legs calls to me like a beacon in a storm, and I drop down between her thighs, setting my mouth exactly where we both want it.

Her taste is even more delectable and addictive than I remember. She shudders and rolls her hips in time with my probing tongue. I delve as deeply into her as possible before spreading her open and slowly licking my way across her wet flesh.

"Oh, God...Gabe..."

Her trembling words make my cock throb and my heart swell. Skye deserves to be worshipped every single minute of every single day like this.

I wish I could be the one who does it.

She grabs my hair and directs me up to her clit. I chuckle against the wet flesh.

Of course, Skye would force me to give her what she wants. She's not a "wait around and hope it happens" kind of girl.

Frankly, I'm surprised she ever let me push her away in the first place. Getting her to let me go now is going to be near impossible.

21

SKYE

*G*abe is torturing me. There's no other way to describe the deliberately slow movements of his tongue on my pussy and clit.

"Jesus, Gabe..."

"Mmm." His hum vibrates against my wet, needy core, and I gasp, digging my nails into his scalp.

A thick finger slips inside me, and I clamp down, desperate for something to fill me and sate my aching need. "More!"

I need more...

I need all of you...

He chuckles against me and slides in another finger while drawing my clit between his lips. The rhythmic sucking and pumping of his fingers winds me tight and high.

Orgasm lingers just outside of my reach. An animalistic, high-pitched whine resonates from my chest, and I pull on his hair, grinding my hips in time with his ministrations.

Fire licks across my skin while Gabe licks and sucks my

core. Release hits me like an atom bomb, tearing me apart from the inside out.

I squeeze my thighs against his head so hard, I think his ears probably leave imprints on my skin. He holds my hips steady as I thrash and buck beneath him, not letting up from his assault or giving me any reprieve from the breath-stealing pleasure coursing through my body.

When I finally sag to the bed, boneless and utterly spent, he kisses the inside of each of my thighs before crawling over me. I'm intimately aware of every move he makes—trailing his fingers over my thighs, up my stomach, across the mounds of my breasts—and even with my eyes closed, I feel his eyes on me. His gaze sears my skin just as much as his hands do.

No one else does this to me. He makes me want to let go of everything—my guilt, my anger, my despair—and just feel again.

He trails open-mouthed kisses up my neck, pausing to suck at the throbbing pulse point there. His lips move across my jaw while his hand slips between us and cups my pussy. I shudder under him at the touch on my sensitive flesh. The press of his lips to mine is soft, and I taste my release on his tongue as he slips it inside my mouth slowly. He pulls away almost immediately and cradles my face in his free hand, softly brushing his thumb across my temple.

"Skye, open your eyes."

I comply with his demand, and his scorching eyes bore into mine.

The corner of his mouth ticks up into a sexy as hell lopsided grin. "That was incredible, I love watching you come."

Love?

Don't read too much into it, Skye.

He's so on-edge right now, with everything that's happening, that anything I say could spook him. This absolutely is *not* the time to say that word back, at least, not the way I want to.

God, I love this man.

I smile back at him, my stomach knotting, knowing I can't tell him how I really feel. So, I'll do the next best thing. "I love you making me come."

Something flashes in his eyes—pain, regret, confusion, who the hell knows. Whatever it is, it's gone before I have a chance to question him about it. He squeezes his hand over my pussy, grinding his palm against my clit and returning my attention to the here and now.

"Keep them open, I want you looking at me when I slide my cock inside you." I groan, wrapping my arms around his neck and pulling him down to me.

Whatever you want, Gabe. I'm yours.

I press my lips to his, trying to tell him everything I can't in words with my kiss. His mouth slants over mine, and he removes his hand from my core, grasping his cock and rubbing the head through my slick folds.

My legs quiver.

My heart races.

Then he pushes into me on one long, languid thrust until he's seated to the hilt.

A gasp tumbles from me into his mouth, and his groan vibrates in his chest against my breasts. His eyes darken, and I'm stripped bare, as if he's seeing all the way to my soul, and I, his.

There's something buried there, behind the impassioned depths of his gaze, that I can't place. He doesn't give me time to ponder it before he slides his tongue across my lips and rolls his hips, grinding his pubic bone against my clit.

"God..." I close my eyes and drop my head back as flickers of electricity skitter through my pussy with his movements.

He stills, and I groan in frustration.

"Keep them open." His voice is rough and the command clear.

For some reason, his need to lock eyes while he fucks me gives me hope. Maybe he's finally understanding this isn't going to go away. Maybe he's finally accepting where this is going.

His hips draw back slowly, and he pauses, his eyes on mine before he buries himself in me again.

And again.

And again.

Never looking away from me.

I'm drowning in the depths of those dark pools.

He sets a gentle, measured pace, and we both fall into it. My hips rise to meet his. We pause occasionally to kiss slowly and breathe in each other.

This is different.

There's no rush or struggle to unleash our unbridled need for each other. This is a slow, building burn.

This isn't fucking. This is making love.

Gabe fucking Anderson is making love to me.

Finally.

GABE

It's tearing me apart to peer into her eyes knowing this is the last time I'm going to be with her, knowing I'm going to shatter her as soon as we both come down from the incredible high we are building toward.

Christ, she feels so good.

The muscles of her cunt grip my cock with every retreat, and she grinds her hips against mine on every thrust, gaining the friction she needs against her clit.

Her eyes roll back, and I want to tell her to look at me again, but I don't want to interrupt her moment of bliss. Skye has been through too much, lost too much, to have to go through losing me. I need to let her enjoy this however she wants to and stop being so God damn selfish.

As much as I need to see the blue of her eyes while I bury myself in her for the last time, I need to see her lose herself in me more.

How can the most perfect moment of my life also be the worst?

Because I'm a fucking asshole who doesn't deserve a woman like Skye.

Skye needs to be with a man who can worship her—the way she *deserves* to be worshipped—a man who doesn't ask her to sneak around and hide it from her friends and family —a man who isn't a fucking broken shell of who he used to be.

I would do anything for this woman, even if it means breaking her heart.

She shudders beneath me and presses her heels into my lower back, urging me to move faster. Her nails dig into my shoulder blades and a moan slips from her perfect lips. "Please, Gabe, I need..."

I capture her face in my hand, tipping it forward. "Look at me and tell me what you need."

Her eyelids flutter open, and her lips tremble. "You...I just need you. All of you."

My rhythm falters.

If only I could give her that.

"Please." Her plea goes straight to my heart, shredding it apart until the pain in my chest steals my breath.

I pull back my hips and slam into her while I take her mouth with mine, claiming with the kiss what I can never have again—her.

Thrust after thrust, over and over, I hammer into her. Our tongues tangle and our panting breaths and moans mingle to form an erotic chorus.

It's the most exquisite sound I've heard in my entire fucking life.

A low, keening whine emanates from her, and I know she's close. Watching Skye Hawke fall apart with my cock buried inside her is the most beautiful thing in the world. Every single detail of tonight will be etched into my memory forever.

The walls of her pussy quiver and ripple around my cock. I press my lips just below her right ear and kiss her, then suck on the skin there. She groans and pumps her hips up to meet mine even harder.

"Come for me, Skye. Just let go."

Her head thrashes from side to side. "So...damn...close..."

I pull back from her face and back onto my knees, changing the angle and driving my cock into her even deeper, dragging the ball of the piercing along her G-spot. A strangled groan rips through the room and she comes—hard. Her body lurches from the bed, and she claws at my biceps, digging her heels into my back and grinding her pussy against me.

Her cunt pulls and contracts around my cock, and I can't hold back any longer.

My orgasm is ripped out of me. I come harder and longer than I have in my entire life, emptying into her hot, wet core, and losing my breath and heart in the process.

I collapse on top of her, burying my face into the side of her neck.

Fuck. I'm in love with Skye Hawke.

22

GABE

*H*er scent envelops me. Every breath I take sucks it into my lungs and warms me with contentment. I could lie here all day, just breathing her in and relishing her warm skin pressed against me.

But I can't.

I crack my eyes open and muted light from the windows hits my eyes. With a groan, I move my face away from Skye's neck and glance at the clock. 6:15 a.m. Rain pings against the window and the howl of the wind outside warns of the impending threat.

Last night was...

Jesus, I don't even have a word for it.

Sex has always been a means to an end—a way to relieve my stress and quiet some of the voices in my head. But that wasn't sex. At least, it wasn't the kind of sex I have. That wasn't fucking. That was something completely otherworldly, and the fact I can never have it again causes bile to rise up my throat and my chest to constrict so tightly, I can barely breathe.

The fact I didn't have a nightmare last night does not go unnoticed, but I can't lie here and consider why. Why doesn't matter anymore. After what happened with my father, I was fairly confident more restless, haunted nights were in my future, so sleeping soundly is almost as shocking to me as what he did. Although, knowing what I have to do now may have played a role in my uninhibited sleep. Maybe finally making the decision was all I needed.

I try to extricate myself from Skye without waking her, but we're too tangled together, and when I unwrap my arm from around her chest, she stirs, shifting against me and moaning softly.

Shit.

She's not going to make this easy for me.

Her head turns toward me, and she studies me over her shoulder—her eyes still slightly glazed and lids heavy with sleep.

"Hey."

Fuck.

That gravelly, sexy morning voice goes straight to my cock.

Down boy.

Morning sex is not an option. Having sex with her ever again is not a possibility.

It's better to end things now than to let them get further complicated by burying myself inside her one more time.

I force a small smile. "Good morning."

She rolls over until she's facing me and slides her hand under my bicep so she can wrap her arm around my rib cage. My skin is still sensitive and tight there, but it doesn't hurt. I almost wish it would.

Her breasts push against my chest, and my morning wood is wedged into her belly.

This is not fucking helping.

Nails lightly graze the skin on my back across my spine. I relax into her touch, closing my eyes, and relishing the caress. My mind clears. This is the most at peace I've felt in a long fucking time, but it's only because my mind is made up. There will be no more worrying about what our actions mean for all the relationships involved. No more lying to my best friend. No more avoiding him at all costs.

Her lips press against my pec, just above my nipple piercing and a shudder rolls through my body. She traces her tongue along my skin, slowly making her way closer to that little piece of metal.

Fuck...that feels good.

Too good.

If I let her get my nipple into her mouth, there's no hope of this ending any other way than with me fucking her brains out again.

Gathering every ounce of will-power I possess, I pull back from her, putting much-needed space between our bodies so I can clear my head and think with the right one.

But shifting away from her does nothing to ease the pain in my chest. I prop myself up on my elbow and study her.

She stares at me with hunger and confusion in her eyes, and my mind flashes back to the last time she looked at me like this—the wedding. God, she was so beautiful in her brides-maid's dress. The way the jet black curls of her hair cascaded down her back and over her shoulders had reminded me of ocean waves during a hurricane. She was absolutely stunning that night—flawless.

How had I ever been so fucking blind? How could I not have known how much I watched her before?

It took her looking at me like this and forcing me to kiss her to bring any hint at self-realization forward. But it took what happened last night for me to comprehend how deep my feelings for her truly are.

Maybe in a parallel universe, one where the accident never occurred, things could be different. But we're here, and they aren't.

The words are lodged like boulders in my throat. I close my eyes, breaking the spell she has cast on me; it's the only way I'll ever get them out.

"There's something I need to tell you."

Her warm palm flattens against my chest. "I need to tell you something, too."

SKYE

He's calm this morning.

Resolved.

It's readily apparent in his eyes. The way he's marking me with his gaze tells me everything I need to know. He feels the same way. How could he not after what we did last night? No man makes love to a woman like that unless he *actually* loves her.

His eyes close.

I wasn't going to tell him, but seeing him this morning, it just feels like the right time. Maybe what happened with his father finally made him realize he needs to hold onto something as amazing as what we have.

He takes a deep breath and opens his eyes.

It's so adorable that's he's nervous about telling me he loves me.

"We can't see each other again."

"I love you."

We speak at the same time.

When his words register, I freeze. I must have misunderstood what he said, because there's no fucking way he just dumped me.

"Wait...what?"

With a groan, he pushes off the bed until he's sitting and then moves to the edge. His feet hit the floor with a *thump*, and he rests his elbows on his knees, dropping his head into his hands.

"I'm sorry, Skye. I just...can't do this anymore. It's not fair to you, or me."

What the ever-loving fuck is he talking about?

I slide up onto my knees behind him. "You're joking, right?"

His hands move back through his hair, and he heaves out a sigh. "No, Skye, I'm being serious. We have to stop this."

"You're really doing this, after last night...I'm just..."

Speechless.

And I am *never* out of words. No one has ever accused me of biting my tongue or having a filter, but Gabe has literally sucked away my ability to speak.

The mattress creaks as he stands and turns to face me. His semi-hard dick hangs between his muscular thighs, directly in my line of sight, and I wish I could appreciate its beauty. But right now, the only thing I want to do is go all Lorena Bobbitt on him.

He's lucky there are no knives within reach.

"Skye, you know this is for the best."

The fuck it is!

I fly off the bed and am in his face in an instant. "The best for whom? You? Me? Fucking Savage?"

"It's not—"

"Oh, fuck you, Gabe. You are so worried about pissing off my brother, you're willing to throw away what you really want. And don't try to tell me you don't want me...want this." I take the last step separating us and press my hands against his chest.

His heart beats wildly, and his cock hardens all the way, digging into my belly.

Instead of wrapping his arms around me and capturing my mouth in a savage kiss like I expect, he shakes his head and takes a step back. Then another. And another.

"No, Skye. I don't want this..."

There it is. That resolve is back. His usually warm eyes are cold and haunted, and it's clear there's no room for debate.

"...and if you really think about it, you will realize you don't want it either."

Unfucking likely.

I can't look at him anymore. I can't look in his eyes knowing he's lying to me, and to himself.

So, I turn my back on him and begin to search for my clothes. Either he's full of shit or everything up to this moment has been one giant mind-fuck.

I know what last night was and so does he.

His eyes follow me around the room. My underwear peeks out from under the bed, and I snatch them up and jerk them on with my back to Gabe.

Cocksucking motherfucking prick!

The rest of my clothes are scattered around the room, and I manage to keep from facing him as I dress. If I look at him now, I'll either break down and cry or grab that gun he keeps behind the headboard and do something rash.

"Skye..."

I slip my shirt on and pull my hair back into a ponytail with the hair tie I always keep in my pants pocket. Several deep breaths later, I turn to face him.

He doesn't even have the decency to look contrite. Instead, he stands buck naked, stock-still, and with zero emotion in his handsome features. His cock has gone down, but it does nothing to change how fucking beautiful he is.

When my eyes meet his, he firms his lips into a thin line

and nods. "You know I'm right. You should be with someone who can give you everything. Like that guy, the one from the picture you sent me."

Lucas?

I roll my eyes and round the bed on my way to the door. My arm brushes his as I push past him. He doesn't reach out to try to stop me, but he follows me out to the living room where I search for my purse. "Lucas is out of the picture. He's a little overly obsessed. I ended it."

"What do you mean, obsessed? Do you need me to talk to him?"

Wheeling on him, I shoot my best death glare his way. "You can't be fucking serious." True concern mars his face. "You're a fucking selfish prick, you know that? I don't want anything from you anymore, least of all your concern or involvement in my life."

"I'm not selfish, Skye. It's the opposite. I'm choosing your ultimate happiness here. You'll thank me later."

"Ha! Whatever, Gabe. You're just a chicken shit. You would think someone who has killed so many people would have bigger balls."

He recoils as if I slapped him, but I can't feel bad about what I said. I need to stay mad so I don't fall apart.

I grab my purse off the chair next to the sofa and storm out the door, not giving two fucks if Savage or anyone else sees me leaving Gabe's place this early in the morning.

It doesn't matter anymore anyway.

By the time the elevator doors slide open, the tears are coming so fast, there's nothing I can do to stop them.

23

GABE

"*A*re you sure you have everything ready?"

I'm not always totally confident when somebody tells me they're prepared for a storm. Especially when it's my mom, or the woman who is the only mother I've ever known. The governor declared a state of emergency yesterday when the National Hurricane Center increased the hurricane watch to a warning. Hera is coming, and we need to be ready for her.

Sunday dinner had been cancelled last night so the house could be prepped.

Thank fuck!

I don't know what excuse I would have given for my absence, but there was no way I could show my face anywhere the Hawkes were gathered after what happened with Skye in the morning.

Guilt tells me I should still have shown up to help Ben get the house boarded up and ready for the storm, but I couldn't bring myself to go and look anyone in the eye knowing what I did to Skye.

Plus, after Skye flew out of my place, I had to deal with my father's lawyer. He called an hour after she left and wanted to discuss my father's will and funeral arrangements. I assured him I didn't want anything from Brian Dunne—except a few items that had belonged to my mother that I remembered being in the house while I was growing up—and informed him they could toss my father's body in the Mississippi for all I cared.

After I hung up on him, I briefly spoke with Savage about it, then spent the rest of the day drinking and contemplating every awful decision I've ever made in my life.

But one decision I can never regret, no matter how painful things might be right now with Skye, was cutting myself off from that awful man and letting the Hawkes be my true family. That's precisely why I worry so damn much about all of them.

"Yes, Gabe, Ben took care of everything yesterday. I am going to run out to the store right now to grab a few last minute items, but I'm otherwise totally set."

Riding out the storms at the Hawkes had always been somewhat of a tradition. But now that Savage had Dani and was remaining at the condo, and I was in this weird situation with Skye, who I know will be there, I've decided it's best if I just stay at home.

"Did you get the extra gas for the generator?"

She sighs, and I can picture her rolling her eyes at my overprotectiveness. "For the third time, yes. I'm ready."

"I know you told me, but that doesn't mean I don't need to check again just for my own peace of mind."

A light chuckle filters over the line. "Well, thank you for checking, Gabe. Between you, Ben, and Savage, I've spent more time assuring everyone I'm all right than I have actually doing any prep for the storm. I'll be fine. Skye says she will be here by midafternoon tomorrow, and she's going to stay until the warnings expire and the streets are safe again."

My stomach turns thinking about Skye trying to drive over there in deteriorating conditions. "Why isn't she there now?"

"Because she volunteered to go into the hospital today and tomorrow morning to help them prepare before the storm hits. They are saying landfall will be later in the evening, so she'll be fine heading over here earlier."

It doesn't appease my worry for her. She'll probably be pissed when her mom tells her I was so concerned. But that's only because she doesn't understand why I ended things. She doesn't get that it's the best thing for everyone. One day, maybe, she'll understand and forgive me.

"Okay, well let me know if you guys need anything. I'm just finishing up some things at the club and then I'm heading home."

"Are you sure you don't want to come over with us?" I let out a sigh. I would love nothing more than to be there to ensure Skye and her mother are safe. But God knows I cannot be in a confined space with Skye right now.

Every time I think about the look in her eyes when she left my place, my body shakes and my chest tightens so much I can barely breathe. If the storm wasn't about to rain down on the city, I'd be making another appointment with Doc just so I could talk about what I did and have somebody assure me I did the right thing. Then again, Doc would never say that. She would talk me in circles until I finally figured out for myself whether I'd done the right thing or not.

"Yes, I'm sure. But give me a call and let me know if you need anything. It's not impossible for me to get there with the Hummer if there's an emergency."

"Okay, I will, Gabe. Stay safe. I love you."

"I love you, too."

Shit.

Why couldn't I have said that to Skye yesterday instead of ending things? I've never said those words to a woman, other than the one I just hung up with. They are too powerful to be thrown around. Hearing them from Skye was the ultimate blow to the gut. I thought I could get away relatively unscathed, but now, that's out of the question.

I stare out the window of my office. The tumultuous sky outside confirms everything the National Hurricane Center has been saying. The storm is going to hit hard soon. With all the flooding and destruction it's already caused in Florida and the Caribbean, I'm not so sure we'll get through this one unscathed.

The check-list on my desk is complete; it's the same one I've used every time a storm has hit since we opened this place. Byron and I have already touched base with all the girls to make sure they had somewhere safe to ride out the storm, but I needed to double-check the list to make sure everything was taken care of before I could relax.

My eyes wander over to the couch on the far side of the office. Christ, I can't believe Skye was over there touching herself while I jerked off. Blood rushes to my cock just thinking about it.

You did the right thing.

It hurts now, but this is for the best.

That's what I keep trying to tell myself. Because while she may be pissed and hurt now, and while it fucking kills me, it's ultimately going to be the best for everyone.

There's a knock on my door, and Byron pops his head in. "Hey, I just got everything finished up downstairs. I'm going to take off and head home."

"Where you riding out the storm?"

Byron eyes dart away from me, and he shifts uncomfortably before returning his gaze to mine. "At a friend's house."

I smile and chuckle even though I probably shouldn't. I'm

pretty sure the "friend" he's referring to is his boyfriend, but if he doesn't want to share that with me, I'm certainly not going to make him uncomfortable by pressing it.

"Be safe. I'll see you in a couple days."

"You too, man."

The worry I have for Skye forms a knot in my stomach. I know I shouldn't, but I need to make sure she's all right.

SKYE

"Are we all set on this floor?" I peer over Brenda's shoulder at the emergency storm protocol checklist on her clipboard.

She runs her pen down the column on the left, checking off the items we just moved down to the ER from the supply closets on some of the upper floors. "Yep, it looks like that's everything on this page."

The next page contains additional items we need to locate from other departments. "All right, Brenda, you take the first ten, and I'll take the last ten. Does that work?"

"Sounds great." We split off in different directions.

The hospital is already a madhouse and the hurricane hasn't even hit yet. After Katrina, the entire protocol for storms was revamped. Everyone on staff at the hospital who deals with patients directly is called in for two days. The only reason I'm going to be able to leave and go to Mom's tomorrow is I'm not an employee of the hospital, and we close our offices during storm warnings. But I'm going to volunteer as much of my time as possible before I have to head out to her house.

Staying busy helps me keep my mind off Gabe and what happened yesterday. After I left his place, I went straight home and spent the rest of the day in bed alternating between feeling sorry for myself and being enraged with Gabe. If homicide didn't carry such a steep penalty, it might actually be on the table.

Part of me wants to call him to give him a chance to change his mind, but the other part screams at me that he had his chance and he couldn't be a fucking adult.

Let him be.

I repeat it to myself a thousand times every hour as I carry box after box around the hospital.

My phone vibrates in my pocket; it's probably Mom or Savage texting to confirm something for tomorrow. He's opting to stay at his place with Dani because he thinks she'll be more comfortable there, but he's already freaking out about me being alone with Mom out at the house. This is the first major storm since Savage and Dani got together and the first time he won't be with us. I understand his concern, so I've been trying to placate him with assurances we will be fine.

When I see the text from Gabe, I'm tempted to toss my phone in the nearest trashcan.

> Are you okay? <

Yes, I'm just fucking wonderful.

What does he expect me to say? That things are lovely? That I haven't cried a thousand tears in the last twenty-four hours, that I don't wish I could take back the words I said to him as he tore my heart out?

I take a deep breath and try to be as adult as I can, given the situation.

< I'm fine. At the hospital >

> Is there any way you can go to your mom's tonight instead of tomorrow? <

My face heats as my temper flares. What business of his is it when I get to Mom's? I'll get there when I get there. I'm not going to abandon the staff here until I absolutely have to leave.

< Why does it matter to you? >

> Because I need to know you're safe. Will you please leave

the hospital as early as you can and text me to let me know you left? <

Should I be pissed or ecstatic at his reply? I know he loves me. I understand he's lying to himself when he says he doesn't want me, doesn't want us. Can I really be mad at him for wanting to make sure I'm all right and worrying about me? Aren't I going to worry about him, too, no matter what happened?

I sigh and type out my response.

< I'll text you when I leave >

> And when you arrive at your mom's? <

Demanding, isn't he?

< Yes, and when I get to Mom's >

There are a million other things I want to say to him, but I hold them all back. They won't change anything, especially now when we all have other stuff to worry about.

We can talk after the storm passes. I can make him see what he's doing to himself and to me and why it's so fucking asinine.

"Hey Skye?"

I turn toward my name. "Yeah?"

"Brenda is looking for you. She's over in the intake area."

"All right, I'll be right over."

Keep busy.

Get shit done.

Stop thinking about Gabe.

I pray this hurricane won't do any more damage to the city, to Gabe, or me. I'm not so sure any of us can survive if it does.

24

SKYE

*R*ain pelts my windows as I work on packing up my bag to take to Mom's. I should have been there hours ago, but I ended up staying later than I had planned at the hospital last night and slept for a few hours in an on-call room so I could continue to assist this morning. It would have been prudent to pack my stuff days ago too, but I had other things on my mind at the time—mostly Gabe.

I almost wish Savage and Gabe were coming to Mom's, so I could just tell Savage what's been going on with me and Gabe. The more I thought about it over the last two days, the more I'm confident that despite what Gabe said, and as fucking pissed as I am, if I just tell Savage and get everything out in the open, it will spur Gabe into action.

He will come back to me and take what he wants. I have to believe that.

Waiting for the storm to pass is probably the smartest game

plan. But I won't wait any longer than that. The moment it's safe, I'm telling him.

Gabe loves me, and not just the kind of love someone has for someone who's been part of their life for a long time. No, he *loves* me loves me. He just can't or won't acknowledge it.

Fucking men.

The knock on the door startles me momentarily, but then my blood pressure jumps thinking it might be Gabe. Maybe he changed his mind and decided we should hunker down for the storm together. It would certainly be more fun than doing it with Mom...assuming he's changed his mind.

Hope makes you do stupid shit, like open the door without checking the peephole first.

"Skye..."

"Oh, hi Lucas. What are you doing here?"

Shit. Shit. Shit.

"I didn't like how things ended at the bar the other day, and I wanted to check on you and make sure you were okay. This storm looks like it may be bad."

Aww, well, that's actually really sweet of him to come check on me. The anger he had seems to have dissipated. Maybe he can be an adult about this whole thing, and we can somehow manage to be friends.

It would certainly make work a lot less awkward.

"I really appreciate you stopping by, Lucas, but I'm fine. I'm just about to head out to my mom's."

He frowns slightly. "The roads are really bad already, lots of flooding. Why don't you let me drive you over there? There's no way you'll get there in your car."

Fair point.

While practical for getting around town, my Corolla isn't exactly designed to deal with flooded out streets and high winds. The drive back here from the hospital two hours ago was already a little precarious, and it's been pouring non-stop since then. Lucas' Jeep is a much better option for getting across town to Mom's house.

"Okay, thanks. Come on in while I finish getting my stuff together." I step back, and he follows me into the apartment, shutting the door behind him.

It's weird to be in my apartment alone with him when the last time we were here he was fucking me and I was screaming Gabe's name. Awkward is quickly becoming the word to describe all my experiences with men lately.

I walk through my bedroom to my bathroom to grab my necessities. Lucas follows me, and I watch in the mirror as he drops down onto the bed.

My skin prickles. Gabe was in that bed. It probably still smells like him...it sure did Sunday when I came home from his place utterly devastated. Sleeping in the on-call room at the hospital last night was a respite from being immersed in Gabe's scent. I don't know if I could have made it through another night alone in that bed with the smell of him, of us, lingering there.

Shit. Did I ever pick up the condom wrappers from the floor?

What a crappy time to remember I'm a terrible house-keeper. If I ever move into a real house, I'll have to spend twenty-five percent of my income on a maid just to not end up on an episode of Hoarders.

I better wrap this up quickly and get him, and me, the fuck out of here.

His eyes meet mine in the mirror, and he grins at me. That mouth used to give me orgasms. Now, it makes me cringe. Not because he wasn't amazing in bed and to me, but because there's only one mouth I want on me and the thought of any other is appalling at this point.

It probably isn't fair of me to have him in here. I should have rejected his offer. I know he's in love with me. This is basi-cally abuse, but I can't turn him down now.

"I'm all set." I drop my toiletries in my duffel bag on the floor and hike it up over my shoulder.

Lucas jumps off the bed and invades my personal space.

Shit, is he going to kiss me?

I step back, but he just moves in closer and pulls the bag from me with a smile. "I got it."

Whew.

He follows me to the door. I can actually feel his eyes on me the whole time. I shudder. I've never felt this uncomfortable with Lucas before. I never realized my feelings for Gabe would make me react so differently to someone I spent so much intimate time with. It feels like being with a stranger now.

We pause just inside the door to the complex. The wind whips the driving rain practically sideways. I'm surprised the trees in front of my building haven't snapped in half yet.

There's no way we'll make it to his Jeep without getting drenched.

When we step outside, I can see why Lucas suggested he drive me. The road in front of my apartment building already has several inches of standing water, and there's a car stuck in even deeper water where the road passes under the railroad tracks further down.

"Damn, I didn't realize it was this bad already." Things are even worse than when I came home from the hospital only a couple hours ago.

Lucas places his hand on my lower back and ushers me toward his Jeep parked several spots down from my building. "I know, and it's only going to get worse."

∾

GABE

Where the hell is she?

Skye hasn't answered any of my five calls today. I got a short text from her around noon telling me she was leaving the hospital. But since then, nothing.

The weather's getting worse and phone reception has been spotty, at best. That's just what I fucking need—to be completely cut off from Skye and everyone else during a fucking hurricane.

I know she's not at her mom's. Neither her mom, Storm, nor Savage had heard from her when I was able to get through to them earlier. Maybe she hasn't left for her mother's yet, but if she thinks she's driving there herself, she's insane. The roads are atrocious, and her car will sink in the first big puddle she hits.

We'll just have to hang tight at my place and pray to God Savage doesn't notice the sexual tension between us and the animosity she's sure to be throwing my way.

I try calling her one more time as I turn down the already-flooded road to her apartment. The same error message telling me to try my call again later rings in my ears. Her car is still parked out front. At least she wasn't dumb enough to try to drive herself.

She better be ready to go, if we wait any longer, we may get stuck here, and she doesn't have a generator like Savage and I do. I park in front of her building and race through the rain to the front door, which is thankfully unlocked.

I climb the stairs to the second floor two at a time and make my way down the hallway to her apartment.

My pounding on her door garners no response so I try to call her again.

Nothing.

Something is not right.

Skye doesn't go dark. Even after Star died. Even when she's at her worst, she's always in contact with someone.

She's pissed at me, and she has every right to be, but with the hurricane bearing down on us, I doubt she would willfully ignore my calls and text messages. One thing Skye is not is stupid.

So, where the fuck is she?

Is she with that guy?

No, Skye wouldn't go to him. Not after what she said about him at my place. She called him "obsessed," and remembering that word coming from her lips sends a shiver down my spine.

Obsession can make people do really fucked up things.

Like sleep with your best friend's little sister.

Fuck.

I don't care, her landlord will just have to bill me.

With one swift front kick, her door breaks away from the frame, and I push my way in. I make a mental note to talk to her landlord about installing stronger door frames and better locks. That was way too easy.

Everything seems normal but it's eerily quiet except for the sound of the storm raging outside. She's not here. One glance in her bedroom and bathroom tells me she already packed up too.

So where did she go, and how the fuck did she get there?

"*Fuck!*" My bellow echoes in her apartment, and there's a yelp from the hallway.

An elderly woman with wide eyes sticks her head around the doorjamb. When she sees me, she yelps again and disappears.

"Wait!" I run to the door and find her shuffling down the hallway away from me as fast as her short legs and walker can take her. "Ma'am, please stop."

I get a quick, frightened look from over her shoulder.

"Ma'am, I just need a minute." I catch up with her and

move to block her path. The poor woman is probably scared shitless. A broken door and a big, unknown man screaming profanities in the middle of the apartment. "Do you know Skye Hawke, the woman who lives in that apartment?"

The old lady examines me slowly and nods.

"Okay, great. Look, I'm a friend of hers, and I can't find or reach her. Do you know where she went? She's not home, and her car's still here. I'm worried about her."

She considers me for a moment and reaches a hand into a bag attached to the side of the walker. "You broke into her apartment." I see her small hand close around something in an aerosol container.

Mace.

Can't say I blame her for being leery.

I step back and hold my hands up in a non-threatening manner.

"I told you, I've been trying to get in touch with her all day, and no one in her family has heard from her. She's not where she's supposed to be riding the storm out, so I came looking." I glance back at the busted door and then return my attention to the old lady. "I'm going to pay to have that repaired. Please, just tell me if you know where she is."

Her narrowed eyes open slightly, and she pinches her lips together before she gives me a sad smile. "She left about half an hour ago with her boyfriend."

Her boyfriend?

My blood runs cold, and I clench my fists together to keep from punching the wall and further terrifying the poor creature.

"If he's her boyfriend, who are you?"

Fair question.

"Just a friend. A friend who's worried." I try my best to appear completely sincere and not show her the rage simmering just below the surface.

With a knowing look, she gives me a half smile. "Good luck."

I step to the side to permit her to pass, and she shuffles around me toward the apartment at the end of the hallway.

If Skye left with Lucas, it couldn't have been unwillingly.

Neighborhood watch lady seems the type to have called the cops or at least told me if she thought Skye were in any danger. But why the fuck would she be with Lucas? And where the hell did they go?

Maybe Savage has heard from her by now. I call him as I try to put her apartment door back in place. I manage to get it back in the frame but if anyone bothers to try pushing it, gaining entry would be simple.

Shit.

I hope no one steals anything, but I don't have the time to locate the super and, with the storm, I doubt he would fix it immediately anyway. My call to Savage fails.

Fuck.

The drive to my building takes twice as long as normal with the awful roads. My stomach twists with each passing block. By the time I push open the door to Savage and Dani's, I'm almost doubled-over with the pain. Princess charges me, yapping and jumping against my leg to get me to pick her up.

"Down, girl."

Dani emerges from the hallway, her hand placed protectively on her protruding belly. "Gabe? What's wrong?"

"Have you or Savage heard from Skye recently?"

Savage appears next to her. "No, I haven't spoken with her since the last time you called to ask."

"Fucking shit!" I kick the end table next to the couch and the metal reverberates. Dani flinches and moves closer to Savage. He turns his head and kisses her belly, and then moves toward me, concern etched in his features.

"Gabe, what the hell is going on?"

This isn't going to end well.

"Skye is missing. I haven't heard from her since noon when she said she was leaving the hospital. She was supposed to go home and grab her bag then head to your mom's. Since then, she hasn't answered my calls or texts. She's not at your mom's, and she wasn't at her apartment. Apparently, according to one of her neighbors, she left with that douchebag, Lucas."

Dani comes over to us and rests her hand on Savage's shoulder. "Are you sure you're not overreacting? So what if she left with Lucas. Isn't she dating the guy? Maybe he decided to go to Mom's with her."

I growl and stomp my foot. "You aren't listening to me. Something is wrong. She would have responded to my texts or answered my calls if she could have."

He narrows his eyes at me. "Why are you so worried about where Skye is, or who she's with?"

Savage is never going to believe she's in trouble unless I tell him the truth.

Christ, here it goes.

"Because we've been sleeping together."

25

GABE

I barely escaped alive.

If Savage could have gotten his hands on me, I'm pretty sure he would have strangled me. He damn near tried. Only Dani stepping between us finally stopped his tirade. That might be as close to death as I've ever been, and I spent eight years in and out of war zones.

Dani convinced Savage to table the much-needed conversation until after we locate Skye. If the look in his eyes is any indication, the "conversation" will not be going well.

But I won't, *can't,* worry about that now. The only thing that matters is finding Skye.

Thank fuck for Dani.

Not only did she wrangle Savage, she also told me I should check the hospital. Even if Skye didn't go back there, she knew Lucas worked there based on something Skye mentioned at a family dinner a couple weeks ago. Maybe someone there knows how I can find him.

The city is already in chaos. Even though Hera is only expected to make landfall as a category one hurricane, she's already causing massive flooding and other problems throughout the area.

I've never been more thankful that I wasted money on my Hummer. I know people see them and assume the person driving it is overcompensating for something and a total douchebag, but mine is a legitimate off-road vehicle, complete with snorkel, so any flooding doesn't stop my progress.

By the time I arrive at the hospital, it's been over five hours since anyone has heard from Skye. The longer I go without hearing from her, the worse the churning in my stomach and the greater the feeling of dread weighing on my shoulders.

I enter through the emergency entrance and wander the main hallway of the hospital until I find a directory for the departments. The office where Skye works is in an adjacent building; I'll need to go up a level and across the skywalk to get there. But I'll check there first; it's the most logical place she would be.

Deserted. The place is completely empty, with all the lights off and the doors locked tight.

Shit.

I guess it makes sense they would be shut down during the storm. But maybe she's helping in the ER.

The entire hospital is a clusterfuck. People on gurneys are pushed past me, heading off in all directions. The storm is already taking its toll based on what I'm seeing outside and in here.

That doesn't make me feel any better about Skye potentially being out there. And with Lucas.

I head directly for the nurse's station. A young red head seated at the desk with her nose in a chart flicks her eyes up to me. "Can I help you, sir?"

"Yeah, I'm looking for Skye Hawke."

Her eyebrows shoot up, and she examines me, her dark brown eyes moving from my face down over my chest where my wet t-shirt clings to me, until the top of the desk blocks her view. The corner of her mouth quirks up. "And who are you?"

An impatient man...

"I'm her brother's business partner, Gabe Anderson. We've been looking for her all afternoon. Have you seen her?"

The playful and flirtatious demeanor she had a moment ago are replaced by concern. "Oh, no, I haven't. I know she was here helping this morning, but I think she left several hours ago. Is she okay?"

Dammit. Where the hell is she?

I slam my palms down against the top of the desk. "Fuck! I hope so. Do you know this Lucas guy she was seeing? I guess he works here?"

"Lucas Oliver? Oh, yeah, he works in HR."

The moment the words are out of her mouth, I'm running down the hall. I remember passing the HR office on my way to the elevator earlier.

I'm relieved to find the hallway in front of the human resources department deserted.

I can see the lights are off through the frosted glass window on the door. I'm counting on everyone being too distracted by injuries from the storm to worry about me lingering suspiciously in the hall.

It's been a while since I've had to pick a lock; I'm hoping it's just like riding a bike. After a quick check to make sure I'm still inconspicuous, I grab my wallet and slide out a credit card.

Thankfully, it appears the hospital isn't too concerned with anyone breaking into their H.R. department. They didn't even bother to put a deadbolt on the door.

Please let this be easy.

If I can't get it open, the only way to get in would be to kick the door down, and that's sure to draw attention. Getting arrested isn't on the top of my "things to do" list today, so I'd like to avoid committing another felony if at all possible.

I wedge the card in between the door frame and the handle then jimmy it up and down until I feel the lock release.

A quick glance down either side of the hall tells me I'm still in the clear, and I duck inside and shut the door behind me.

Thank fuck for lax security.

The flashlight function on my cell is going to have to do. I can't risk turning on any lights.

I survey the office, making my way past the receptionist's desk and toward the back, down a main hallway with offices branching off either side. *Lucas Oliver* appears on a door to my left, but I move past it toward my target.

The file room is exactly where I thought it would be, all the way in the back corner.

Get what you need. Get out. Get Skye.

Metallic file cabinets line the walls all the way around the room and two rows of them run up the middle. It only takes a moment to find the "O" cabinets.

Why the fuck are there so many O names?

I flip through them, listening carefully for anyone entering the office behind me. Oakton. Oats. Obermeyer. Odell. Ogden. Olan. Oldham. When "Oliver, Lucas" touches my hand, my heart actually stops for a moment.

His address is printed right on the first page below his name and date of birth.

I'm coming for you, Skye.

∾

SKYE

The storm rages as we inch our way through the flooded streets and around downed trees.

We haven't been hit like this since Hurricane Isaac back in 2012. It was the summer before the accident, and the last time Star and I rode a storm out together. We were at the house with Mom, Gabe, and Savage. Stone was away at school, and Storm was at her house with Ben and Angelina, who was a newborn at the time.

Star always loved storms. The energy and power of them fascinated her. I always thought she should have gone into meteorology instead of nursing, but she shared my love of helping people and didn't think predicting the weather would fill that need in her.

I remember her sitting at the back window, peering out of the small crack left between the boards Savage and Gabe had used to reinforce the window. Her eyes lit up every time the sky did. "God's fireworks" is what she always called it. I thought her love for storms was a bit odd, but I never told her that. I didn't need to, because she knew and she didn't care at all.

Thinking back, Gabe's behavior should have been a clue something was wrong even back then. Each crack of thunder made him flinch slightly, and he avoided going anywhere near the windows.

He had just been discharged a few months earlier and had returned to New Orleans to work with Savage. Their dream was always to run the Hawkeye businesses together, and Savage was thrilled to have him back, assisting him.

Growing up, we would always play board games and listen to the radio during storms, a tradition we continued into adulthood. But that night, Gabe disappeared into one of the back bedrooms and shut the door instead of joining us.

I didn't think it strange at the time. I was too busy being pissed at him for continuing to treat me like a sister and sleeping with a never-ending string of girls to recognize he was struggling. Maybe things would have been different if I hadn't been so blind to what was happening with him then.

Star hadn't been blind, though. She had wandered back at some point to check on him and didn't return for almost an hour. When she did, her eyes were red as if she'd been crying. Gabe came out and joined us a few minutes later, with a plastered-on smile and fake enthusiasm. At least, that's what I know they were now. At the time, I never suspected there was anything wrong.

If only I'd been paying better attention instead of being so focused on what I wanted...

"So, what have you been up to the last couple days?"

Lucas' question brings me back to the present.

Working. Fucking Gabe. Avoiding my brother.

"Oh, you know, working and prepping for the storm. I was at the hospital yesterday and this morning chipping in."

He nods but keeps his eyes on the road. "Did you give any more thought to what we discussed at the bar the other night?"

Wow. He can't be serious. That conversation could not have been misconstrued to be anything but a total and complete break up, without any hope of a reconciliation. This time, I know for a fact I didn't say anything he could have read more into.

"Uh...not really. I thought I was pretty clear about how I felt."

An odd chuckle comes from his side of the car. Does he think this is funny?

"I know that the other night you seemed confused. But I know that, given time, you'll realize we both want the same thing."

I stifle a laugh. I probably shouldn't piss him off while I'm still reliant on him for a ride, but his inability to accept what I'm telling him is bordering on comical. Has he never been dumped before?

"And what is that, Lucas? What do you think we both want?"

He grins. "To be together, of course. The last four months have been amazing. I know we started out just as friends with benefits or whatever, but you can't deny that there are stronger feelings there now. I know there are."

Jesus, this is going to be a long car ride.

"Lucas, of course I care about you. You're a great guy, and we've had a lot of fun. But, I think deep down, we both know this was never meant to be more than a short-time deal."

His knuckles turn white on the steering wheel but he remains focused on the road. "You don't know what you're saying."

I don't bother to reply. Clearly, whatever I say is only going to go over his head and out the window into the storm. I've never had to deal with a clingy guy before. The last boyfriend I had was in college and even after two years, when things ended, they were over. We both moved on.

There's probably some etiquette for this, but I have no idea what it is.

Star was the diplomatic one. She was always reining me in and making sure I didn't put my foot in my mouth. Without her here, I'm constantly floundering to find the right things to say. Maybe saying nothing is the best thing right now.

Instead, I return my attention to the passing city and the destruction already happening. We're moving agonizingly slowly so it takes me almost ten minutes to notice we're going the wrong direction.

What the hell?

"Um, Lucas...my mom's house is the other way."

He glances over at me and gives me a smile that I'm sure is meant to be reassuring, but there's something dark and cold beneath it. Images of Kathy Bates in *Misery* swim through my head.

When did Lucas become creepy?

I've never felt these weird vibes from him before today.

No. Stop.

It's probably nothing. There's a reasonable explanation.

"I know. I just need to run by my place quickly to grab something before I take you over there. Some of the roads are already washed out so going from my place is actually easier."

For someone who was so nervous about me driving and getting me to Mom's safely, it sure seems strange he'd want to detour all the way to his apartment. Something is definitely up.

He has an ulterior motive. Whether that's hoping we get stranded alone together at his place or something else, I'm not about to spend the next two days with Lucas. Not when he thinks he's in love with me, and I can't stop thinking about Gabe.

I grab my phone from my pocket. If I can get ahold of him, he'll come grab me from Lucas'. His Hummer will make it through just about anything, so I'm sure he can get me to Mom's.

Shit. No reception.

The fucking cell towers are probably down because of the storm. Maybe I can get a text out. If it doesn't send right away, it will when service is back up.

< On way to Lucas'. Come get me. Symphony Building, Apt. 1012. Hurry. >

I hit send and pray to God it goes through. I don't want to spend another minute longer than necessary with Lucas.

"Who are you texting?" His voice makes me jump.

I force a smile and turn to him. "Oh, no one. I was just checking to see if cell service was back up."

His eyes narrow at me for a moment before he grins and returns his attention to the road. "Oh, I bet they'll be down for some time. It's really inconvenient to be so cut off, don't you think?"

26

GABE

The Symphony Building looms in front of me, though the top floors are barely visible against the dark sky and through the driving rain.

Things have gone from bad to worse. And the phones still aren't working.

Son of a bitch.

I run through the deluge to the front door of the building.

Locked.

Fuck.

For a brief moment, I consider breaking the solid glass door pane, but then someone exits the elevator inside and walks toward the mailboxes to the left of the front entrance.

I pound on the glass to get the guy's attention and smile as friendly as I can when he turns toward me. He moves to the door and opens it for me but doesn't move out of the way.

"Who are you here for? You should just use the buzzer." He

points toward the list of residents near the door over a small buzzer box.

Shrugging, I try to look as innocent as possible. "I know, I've been buzzing my friend Lucas up in apartment twelve for a while, but he hasn't been answering. He must be in the shower or something. Can you let me in?" I'm absolutely drenched, and I force my body to shake in hopes he'll feel pity on me.

Come on, dude.

Dropping Lucas' name and apartment number apparently does the trick, or maybe it's my stellar "woe is me" performance, because he moves to the side and lets me enter the lobby.

"Thanks, man. It's nasty out there."

He looks out and nods. "No shit."

I clap him on the shoulder and mumble another thanks before jogging to the elevators. Just as I press the "up" button, the lights in the lobby flicker out, as does the light on the elevator bottom.

Shit.

The power is out.

A red exit sign at the end of the lobby catches my eye. I run to it and shove it open before racing up the stairs. By the sixth flight, I'm cursing the fact Lucas lives on the tenth floor and wondering if I need to do more cardio at the gym, but I eventually make it.

Apartment 1012 is at the end of the long, dark hall. The only illumination is the red exit sign and one emergency flood light that probably runs on a generator.

I pause outside Lucas' door and listen for any signs of someone inside.

There are two possible approaches here. One—I could go in guns blazing. Literally. Two—I can knock and hope he answers. He doesn't know who I am. There's no reason for him to suspect anything more than me maybe being a neighbor he doesn't know.

As much as I want to shoot the fucker, option two is probably the most prudent.

I rap my knuckles against the door and listen for a response. Silence.

I pound harder.

Silence.

The dark hallway is empty. I have only one option at this point. I'm not leaving without getting inside this apartment.

There's a deadbolt on this door, and I don't have time to get what I need to pick it.

Damnit.

I'll have some explaining to do when this is all done. I'm probably going to end up back in a jail cell, but I don't care. He has Skye, and I'm getting her back.

Two kicks is all it takes before the door releases from the frame. I won't have much time before a neighbor comes to investigate.

Work fast.

It's immediately clear no one's here. I search for any sign of Skye as I make my way through the small apartment.

My heart races and my vision turns red when I open the last door. What should be a guest bedroom is instead some sort of sick shrine.

Photos of Skye plaster the walls and range from close-up shots in bed where she's clearly posing for the camera to ones that were taken from a block or two away with a telephoto lens.

The latter appear to be very recent, maybe even from the last couple of days.

Fuck. Fuck. Fuck.

He's more of a psycho than I ever thought.

I check my phone again.

No service.

But a text came through...from Skye.

The words make my blood run cold. He fucking has her. There's no question about it now, and they aren't here. My worst fear is a reality.

The wooden desk chair splinters as I slam it against the wall. I reach under the desk and flip it, tossing the contents of the drawers onto the floor.

I rummage through the papers, searching for anything that might give me a hint where he took her.

My eyes land on the bottom drawer of the sick psycho's desk, which managed to stay closed. I yank it out, and its contents take my rage to a level I never thought possible.

You've got to be fucking kidding me.

A drawer overflowing with women's underwear I can only assume belong to Skye tells me all I need to know about this fucker. He's not living through this.

There's plenty of Skye's things in here, but no sign of Skye actually being here any time recently.

Where the hell are you?

Returning to the living room, I search for absolutely anything. His mail sits unopened on the kitchen counter. I tear through, praying for anything to give me a clue to where he may have taken her.

First, breaking and entering...three times. And now, federal mail fraud.

It's been a real banner day for me.

A notice from St. Tammany Parish Assessor's office catches my eye.

I rip it open.

Dear Mr. Oliver,

We have made repeated attempts to contact you regarding

your property located at 35305 Laurent Drive, Slidell, St. Tammany Parish, Louisiana 70458. As you know, the property taxes for this location were due on January 1, 2017 and have yet to be paid. Please contact us immediately to avoid any further legal action being taken against you in regard to this matter.

  Parish Assessor

He has another house.
Fuck!

~

SKYE

The darkness and bone-chilling cold of the room are suffocating.

Wind howls outside and thrashes rain against the windows. The entire house shakes violently with every gust.

I shudder and snuggle down deeper under the blanket.

I've weathered worse storms and been through some serious shit the last few years. But this takes the cake.

Shit.

Trying to stay positive and not let my mind wander down the road of worst-case scenarios is nearly impossible.

I'd give anything to have Gabe here right now. He's always been there for me, for Star, for all of us, whatever we needed, whenever we needed it. And I need him now, more than ever.

Where are you, Gabe?

You promised you would always come…

FALL 2004

"Where's Star?"

Christy glares up at me from where she sits on the couch,

talking with her boyfriend, Greg, with a red Solo cup of shitty beer in her hand, and shrugs. "How the hell should I know?"

"Because I left her here with you, and you promised you would keep an eye on her!" My head throbs, and I pinch the bridge of my nose. I can't believe she would let Star wander off. Christy knows how wasted and upset she is and that she shouldn't be left alone.

My stomach roils even though I haven't drunk enough to get sick. It just tells me what I already know—somewhere, Star is really not doing well. While the constant feeling of being connected to her is comforting on many levels, one of the downsides of the whole twin thing is the pangs of pain and discomfort I feel when she's sick or hurting. And right now, she is definitely both.

I peek at my watch.

It's after midnight. Mom will flip a fucking lid if Star and I don't make it home before one. The only reason I even left Star was to try to find us a sober ride.

My search was unsuccessful and, as the seconds tick by on my watch, I can already hear the lecture not only from Mom, but Savage, too. Words like "irresponsible," "reckless," and "immature," echo in my ears—the same ones I've heard at least a dozen times from them in the not-so-distant past.

And now, I let Star get drunk. Star, the one who never drinks. Star, who is usually jumping on the "Skye is careless" bandwagon and mothering me when we are out.

To be fair, she really needed it. After what that little twat-waffle Mike did to her—telling her he needed "time to be alone" and breaking up with her this morning only to show up here tonight with that slutbag Audra—she deserved to unwind and drown her sorrows.

But Savage and Mom won't see it that way. Never.

I need to get her sobered up and home. STAT.

So, I swallow my anger at Christy and focus on what needs to be done. "At least come help me find her."

She sighs and pushes herself up from the couch, bringing her cup and bad attitude with her. Greg grabs her hand. "Where are you going?" The pout he gives her makes me want to vomit even more.

Christy bends down and kisses him. "I'll be right back."

With a massive eye-roll, I turn back to the party and start looking for Star again. Christy follows. I make my way through all the rooms on the first floor of our classmate's house asking people if they've seen her.

No sign of Star.

The yard garners the same result, so we take the search upstairs.

I knock on each locked door I come to and receive some dirty looks from the guys who open them. I'm no doubt interrupting some fumbling attempt to get laid.

High school boys are such fucking losers.

When I reach the last closed door, I send up a silent prayer Star didn't somehow end up alone with one of the less than gentlemanly boys from our school. "Star?" I knock on the door and get a muffled, mumbled reply that sounds vaguely like my name.

A twist of the knob tells me she didn't even bother to lock it.

The hinges creak when I push the door open. A mixture of relief and concern flood me. She's alone in the bathroom, but also laying on the tile floor in front of the toilet, looking as shitty as I now feel.

"See, you found her."

I glance over my shoulder at Christy.

"Can I go now?"

"No."

She rolls her eyes at me. I ignore her and step into the bathroom to kneel down next to Star, brushing her dark hair back off her forehead. "Star, wake up."

Star stirs, rolling more onto her side, and turning her face up toward me. "Skye...ugh...I'm sick."

"No shit, Sherlock. We're gonna get you home."

Christy moves into the bathroom and leans against the counter. "I thought you couldn't find a ride?"

"I didn't, but I have someone I can call."

27

SKYE

FALL 2004

Pick up. Pick up. Pick up. Pick up. *Pick up.*

Come on, Gabe. Answer your damn phone.

Christy returns with the cup of water she reluctantly got for Star after I asked her twice. "Who are you calling?"

I take the cup from her and hand it to Star, who I've managed to get sitting against the wall instead of face-planted on the tile, then turn back to Christy. "Gabe."

A spark of interest flares in Christy's eyes. "Ooo, is that the hot blond who's always with Savage?"

My chest vibrates with the growl threatening to emerge.

Back off.

I manage to swallow it down and return my attention to Star. "Star..."

Her glossy, bloodshot eyes try to meet mine, but she fails, and her chin drops down onto her chest.

"Shit."

Just before I'm sure Gabe's voicemail is going to pick up, he answers. *Thank God.*

"What's wrong, Skye?"

A relieved breath rushes from my mouth despite the annoyance in his voice. "I need you to come pick me and Star up."

Shuffling sounds on the line along with an exasperated sigh. "Why?"

"Because I've been drinking and Star is wasted and sick. Please don't make me call Savage." If Storm were in town, I would have called her in a heartbeat. I know she would never rat us out to Mom or Savage. But with her gone at college, my choices for discreet emergency transportation are severely limited.

Gabe may not be happy about it, but he won't say no. He would never leave us hanging or at the mercy of Savage's paternal lectures. I'm just lucky he's home on leave right now, otherwise, we'd be fucked. This time next week, we'd be facing Savage's temper and Mom's disappointment.

"Give me the address." His voice comes out rough and low, and even though I know he would never deny us the help we need, I also know I'm going to get a fucking earful from him that may end up being worse than what I would have received from Mom or Savage.

It's always worse coming from someone you're in love with.

I rattle off the address and hang up before he can say anything else about the situation. I'll hear enough from him about it when he gets here. Assuming he's at home, he should be here pretty quickly.

I lean forward and cup Star's cheek. "Wake up, Star. Gabe is coming to get us."

Her eyes flutter open and she smiles. "Gabe's coming?"

"Yes, he'll be here soon. Can you get up and walk downstairs with me?"

A giggle rocks her body, and she shakes her head side to side. "Nuh uh. Not going downstairs. I don't want to see that jerk. Is he still here?"

Mike had been out on the front lawn when I first started looking for Star, but that was almost twenty minutes ago; he could be anywhere by now. "No, he left. Let's get you downstairs."

I slide my arm under her and try to help her stand, but she immediately lunges for the toilet and heaves. My own stomach turns, and I swallow the bile back. Her hair hangs down around her face so I lean over her and pull it back, holding it behind her head and rubbing her back gently, just like she's done for me a hundred times.

Talk about an ironic swap of circumstances. It feels like I'm in my own version of *Trading Places* in which Star takes on the role of the irresponsible, irrational, drunk twin, and I the role of the careful, trustworthy, reliable twin.

Fucking eh.

Star heaves again, and I pat her back. When she finally stops, I hand her the cup of water and let her wash her mouth out. I've been there way too many times and know how nasty it is.

She falls back onto her butt on the tile and drops her head into her hands with a groan. I sit next to her and wrap my arm around her.

"Skye?"

"Hmm?"

"Why did I drink so much?"

I laugh even though it really isn't funny. "Because men are fucking assholes."

Christy has disappeared. Not surprising. She probably bolted the minute the heaving started.

Star moves her head over against my shoulder and peers up at me with glassy and unfocused eyes. A smile cracks the corner of her mouth. "Gabe's not an asshole." The sing-song way she says it and the giggle that follows make me smile despite the fear churning in my gut that she may reveal something about the way I feel to him in her drunken state.

"No, no he's not." He's fiercely loyal, strong, compassionate, honest—everything anyone could ever want in a man. And I can't have him.

Christy appears in the doorway, her cheeks flushed, and a stupid grin on her face. She steps into the bathroom, and Gabe fills the door behind her. "Look who I found outside." With a giggle, she turns toward him and places her hand on his exposed forearm.

Back the hell off, bitch. I peed on him, he's mine!

He brushes her hand away without taking his eyes off me and Star. "Thanks for showing me where they were. Have a nice evening."

Her face falls at his dismissal, and she huffs and shoves past him, back into the hallway. His luscious lips fall into a deep frown, and he steps closer before squatting down in front of us.

The soft green of his eyes darkens. He reaches out and brushes hair back from Star's face.

"Jesus, Skye...how much did she drink?"

"Enough." I can't bear the disappointment and condemnation in his eyes. He doesn't even have to say the words. I should have protected her. I never should have let her get this far gone. This is all my fault.

His eyes hold mine for another moment. My chest tightens under his stare. The brotherly affection I see there makes my eyes burn with unshed tears.

When will he ever stop seeing me as a child who needs rescuing?

∾

GABE

PRESENT DAY

How the fuck did this happen?

I went from being worried about how Savage would react to finding out about me and Skye, to trying to locate her fucking kidnapper.

I should have known he was a threat. When she told me about how he's been acting, I should have had a conversation with him and made things very clear. Even if I couldn't be with Skye, he needed to know she was off limits. She's only in this situation because I was too stupid to recognize the threat and protect her.

If anything happens to her, Savage will never forgive me. I'll never be able to forgive myself.

Damnit.

This storm is making things a thousand times more difficult.

Washed out roads and downed trees and powerlines impede my progress at every fucking turn. A drive to Tammany Parish should only take half an hour, but after getting across the Twin Span Bridge, I have to take a dozen detours before I finally reach the area where Lucas' property is located.

Just outside Slidell, it abuts Bayou Bonfouca and the Big Branch Marsh Wildlife Preserve. Wind buffets my Hummer, shaking it as I slowly proceed down flooded streets. The driving rain makes it impossible to see street signs or anything beyond a few yards from the road.

Come on.

Where the fuck is it?

I pass a gravel drive on the south side of the main road for the third time. There's nothing marking it, but there are no other signs of civilization within a half a mile in either direction.

This has to be it. There's nothing else out here.

I run through the plan I've already gone over a hundred times during the drive.

Get onto the property.

Recon the building.

Get the fuck in.

Get Skye the fuck out.

Right now, I'm acting on instinct and training. I've never been more thankful for the U.S. Army than at this moment.

I ditch my Hummer near the road and dump my wallet and keys into the glove compartment so I'm totally unencumbered and there's nothing to announce my presence. Then, I proceed on foot into the thick brush and trees leading into the property.

She has to be okay. There are too many things I need to tell her, things I need to explain.

Skye's eyes filled with tears are at the forefront of my mind. I did that to her. I was selfish and let her believe there was a chance for us, then I smashed her to pieces again.

She needs to know how sorry I am for everything; it can't end like this. I can't let her think I don't love her.

Damnit, Gabe, you really fucked this up.

My boots stick in the thick mud and the trees do little to shield me from the pelting rain or thrashing winds. I should be freezing, but the adrenaline coursing through my bloodstream keeps me warm.

Branches slice at my bare arms and water runs into my eyes as I fight my way through the muck.

Jesus.

How far back does this property go? I must have hiked at least a mile and seen no signs of any human activity except the barely-visible drive running parallel to my path. Although, with the wind and thunder, I wouldn't be able to hear much anyway, and the flashes of lightning are my only guiding light. I can't risk using a flashlight and alerting him to my presence.

Deep puddles swallow me up to my thighs in places and suck me down like quicksand. With the bayou and wetlands so close to the property, it could very well be under feet of water before the storm is done.

Why the hell would he come out here?

The million and one creepy, perverted things he could be doing to Skye out in the middle of nowhere with no one to hear her screams pushes me forward through the sludge.

I'm starting to wonder if there is really anyone out here.

If they aren't here, I don't know how I'll ever find her.

That thought makes my stomach knot, and I pause for a moment against a tree to gather my shit together. I have to stop thinking like that and concentrate on completing my mission.

I turn my head and a soft glow appears through the trees in front of me. I approach slowly, creeping along the wet, muddy ground the last several yards until I'm at the edge of the tree-line.

The cabin sits in a small clearing, surrounded by overgrown bushes and low hanging Cypress trees. The mud-covered brown Jeep parked in front of the cabin matches the description Storm gave me the day he picked her up from her mom's house. A hazy light is visible through sheer curtains covering one of the two windows.

There only appears to be one door, at least on this side of the building.

One way in, and one way out.

Movement in the window draws my attention away from my re-con of the surroundings. There's definitely someone inside.

Skye's tear-filled eyes flash before me again. I shake my head.

Get your shit together, Anderson.

I can't concentrate on what I need to do if I have her obscuring my clarity of mind.

He's going down, one way or another.

No way he can fuck with my girl and expect to walk away from this.

The curtain in the front window parts and the motherfucker's face appears, pressed against the dirty glass. I recognize him from the photo on the front of his file at the hospital.

He scans out the window, then up, then back toward the woods just as another crack of lightning rips across the sky, illuminating his face.

And me.

It might as well have been a spotlight falling on me, announcing my presence.

Our eyes meet momentarily, and his widen before the curtain drops, and he retreats into the cabin. No doubt to locate a weapon of some sort.

There goes the element of surprise.

Acting now is the only option.

I move from behind the tree.

A blinding white light flashes and a boom louder than any IED I've ever heard explodes in my ears before the world goes black.

28

GABE

PRESENT DAY

Clarity returns slowly, and with it, searing pain and fuming anger.

Where the hell am I?

The throbbing in my head is only eclipsed by the agony from my left shoulder. I try to lift my right hand over to check it but something restricts my movement. Cold air surrounds me, and I can't stop my body from shaking violently.

What the fuck is going on?

My arms are stuck behind my back. I tug again and white hot pain radiates through my left arm.

"Fuck!"

Shuffling noises come from my left, and I turn my head toward them.

I open my eyes, or at least attempt to, but warm, thick blood flows down into them and obscures my vision. All I get is flashes of light and movement and extreme dizziness as every-thing I can see swirls around me like I'm trapped inside a tornado.

"You're awake. Good. That will make this much more enjoyable."

The voice isn't familiar.

I'm wet. I'm cold. I'm bleeding.

And I'm pretty sure my shoulder is dislocated.

The sound of rain pounding on a roof and wind howling and rattling the windows registers.

There was a storm...I was driving in it...where was I going?

Brief flashes of washed-out streets and flooded roads come to me.

Then in a split second, my brain finally comes back online and everything clicks into place.

Skye.

Lucas.

The cabin.

I made it through the woods. I found the cabin. I saw him.

What I don't remember is how the fuck I got inside.

"That lightning sure saved me a lot of effort. If it hadn't struck next to you and knocked you out, I would have had to fight you. Something tells me I probably would have lost that battle. You are one big dude. It was hard enough dragging you in here."

Fucking lightning.

Even Mother Nature seems to have it out for me. Maybe it's karma for the way I treated Skye. I guess I probably deserve it.

I twist my right hand around and reach my fingers up to feel my wrists. My arms are pulled between two slats in the back of the chair and some sort of rope binds my hands together behind me.

Something cracks me on the side of the head and it snaps back. I breathe deeply and absorb the pain. The room spins when I try to open my eyes. I don't know what he hit me with, but it certainly wasn't his fist. The familiar metallic tang of blood fills my mouth.

"Now, do you want to tell me who you are and why you're here, or do you need some more motivation?"

My only motivation is Skye and getting her out of here safely. I listen to his heavy, ragged breathing and search the room for any sounds to indicate where in the cabin he's keeping her.

He slams something down and grasps my hair, jerking my face up toward him.

"Open your fucking eyes and answer me."

Although it kills me to give in to his demand, I need to see what I'm dealing with. This time, enough of the blood has dripped away from my eye that I can actually see him, although he's fuzzy, and I can't get my eyes to focus.

His snarling face is mere inches from mine and there's just enough crazy in his eyes to renew my fear for Skye's safety. But giving him my name won't benefit me, or her, in any real way.

After a few moments, he grins, one of those creepy smiles you always see in photos of serial killers before they were caught.

"No answer? Well, maybe you thought I was going to be an easy target—all alone out here during a storm. But with the damage the lightning may have done and that dislocated shoulder, not to mention the probable concussion, and the fact that you're probably borderline hypothermic in those wet clothes, I doubt you'll make it much longer before you go into shock without proper medical treatment. So, you're going to need to rethink your plans."

No shit.

He's not wrong about my predicament. There's definitely something wrong with my shoulder, and I've had enough concussions in my life to recognize that the agonizing headache, memory loss, blurry vision, and a spinning room aren't a good sign. I've also been in these wet clothes for hours, and I'm shivering so hard, my teeth are chattering. Who the fuck knows what being struck by the lightning did to me either.

He yanks on my hair again but the pain rippling across my scalp barely registers in comparison to my arm.

"I said, who the fuck are you, and why are you here?"

My eyes lock with his, and I grin. He has no fucking idea who he's messing with.

I clear my throat like I'm about to speak, then spit blood directly in his face.

Red looks good on him. I can't wait to see him covered in it.

SKYE

FALL 2004

Gabe glances at me in the rearview mirror for the tenth time since we got Star in the car. She's already fast asleep with her head in my lap. I run my fingers through her hair and rub her back.

My stomach hasn't settled, but it's no longer from the boozy twin connection. Now, the discomfort is from knowing Gabe wants to say something and anticipating it.

We stop at a red light, and his eyes find mine in the mirror again.

Jesus.

"What? Stop looking at me like that. If you have something to say, just say it."

His lips press into a thin line. "We'll talk when I get you home."

Home?

"No! You can't take us home. Mom and Savage will fucking kill me for letting her get this wasted. Can't we crash at your place?"

He groans and shakes his head. "No, Skye, absolutely not. No way."

"But why? You know what will happen if I bring her home drunk. It won't matter that there's a good reason or that I kept an eye on her. They will just see it as another reason I can't be trusted. Mom will probably take my car away."

His eyes narrow, and he curses under his breath. The light turns green and two blocks pass in silence. I'm convinced he's going to say no. Why wouldn't he? It's not his job to help me deceive Mom and Savage.

"You are damn lucky I'm here and a sucker for a woman in distress."

Did he just call me a woman?

Holy shit.

"Does that mean we can crash with you?"

Please say yes, please say yes.

He growls and grabs his cell phone from the cup holder. I don't get an answer to my question; he just makes a call. "Hey, yeah, I know it's late. No, everything is fine. I just wanted to let you know the girls are with me and are going to stay at my place tonight. No. I met them out for pizza, and we're right by my place. No. They left Dana's house earlier. Right. Yeah. Okay, see you in the morning."

I'm surprised his phone doesn't break with the force he uses to throw it back in the cup holder. "There, now I've lied to my best friend for you. I hope you're happy."

I don't know that happy is the right word. I would prefer if Star wasn't passed-out drunk. I would prefer if I were spending the night at his place because he asked me to, not because I guilted him into it. I would prefer to sleep with him instead of on the couch or the floor where I know I'll end up. I would prefer it if he would stop seeing me as a little girl and realize I am a woman now.

Hell, I'm old enough to be married and already have kids in some countries.

I would love to say a hundred different things to him. But only two words come out. "Thank you."

That won't be the end of the conversation. Not by a long shot. I know he's just biding his time until we can get to his apartment and get Star settled in. Then, he'll unleash on me.

The remainder of the ride to his building is in silence, only the sounds of Star's rhythmic breathing filling the car. When we pull into his parking space, he exits and opens my door.

"I'll carry her in."

I slide out from under her, making sure to gently lower her head to the seat. Gabe hands me his keys with a scowl before he leans in and scoops her up easily. Dejected is probably the proper word for how I feel following behind him. And maybe a little jealous of the fact Star is wrapped up in his arms right now.

We pause at his door so I can unlock it and then he leads me inside.

Gabe's place looks exactly the same as the last time I was here several months ago. The sparsely furnished living room is devoid of any clutter. He isn't here enough for the place to look or feel lived-in. This is only the second time he's been home since he enlisted last summer, so he's lived here all of three weeks in the last year. I don't even know why he bothered to get an apartment, he knows he could have stayed at our house when he's here, but he insisted he needed his own space, despite Mom's protests.

Without a word to me, he disappears down the hallway toward the bedrooms. I drop down onto the couch and tip my head back.

I really fucked this up tonight.

Gabe returns a few minute later and stands in front of me. He has the distinct glimmer of disappointment in his eyes, and isn't that a motherfucking bitch. I wait for him to say something.

Moments turn into minutes. He's waiting for me to talk first.

"I don't know what you expect me to say."

His eyes narrow, and he pinches his lips together. "Why don't you just tell me why your sister is so smashed that she passed out in the bathroom and had to be carried out of the house?"

"Her boyfriend broke up with her today and then showed up with another girl at the party. She was just trying to unwind."

Gabe scoffs and paces in front of the couch. "And you think it's a good idea to let Star, who never drinks, get fucking wasted?"

"I'm not her mother, Gabe. She's a big girl. She can make her own decisions."

He clenches his hands behind his head. "Star is not you, okay? She's not used to indulging the way you do. You and I both know this could've ended very, very badly. What would you have done if I wasn't home on leave right now? Would you have called Savage or your mom? Would you have tried to drive home?"

Gabe's lack of faith in me is really fucking pissing me off. "Jesus, Gabe, do you really think I'd be stupid enough to get behind the wheel of a car after I've been drinking? Give me some fucking credit already. I'm not a total idiot."

He gives a short, sharp laugh and tosses his head back. "No, Skye, you're not a total idiot and that's what makes this even harder. You're just as smart as Star. You're just as capable as Star. But you choose to go off on your own and do whatever the fuck you want no matter how it affects other people. No one can ever rely on you for anything."

Ouch, that one hurt.

Tears well up in my eyes, but I refuse to let Gabe see me cry. If I start crying, he'll only continue to see me as a child.

29

FALL 2004

I don't respond. I just sit and stare at Gabe. Anything I would say right now would probably be regretted later. He has no idea how much what he just said cut me.

I may bleed to death sitting right here on his couch.

"Look, Skye, I'm sorry, I didn't mean that. I just wish you would take things a little bit more seriously."

"I do take things seriously, Gabe. Very seriously. Why do you think I called you when I knew I couldn't take care of her myself? It wasn't just to avoid my mother and Savage. It's because I knew, without a doubt, you would be here for us. I knew you would understand. You might not be happy about it. But you know why I did it."

A storm rages in his eyes, mimicking the one raging inside my heart right now. This is the first real fight I've ever had with

Gabe. We bicker, like any brother and sister do, even though I can never think of him as a brother, and he often steps in to mediate between me and Savage. But we've never actually fought. Not like this.

He knows I'm right.

"Come on, Gabe. You mean to tell me you didn't go out and get drunk when you were my age? If so, that would be a fucking lie. I vividly remember you and Savage coming home late on weekend evenings totally smashed after Mom had already gone to bed. The fact that your curfew was so much later than ours and she didn't bother to wait up for you two just goes to show how much leeway she gave the boys. Storm, Star, and I get treated differently because we're girls."

With a huff, he drops into the chair to my right. "Of course you're treated differently, Skye. You're much more vulnerable than Savage and I were at your age."

I have to admit, he's probably not wrong about that, but I'm not giving him the satisfaction of admitting it. He needs to stop thinking about me as someone who constantly needs a babysitter and protecting.

"You say 'your age' like I'm a child, Gabe. I'm sixteen, and you were my age only three years ago, so don't act like you have some deep wisdom based on how long you've lived, oh ancient one."

That manages to get him to crack a smile, but he sobers almost immediately. "It's different for girls, Skye. Anything could've happened to Star while she was in that state. She could've been assaulted by someone at that party. How would you have felt if she had been hurt?"

The thought had crossed my mind. My stomach had been in my throat when I was checking all the rooms upstairs, and I prayed she wasn't in any of them with a guy.

"Never let your guard down, Skye. Pay attention to your

surroundings and everyone around you. I thought Savage, me, and your father had taught you that."

I roll my eyes. "Gabe, I barely remember my father. I was only seven years old when he died. And Savage spends more time lecturing me than teaching me anything. He treats me like a child, just like you're doing right now."

His eyes narrow on me, and he pulls his bottom lip between his teeth.

I can't tear my eyes away from his mouth. I'd give anything to kiss him and feel those lips against mine. It's the only thing I've wanted for as long as I can remember.

"I'm not trying to treat you like a child, Skye. If that's how it's coming across, then I'm sorry. I just..."

He runs his hands over his short hair; it's still weird to see it like that. When he came home on leave the first time, I did a double-take. I was so used to his longer blond locks that hung around his face. He looks so much more grown up like this even though he's only nineteen.

"You just what?"

"I worry about you..."

My breath catches in my chest. He worries about me? That means he's thinking about me when he's not here.

"...and Star, and Storm for that matter."

His clarification stabs my heart a little.

"If anything ever happened to any of you...I wouldn't be able to handle it. I feel so fucking helpless being so far away from everyone all the time."

That admission silences any reply I'm tempted to make. There's nothing he can do about being away from us. When he made the choice to enlist, he did it knowing where it would take him and what he was sacrificing. I don't need to make him feel worse by telling him how much we all worry about him, and how I lay awake at night praying he's safe.

"We're fine, Gabe. We have Savage here to lord over us like king of the damn castle. You know he'll keep us in line."

The corner of his mouth ticks up, and he nods. "Just remember, I will always be here for you, no matter what. That's what family does. You can always count on me."

GABE

PRESENT DAY

Lucas recoils, releases my hair, and curses, stepping back from me. He wipes his face, smearing my blood across his cheek and temple.

I want to laugh.

But nothing about this situation is funny.

There has been no sign of Skye, and I know I'm in trouble. My body shakes uncontrollably and my vision blurs in and out. I'm fairly certain Lucas is right about shock setting in soon.

He rubs his hands on his jeans and glares at me for a moment before turning his back to me and grabbing something off the table that was behind him.

When he turns back, a familiar sound makes my blood run cold.

Aww...fuck.

He just racked my gun.

My 1911 had been tucked into the holster on the side of my jeans.

The end of the barrel presses into my temple, and Lucas gets into my face again. "You think you're funny? I'm in control here. So tell me who the fuck you are and why you're here!"

SERE training is no fucking joke. I've been prepared for the worst of the worst in interrogation tactics. I can handle being beaten, burned, water-boarded, choked, drowned, and anything else anyone can think to throw at me. And this guy doesn't have a fucking clue what he's doing.

In war, remaining silent is imperative. Other than your name and rank, giving the enemy any information about yourself or your unit would be catastrophic.

But now, the only thing on the line is Skye's life, and I'm not doing her any good tied up here or dead, which I very well may be soon if I go into shock or piss this psycho off enough that he actually shoots me.

Something has to change in this dynamic. Maybe if I get him riled up enough, he'll make a mistake I can take advantage of.

"Look, you psycho motherfucker, just tell me what you did with Skye."

His reaction is unexpected.

He tilts his head and narrows his eyes. His brow furrows as he removes the gun from my head and takes a step back.

"Skye? This is about Skye?"

What the hell else did he think I was doing here?

Lucas paces the squeaky floorboards in front of me, rubbing his left hand on the back of his neck while his right clutches my gun in a death-grip so tight, I can see his white knuckles. When he starts mumbling to himself, my blood runs cold.

Why is he so confused?

The fact I haven't seen Skye sits at the forefront of my foggy mind.

Maybe his mental break is bad enough he doesn't remember what he did with her. Maybe he doesn't even know where he put her.

Shit.

Another shudder rolls through me and the shivering intensifies. I need to keep my shit together if I'm ever going to find her.

Lucas stops midstride and turns to me, his eyes wild and frantic. I come face to face with the end of the gun barrel. "Who the fuck are you, and what do you want with Skye?"

He really doesn't know why I'm here.

Why wouldn't he expect someone to come looking for her?

Answering him when he's unstable and has a gun pointed at me will get me nowhere and may enrage him more. Remaining silent at least buys me some time.

Time for him to hopefully let something slip about what he did with her.

The gun shakes in his hand, and he pulls on his hair with the other one. "If you won't answer me, I'll figure it out myself. I have all the time in the world. You, on the other hand, do not."

He turns toward the door, and with a quick backward glance at me, throws it open to the tempest outside. It slams behind him. An engine starts and lights flood through the front windows before the sound of his Jeep disappears into the roaring storm.

I may be alone, but I don't have much time.

It's only a matter of minutes before he locates my Hummer near the road, and then he'll be back. But I'll be ready.

Lucas has clearly never been trained on how to properly tie up a captive. The chair I'm tied to is old and the wood doesn't seem very stable. I tug my hands forward until they meet the resistance of the slat between them.

"Fuck!"

The pain radiating from my left shoulder overtakes my senses. I grit my teeth and try to breathe through it.

Pain isn't permanent.

Skye.

Think about Skye. She's the reason you're doing this.

I inhale a deep breath, gather all my energy and jerk forward, yanking my hands against the slat as hard as I can. The searing in my shoulder only intensifies and the slat didn't break.

"Motherfucker!"

I repeat the process a second time, feeling a little give in the slat, but again, it doesn't break.

"Son of a fucking bitch!"

The recovery time to catch my breath is longer. The pain makes my stomach roil and taking deep breaths seems to do nothing this time.

I conjure an image of Skye in my head—her black hair fanned out like a halo against the white pillowcase as she stares up at me with a smile on her lips and in her eyes.

Just do it, Gabe.

As long as I don't pass out, I should be able to break it, and I can free my legs from where they're tied to the chair legs.

The sound of Lucas' Jeep on the gravel outside hits my ears; it's now or never.

With a quick, forceful jerk, the slat breaks away and my hands are free. The scream that's ripped from my lungs is deafening to my own ears. I just pray Lucas didn't hear it.

The engine still running outside gives me a glimmer of hope. I have only seconds to free my legs. It would be impossible with one hand, but luckily, Lucas is a true amateur, and didn't remove the knife from my boot.

With a flick of my wrist, my legs are free. I grip my left bicep and hold my arm steady while I try to stand.

The room spins, and I topple sideways, barely managing to catch myself by grabbing onto the small table to the right of me. The knife tumbles from my hand to the floor.

This is going to hurt, but I'll be a lot better off if I can get my shoulder back in the socket. I grip my bicep and shove up as I drop my torso down.

I bite back the scream when it pops back in. The pain immediately ebbs. I won't have full use of it, and it will still hurt like a motherfucker, but at least I can move it now.

The engine stops. I barely have time to get upright before the door swings open.

Damnit.

My wallet in his left hand and the rage in his eyes tell me he's finally made the connection. "You're Gabe? Did you fuck my girlfriend?"

Girlfriend?

I scoff and lock my eyes on his. "She was never your girlfriend."

He growls and glances down to where my gun is tucked into his waistband as he reaches for it with his right hand.

Rookie mistake.

His moment of distraction is all I need to grab the knife from the floor and close the distance between us. I slam into him, pushing him up against the wall of the cabin, and jabbing my knife into his upper arm, straight into the brachial artery.

It hits home, and he cries out, dropping the gun and knocking the knife from my hand when he goes to clutch at his arm. Blood spurts out between his fingers but his eyes return to me just before his knee connects with my stomach, knocking me back.

The moment he has room, he drops and lunges for the gun.

Without hesitation, I dive on his back and reach over his shoulder for the gun but it's already in his hand. In an instant, he rolls sideways under me and fires.

Bang.

I thought I knew what pain was, but this...this is something else entirely. The fire of a thousand suns is centered on my abdomen. I slump to the floor and roll onto my back.

Before I can even take a breath, Lucas is standing over me with the gun pointed at my face.

Well, shit.

This is not how I imagined I would go.

Bang.

30

GABE

A crimson hole spreads on Lucas' chest. He teeters and collapses onto me, sending me into a renewed battle with my new friend agony.

I should be toast. But instead, Lucas is a dead weight on my chest. Breathing is damn near impossible with the combined pressure and pain. I can't hold my head up anymore.

Blackness encroaches on the corners of my vision.

What...how...

Someone's talking...

Who...

Shuffling and grunting.

The weight's gone.

Air floods my lungs.

I can breathe.

Small, cold hands find my face and turn it up, but my eyelids are as leaden as my useless arms.

"Gabe!"

That's my name.

"Gabe, open your eyes." A tearing sound rends the air. Cool air hits my skin.

The hands move down my body to my chest and across my stomach, then up and down my arms, and legs. "Fuck! Dammit...Gabe, don't you fucking die on me. I can't lose you too."

Lose me?

Fingers press into my neck and someone mumbles something about pulse...blood loss...

Banging.

Cursing.

Something warm next to me. Something wet dripping on me, then more burning and searing pain in my abdomen. I reach over to put my hand there, but someone swats it away.

More tearing.

"I'm sorry, Gabe, but this is going to hurt."

Hurt?

Already hurt so much.

I reach out toward the voice but my hand is swatted away.

"Knock it off. Don't move."

That voice. Only one person is that bossy with me.

Skye.

But, how? The blackness surrounding me encroaches rapidly; it's so welcoming...

She shakes me, sending ripples of pain throughout my body. "Fuck!"

"Sorry, but you need to stay awake. I need to pack the gunshot wound and wrap it so you don't bleed out. Don't you dare pass out on me! I need you to help me get you into the car."

Car?

I struggle to open my eyes and reach out until my hand finds her arm. "Where are we going?"

She laughs and squeezes my hand before moving it back down to the side of my body. "The hospital, you asshole."

I force my eyes open. A fuzzy version of her tear-streaked face hovers over me. She shoves something hard between my teeth. The faint taste of wood fills my mouth, mingling with the copper taste of blood.

"Bite down and promise not to hate me after this."

Hate her? Why would I...

Motherfucker!

My scream is muffled by whatever my teeth are grinding into and, despite my delirium, I can still hear her apologizing over and over again while she presses and prods at me.

"Shit, Gabe. What the fuck were you thinking coming out here?"

I spit out whatever she put in my mouth and swallow, trying to find my voice through the pain. "I came for you."

Her hands find my face again, and she holds it steady until my eyes meet hers. "I know you did. You always told me you would. And I came for you."

The words don't make any sense to me...*she came for me?*

I don't have the time, energy, or coherence to analyze them.

Sleep. That's what I need, to sleep.

I let my eyes slide closed and it feels so damn good.

∾

SKYE

"No! Gabe, wake up!" I shake his head until his eyes reluctantly slide back open. His dilated pupils don't react when I shine my flashlight in them and are a sure sign of a concussion. Coupled with the gunshot wound, and the fact I'm pretty sure he's borderline hypothermic, he is in real trouble. And that's just the stuff I can see.

Shit.

How the fuck did this happen?

Only I could end up in a cabin in the boonies in the middle of a hurricane with the body of an ex-fuck buddy I just shot and killed and the love of my life dying in front of me.

Well, I'm not losing him too. I can't. I wouldn't survive it.

I have less than an hour to get him to the hospital before things are going to go from bad to worse. With the roads the way they are and the weather continuing to deteriorate, there's a very real chance we won't make it in time.

No. Fuck that, Skye.

Just get it done.

"Gabe, I need you to tell me where else you are hurt. I need to know what else I need to triage before we get you to the car."

He groans and lets out a rattling, painful-sounding laugh. "Everything hurts."

"Be specific."

"My head, my shoulder, my foot..."

I move the beam of the flashlight up over his right shoulder but don't see anything. On his left, I find what appears to be another entry wound and very distinctive pink, fern-shaped burn marks. Lichtenberg figures are only caused by one thing. "Jesus, Gabe, did you get struck by lightning?"

He nods and winces at the movement.

You have to be fucking kidding me.

I crawl down to his feet and check the bottom of his combat boots. The soles are melted and the leather singed. A very distinct smell of burned hair and rubber lingers.

"That's how...he got me in here...in the first place...I was... knocked out. Shoulder was dislocated."

"Was?"

"I...put it back."

The gasping breaths he takes between words spur me back into action. He's in far worse shape and even more danger than

I thought. A lightning strike could have done major damage to his heart and brain.

I grab his right hand and put it over the wound in his abdomen just below his ribcage on the left side. "All right, Gabe. I need you to press here with as much force as you can. Keep applying pressure. We need to get you vertical and to the car. You need to help me here."

He mumbles something unintelligible.

He's incoherent, which makes sense considering the concussion and lightning. Another bad sign. I kiss him gently on the lips before I slide my left arm under his shoulders so I can get him sitting up.

"Here we go." I pull, and it's like trying to lift a two-hundred-and-twenty-pound dead weight. He barely budges an inch from the floor, and his hand falls away from where I placed it. Maybe I should be spending more time at the gym instead of drinking.

Shit.

I turn his head to the side toward me. "Gabe!" I slap him—hard. He jerks and groans.

"What the fuck?" His slurred words shake along with his body, and his wide, unfocused eyes meet mine.

Knowing how painful this is going to be for him gives me pause for a second. I hate doing it to him, but it's our only option. I grab his right hand and press it against his wound again. "Sorry. I need you to help me here. Keep your hand pressed against that and apply as much pressure as you can. We need to get you up."

This time, I pull on his shoulders, and he moves up, grinding his jaw and clenching his eyes shut until he's sitting up. His head and body sway, and I tighten my grip on his shoulders, steadying him.

"Just take a couple deep breaths, Gabe."

He turns his head and glares at me. "You make...that...

sound...easy..."

My vision blurs as the tears I managed to turn off return in full force. "Come on. Suck it up, Gabe. We need to move now. On three. One...two..."

A strangled groan accompanies my "three," and I help him to his feet, doing most of the work and supporting almost his entire weight. He wobbles and tips toward me, dropping his head against mine.

"Skye...I can't..."

Oh no.

I grip his jaw in between my thumb and finger and force him to meet my eyes. "Stop it. You can, and you have to. Let's go."

Being commanding and overbearing generally doesn't benefit me in my daily interactions, but it's paying off now. He nods and takes a step forward.

Lucas' body lies on the floor where he fell after I shoved him off Gabe. I try not to inspect the red stain on his shirt, but my eyes naturally drift there, then up to his face. It's too soon for him to have the pallor of death. With his eyes closed and his mouth open slightly, someone might even think he's sleeping peacefully.

How did things go so horribly wrong?

How did I not see what a psycho Lucas was until it was too late? I never in a million years expected to find Gabe in this condition. Lucas was a little off and a lot obsessed, but violent? The possibility never crossed my mind.

This is all my fault.

Being with Gabe has caused nothing but problems, and we haven't even told Savage yet. Maybe he's right; maybe this was never a good idea. Maybe there are too many reasons to stay away.

I tear my eyes away from Lucas for the last time and help Gabe inch toward the open door. Rain pours, and the wind practically topples us over. I urge Gabe forward past Lucas' Jeep and toward Mom's Tahoe.

Gabe is fading fast. I open his door and help him slide in. His teeth grind together so hard, I can hear it above the storm.

Even if I had something to give him for the pain, I can't risk him passing out. They're going to need to operate as soon as we reach the hospital. I need him alert, no matter how painful it is for him...and me.

31

GABE

*B*eep. *Beep. Whir.*

The sounds echo in my head, combining with vise-like pressure that's enough to make me want to scream.

Every muscle and bone in my body throbs.

When did I get hit by a truck?

Beep. Beep. Whir.

Heat licks across my skin like a raging wildfire.

Why is it so hot in here?

I try, unsuccessfully to open my leaden eyelids.

Why are they so heavy?

A heavy fog drowns me, threatening to pull me under. I fight it.

Beep. Beep. Whir.

Why doesn't someone turn off that damn noise?

Something brushes my hand. Tugging. Burning pain slithers up my right arm into my shoulder and then throughout my body.

Beep. Beep. Whir.

The darkness creeping in is so damn inviting.

It will take me away from the damn noise.

Beep. Beep. Whir.

"Gabe, can you hear me?" Soft, cool hands cup my cheeks and the scent of vanilla wraps around me.

Skye.

I try to turn into her inviting touch, but my body won't cooperate.

Something wet hits my face, and I hear a sob.

Why is she crying?

Beep. Beep. Whir.

All I want to do is drag her against me and fix whatever's wrong, but my body won't cooperate. I can't move.

A stinging burn and that beautiful, black fog clouds my head.

I try to take a deep breath to immerse myself in Skye, but pain tightens my chest.

Her fingers move soothingly over my face.

There's something mingled with her scent. Something familiar.

What is that?

Beep. Beep. Whir.

Another deep breath brings more of the cloying smell.

Antiseptic. That's what it is.

Beep. Beep. Whir.

That sound, coupled with the scent, finally clicks.

Shit.

I'm in the hospital.

What the fuck happened?

Beep. Beep. Whir.

A black wall of nothing pops up when I search my memory.

I was at the club alone. The storm was getting worse. Skye sent a text saying she was leaving the hospital.

Warm breath flutters against my neck. "I really need you to wake up. I'm so sorry."

Skye's whispered words open the flood gates.

Her apartment...Savage and Danika...Lucas' place...driving through the storm...the cabin...the lightning...the gun...the pain...Lucas falling...Skye...

I try to speak, to tell her that I'm okay.

Something's very wrong. I can't move or talk to her. Even after the RPG incident in Iraq, when I was knocked unconscious, I wasn't like this. Something is very, *very* wrong.

Am I dying?

Cool, familiar lips press against mine. "Everything will be okay. It *has* to be."

~

SKYE

"How's he doing?"

Storm's voice makes me jump in my seat.

"Shit. You scared the crap outta me."

"Sorry." She sets her purse on the chair in the corner and comes over to where I sit next to the bed. "I thought you heard me come in."

It was only a matter of time before the rest of the Hawkes swooped in to give me the third degree about what happened to Gabe. Frankly, I'm surprised it took this long. I expected everyone to come running once they got my text about what happened.

They know.

Between bouts of moaning and passing in and out of consciousness while on the drive back into town, Gabe managed to tell me how he ended up at the cabin—including the long list of felonies he committed trying to track me down.

Mom and Stone have been texting for updates, but not a peep from Savage.

What a clusterfuck.

Storm leans over and kisses Gabe on the cheek. "He looks like shit."

"I know."

I contemplate his sleeping form, cataloguing his injuries for the hundredth time in the last two days. The angry gash on his head, now sealed with staples, and the magenta and purplish bruises surrounding it and scattered over other parts of his face are hard to look at. The rest of his body is covered by the blanket except his arm in the immobilization sling on his left side. Every time one of the nurses comes in to check his drain and surgical sites, I end up sobbing again. I didn't think it was possible to cry this much.

At least his color is getting a little better. His eyes shift under his lids, bouncing around while he's trapped in a Propofol-induced dream.

Is it a good one or a nightmare?

Now that his fever finally broke, he should be improving. But, thus far, there's been little change. My gut twists, and I brush away tears from my eyes for the millionth time since I brought him here and return my gaze to Storm.

With a brief glance between us, she drags the empty chair over to the other side of the bed and begins her stare-down. I know what she wants but I'm in no mood to rehash what happened.

"Were you ever going to tell us?"

I return my gaze to Gabe's face and keep it locked there so I don't have to make eye-contact with her when I answer. "I wanted to, but Gabe..."

My vision blurs. I swipe at my eyes and bite back a sob.

"Gabe what?"

I don't really know what to say. If I tell her the truth, that

Gabe never wanted this, and that he didn't want anyone to know because we were never anything to begin with, that will be admitting to myself it's over.

And I can't do that.

Not yet.

Not before I get to talk to him again.

I squeeze his hand and go with the obvious. "He was just worried about what Savage would think, and we aren't even sure what's going on with us yet."

After the semi-truth leaves my mouth, I turn to Storm. She narrows her eyes on me and crosses her arms over her chest. One of the biggest problems with sisters is they can read you like a fucking book and see through any bullshit. Storm is good but Star was great. Words wouldn't even fully leave my lips because she would call me out.

My heart aches more than I thought possible. Losing her and Savage being injured was as bad as I thought it could possibly get. But now I might lose Gabe too, and that would be the trifecta of fucked up shit and too much for me to handle.

Please. Storm, just let it go...

Maybe she senses my distress or maybe she just doesn't care. Either way, her expression softens, and she gives me a half smile. "Yeah, Savage was not pleased when I spoke with him."

"He's not here, is he?" I check the closed door, and my stomach sours imagining how that conversation will go.

"No. He didn't want to drive with Dani yet. Once the roads are better though, you can expect him."

I return my attention to Gabe and watch his chest rise and fall rhythmically under the power of the ventilator.

Between the blood loss and shock to his system from the lightning strike and hypothermia, he was practically dead when I finally got him here. Three hours of surgery later, I was told he went into asystole twice, and they had to revive him.

Gabe literally died. And it's all my fault.

They had to transfuse so much blood into him, fluid built up in his lungs, and he went into accurate respiratory distress within twenty-four hours of surgery. They can't seem to get his lungs to oxygenate properly. They've been pumping him full of antibiotics to try to prevent him from developing pneumonia, but they keep telling me we just have to wait to see how he's doing in another day or two.

Like I needed to be told that.

That's what made the last two days a hundred times worse —knowing how bad it was and how there was a good chance it could go either way.

There were so many times I almost lost him.

I wasted so much time.

And who knows what will happen even if he survives this. Both of us could be facing criminal charges. I provided a very lengthy and detailed statement after I brought Gabe in, but there wasn't much they could do to investigate until the flood waters receded.

I'm fairly confident I would have ended up in cuffs if the shit with Lucas had occurred any other day. For once, the hurricane worked in my favor. If they had tried, I would have gone kicking and screaming, because there was no way anyone was going to take me away from Gabe.

"I never should have let him push me away at the wedding."

"So this has been going on that long, huh?"

I turn back to her and shrug. "I guess. Maybe longer? I kissed him at the wedding."

Storm nods and warm sympathy shines in her eyes. "As happy as it was, that was a hard night for all of us—you especially. I think we all may have done things we wouldn't have normally."

"He said something very similar." *Actually, I think he called me a train wreck at some point.*

"You were also pretty drunk, weren't you?"

I roll my eyes and nod. Who wasn't? We never thought we'd see Savage that happy, nor did we imagine having to celebrate without Star.

"Stone disappeared for a while, too."

She says it like a statement, but there's an underlying note of question there. Maybe she thinks I know where he went. We comforted each other earlier in the night, but once I hit rock bottom with Gabe, I never returned to the festivities. So if she wants info, she'll have to get it from Stone.

"He may have, I never went back after Gabe brought me to his room and left."

"So you two have been dancing around each other since then, huh?"

That's one way to put it.

"I guess you could say that. I'm frankly surprised no one noticed something."

She shrugs and smiles at Gabe. "I guess I just figured you had done something to piss him off. It certainly wouldn't be the first time."

I smile, probably my first real smile in three days. "I definitely did that."

32

SKYE

*T*he hospital coffee tastes like piss, and my back is starting to cramp up from sleeping in this chair for four straight days. They offered me a cot, but I couldn't touch him if I slept there, and I can't bear to release his hand.

I thought I felt him squeeze it earlier, but when I looked up at his face, it was still frozen in the same position it has been since the moment they brought him out from surgery and into the ICU. They finally removed him from the ventilator this morning and stopped the Propofol. Now, it's just a matter of waiting for him to wake up.

Storm has stopped in two more times, and Mom promised she would be coming in person today since the roads are finally mostly cleared. The widespread flooding and downed power lines were causing a lot of problems moving around the city, and she has never been comfortable driving in these post-storm conditions. Stone has called three more times for updates.

But still no word from Savage.

I've spoken with Dani five times, but it's clear from my conversations with her that Savage doesn't know she's been talking to me. I feel for her, I really do. She's stuck in the middle of Gabe and Savage—the man who saved her life and the man who is the love of her life.

Regardless of how angry Savage might be about what happened between me and Gabe, I know Dani could never harbor any bad feelings for Gabe, no matter what he did.

But the fact that Savage still hasn't made an appearance makes my blood boil, especially after Gabe spent so much time by his side after the accident.

I close my eyes and rest my head on the bed next to Gabe, his hand still clutched in mine.

The door opening doesn't even faze me. Nurses come and go and have come to expect me here.

"How's he doing?"

Savage's voice breaks through the constant beep and whirring of the machines in the room. I pause for a moment before I do or say anything. This isn't the time to fly off the handle and say something I'll regret later.

Really, I'm not ready for this.

Things are still too raw. I can't worry about Gabe and also worry about not pissing off Savage.

I pull my head up to find Dani standing just behind him, holding the door open for him as he enters the room. She gives me a sympathetic smile and mouths, "I'm sorry," before she ducks back into the hall, leaving me alone with two of the three men I love more than anything in this world.

"Like you fucking care."

So much for not flying off the handle.

Savage's body tenses and his eyes narrow on Gabe's sleeping form. "Of course I care, Skye."

"If you really cared, you would have at least called to check on him days ago."

His cool blue eyes whip over to mine, and his mouth presses into a hard line. "I've been getting updates from Mom. She said he's going to be okay?"

Wow. He must really be pissed if he wouldn't even talk to me.

"Well, he's alive. His vitals are steady. The surgery went well, but he developed an infection and some complications with his lungs. He's been on antibiotics. So now, we just wait."

Savage moves up next to the bed and examines Gabe's prone figure. I can only imagine what's running through his head right now. No doubt he's remembering when their positions were reversed after the accident not so long ago.

It's probably better to just get it over with quickly. Prolonging the confrontation with him will do none of us any good.

"I know you're mad..."

He scoffs, and his eyes flit from me to Gabe before his hard stare returns to me. "Mad doesn't even begin to cover it, Skye. What were you two thinking?"

"Well—"

I'm silenced with a shake of his head and a held up hand. "No, don't bother. I know. Gabe thinks with his dick, and you haven't thought straight at all since the accident."

My temper flares, and I clench my fists to keep from clambering across the bed to smack him.

"Wow. Is that what you really think?"

Asshole.

Savage has always been protective of me, and all the Hawke siblings, but this goes beyond being protective and straight to judgmental dickcheese.

His eyes narrow on me. "What else am I supposed to think?"

"How about you give us some fucking credit, Savage? Do you really think Gabe or I would jump into bed with each other without knowing what a fucked up situation we would be creating? What we would be risking? And you think we did it just because we wanted to get laid?"

I shoot from the chair, unable to remain seated while I'm so fuming mad. Plus, as awful as this sounds, being physically taller than Savage always makes me feel like I have some power, the illusion of the upper hand. I never had it with him growing up, but in this instance, I deserve to use it.

"Skye, you are my goddamn baby sister, and he's my best friend...I mean, fuck, he's practically family. It's just...wrong."

"Why is it wrong? You, of all people, should understand that when you find something good, you have to hang onto it."

He barks out a sardonic laugh. "Don't compare my relationship with Dani to you and Gabe fucking."

Whoa. Knife to my heart, much?

"That's what you think this is? That we're just fucking?"

Savage glances to Gabe before answering. "You tell me differently, Skye. I know Gabe, probably as well as I know myself. He's not a relationship guy, and you have been vulnerable since Star's death, don't try to deny that."

"Holy shit!"

Now, I get it.

"You think he took advantage of me?" I charge around the end of the bed until I'm directly in front of Savage. "How the hell can you possibly think that of your best friend...of me?"

My blood isn't boiling, it's ready to burst out of my veins. How the hell can Savage think Gabe would take advantage of me or that I would ever *let* anyone, let alone Gabe, do that in the first place? Doesn't he know us at all?

Savage doesn't respond. He just stares at me with the eyes so similar to mine—filled with fear and pain. I know he feels betrayed. I get it, I really, really do, but what happens between me and Gabe is none of his business.

I run my hands back through my snarly, dirty, matted hair

and sigh. "I don't even know what to say to you, Savage. If you really believe that, then you never knew Gabe or me at all."

"He's my best friend, Skye."

"Then fucking act like it, Savage."

GABE

I've never heard Skye so angry before, and that's really saying something. That woman is like a cobra—coiled and ready to strike at any time.

I feel sorry for whoever the sucker is she's tearing into.

The visual I bring up in my mind of her angry—blue eyes flashing, skin flush, body tense—is so fucking hot, I smile.

Fuck, that hurts.

Her last words ring in my ears along with the constant noise of the machines near my head and the synapses finally fire and connect.

Shit...Savage.

"Why don't you back off a little, Skye?" The voice that comes out isn't mine—it's harsh, and scratchy, and sounds like it comes from someone who smokes four packs a day. I never smoked more than two at my worst.

"Oh, my God...Gabe!"

Pain shoots through my abdomen and arm as something warm, firm, and curvy falls against me.

A gasp slips from my lips, and I clench my eyes and grit my teeth against the fire burning through my body.

"Oh, shit, I'm sorry."

Skye. Fuck, I love this woman. How did I not tell her before?

I force my eyes open against the harsh lights of the hospital room and see her standing back from the bed, concern and guilt etched on her beautiful face. "Don't be sorry, just get back here, and be gentle this time."

She smiles and moves toward me, taking my hand in hers and leaning in to press her trembling lips to mine gently. "You're going to be okay." Her whispered words soothe me, and I relax back into the bed.

"You wanna tell me what happened?"

The joy in her eyes and her smile vanish, quickly replaced by tears and a quivering lip. "I'm so sorry, Gabe. It's all my fault. I never thought Lucas would go this far."

Neither did I.

"How did you get away? Where was he keeping you?" Every word I speak is like dragging razorblades down my throat.

Confusion flits across her face, and she backs away slightly. "You don't remember what I told you in the car?"

Broken memories of the ride from the cabin to the hospital flit through my head. Most involve pain and screaming. But nothing about how Skye escaped.

I shake my head but immediately regret it when pain stabs at my temples. "Shit." My eyes close again, and I try to breathe through the pain, but the tightness and sharp stabs against my rib cage prevent me from taking more than a shallow gasp of air.

"Crap, I need to let them know you're awake." A voice crackles from somewhere off to my right and Skye tells whoever it is that I'm finally awake. I don't bother listening for the reply. I'm more interested in what Skye has to tell me.

When she's done and retakes her place next to me, I open my eyes again and look up at her. "So?"

She chews on her bottom lip.

Fuck, that's hot.

"Um, shit..." Fear flashes in her eyes.

Why is she afraid to talk to me about this?

"Gabe...Lucas never had me."

"What?" I jerk up in the bed but immediately fall back and clutch at my abdomen. "Fuck..." It feels like I've been ripped open from my ribs to my belly button. What the hell did they do to me?

"Shh." A soothing hand finds my forehead. "Just lay back. Don't try to move. The nurse will bring more pain meds for you."

I grit my teeth and turn my face to hers. "I must have heard you wrong. Tell me."

She hesitates and curses under her breath, examining the ceiling briefly before returning her gaze to me. "Lucas dropped me off at my mom's, *after* I sent you that text. I didn't even know the message went through to you, or that you had been looking for me. I did try to call you, several times, but the calls wouldn't go through. Fuck, I'm so sorry."

She was never there.

You have got to be fucking kidding me.

I know better than to go off half-cocked. Yet, I did. In a big fucking way. And now, Lucas is dead. He was a fucking psycho and deserved it, but still.

"But, how did you find me at the cabin, then?"

The corner of her mouth twitches up and her eyes twinkle with affection. "Because I didn't want to leave things the way we did. I was at Mom's and her electricity went out. We couldn't get the generator going. It was cold and miserable, and I wanted to be anywhere but there. I was thinking about that time you came to get me and Star from that party sophomore year. And I just couldn't imagine not being with you just because of Savage. So, I went to tell him and brought Mom with me. I thought you would be at your place. Dani told me you went looking for me and that you thought I was with Lucas before I even had a chance to talk to Savage. I went to Lucas' apartment and found it...let's just say...in some disarray and realized what you must have thought after you got my text. I've been to the cabin with

Lucas before, and he told me he had to go out there to do some prep for the storm. I knew you must have gone there when I saw the ripped open mail and letter."

She takes a shaky breath and closes her eyes briefly. "Thank God I had my gun in my purse...I'm just so sorry I didn't get there sooner."

Sorry?

There is absolutely nothing for her to be sorry for.

"But you still shot Lucas and managed to get me here in the middle of a fucking hurricane."

She smiles and nods as tears roll down her cheeks.

It shouldn't surprise me she turned out to be a total badass.

It's kind of a Hawke quality.

33

GABE

Someone clears their throat, and I manage to move my head so I can see who is to the left of my bed.

Fuck. Savage.

I forgot he was here. He heard all of that, and saw Skye throw herself at me.

His cold, hard eyes meet mine, and he gives me an awkward nod. "I'm glad you're okay."

Without another word, Savage turns and disappears out the open door.

Well, fuck.

I can't remember a single time since I met Savage at age six that he treated me with such cold disdain. He can be a real asshole, but underneath it all is always the warmth of my best friend. There was none of that just now. That man was not the man I know. And that fucking terrifies me.

Skye's eyes follow him out just as a nurse bustles in with a bright smile, bee-lining for the IV stand and machines next to Skye.

Maybe I will be okay, but things are definitely not okay with Savage.

We've never had any kind of test of our friendship before, unless you count the accident. But for me, there wasn't even a question I needed to step up and help him with whatever he needed. I would have done, and did give, anything and everything to help him and bring him back home. Things would never be the same, we both knew that, but I wasn't about to let what happened to him change our friendship.

Nothing has ever come between us before, and the fact it's his sister makes this different. This may be something we can't overcome. And that breaks my fucking heart because, after the accident, at least I still had him. Now, I have nothing.

When Skye returns her attention to me, the tears are still falling and the guilt overwhelms me.

It's all my fault.

I drove a wedge between her and Savage all because I wasn't strong enough to push her away permanently.

"Mr. Anderson, how are we feeling?" The nurse smiles at me as she fiddles with something on the IV stand.

Might as well go with honesty here. Maybe it'll get a laugh.

"Like I got shot."

Skye winces, and I instantly regret my attempt at honesty as humor.

The nurse tosses me a dirty look. I guess she didn't like my joke either. "Well, that's to be expected. What's your pain level like?"

I instinctively check Skye before answering.

It fucking hurts. A lot. Like, more than I ever thought possible. But, if I tell the nurse that, it will only make Skye feel worse.

"Uh, not too bad."

Skye's eyes narrow on me.

She's not buying it.

I look to the nurse, who's now hanging a new bag on the IV stand. She mimics Skye's reaction.

Guess I'm not fooling anyone.

Without returning my eyes to Skye, I close them and drop my head back against the pillow, letting out a sigh of resignation. "Okay, it's bad."

"I would imagine so, Mr. Anderson. The doctor is on his way, and once you're done talking to him, we'll get you something to make you feel better."

I hate pain meds. Really, really hate them.

The mindless fog they put you in and the very real potential for abuse has always made me leery of taking anything if it isn't absolutely necessary. But the last few minutes awake have convinced me this is one of those times.

Who would have thought, I make it through six tours without getting shot and then come here to get blasted by Skye's psycho fuck buddy. I should have known pussy would be the harbinger of my demise.

Skye squeezes my hand, and I explore her stormy blue eyes. She wants to say something, probably apologize again, but I won't let her. It wasn't her fault. None of it.

If I hadn't been such a fucking asshole, we would have been talking, and I would have given her a ride to her mom's house and ridden out the storm with them. I never would have had to search for her, there never would have been the misunderstanding, and I wouldn't have ended up here. None of it was her fault, not a single fucking thing.

All she's ever done is want me and love me, and all she requested in return was for me to do the same. And I couldn't.

I can't.

There's no way I'm going to be the reason she destroys her relationship with Savage. It may be too late for me to salvage my friendship with him, but she doesn't have to lose her brother because of my stupidity.

I have to let her go.

The pain of making that decision tears through me stronger and harder than the bullet did. I love her more than I ever thought possible. But I was never meant to have her. It's the only possible way to start to repair what's been broken.

~

SKYE

The look in Gabe's eyes turns the blood in my veins to ice. Something's going on inside his head and it isn't good.

Savage didn't help things. I don't know how much Gabe heard, but the fact Savage could actually think so little of him was heartbreaking for me, so I can only imagine what it would do to Gabe if he knew how Savage felt.

But this isn't the time to broach the subject with him.

The doctor strolls in and grabs the chart from the nurse. "It's nice to see you awake, Mr. Anderson. I'm Dr. Schaefer. How are you feeling?"

"Shitty."

I flick my eyes from Gabe to the doctor and he smiles. "Mr. Anderson, you were struck by lightning and shot, so feeling shitty doesn't surprise me."

Gabe manages a weak smile, and Dr. Schaefer leans against the end of the bed. "The bullet tore through your spleen. We had to perform an exploratory laparotomy with splenectomy, which basically means we opened you up, looked around to make sure there wasn't damage to any other organs or major vessels, removed the spleen, and sealed you back up."

"Don't I need a spleen?"

The doctor chuckles and smiles at Gabe. "Fortunately, the

spleen is one of those organs you can actually live without and pretty much maintain your regular lifestyle. It's kind of a supporting player, so to speak, and helps the immune system filter blood. The biggest concern with removing the spleen is that it helps fight off certain types of bacteria, so without it, you are more susceptible to certain infections, like pneumonia and meningitis. Your body was having a tough time fighting off an infection you developed post-surgery and you had some issues with your lungs. We had to do several rounds of IV antibiotics before you finally started showing some improvement."

Gabe's worried. I don't blame him. Without the medical knowledge I have, I would probably be freaking out if I were in his place.

"But I'm okay now?"

I squeeze his hand. The doctor gives him a reassuring smile. "You will be very soon. We're going to keep you here for another week or so to give you some more antibiotics and to make sure all your systems are operating properly after the lightning strike and major surgery.

"When the lightning struck you, it caused the muscles in your body, especially your neck and shoulders, to convulse so forcefully, it actually caused your shoulder to dislocate. You're very lucky. Your clothes being wet may have actually saved your life. Most of the charge from the lightning likely conducted through your wet clothes rather than your body. I know you were able to pop your shoulder back into place, which definitely is something we would have preferred to be left to a professional." His eyes meet mine, and he gives me a knowing smile. "But luckily, the ligaments and muscles were just stretched, there was no tearing or major damage. That means you won't have to spend a great deal of time with it immobile. Keep it in the sling at least eight hours a day and no lifting with that arm or anything else that will put any strain on it. Can you manage that?"

He looks from me to Gabe, and Gabe nods. I'll no doubt be monitoring to make sure he's not overdoing it. God knows it's going to be a pain in the ass to get him to slow down and admit there are things he can't and shouldn't do.

"Good, as long as there are no other complications, you should have full normal function within twelve to sixteen weeks. But for now, I'm guessing you need some more pain meds."

Gabe shifts uncomfortable. "I wouldn't turn them down."

Seeing him miserable and knowing it's all my fault makes the tears well in my eyes again. I swear, I've cried more in the last couple days than I did after Star died. The nurse grabs a vial of morphine and hooks it to the IV, setting the drip.

The doctor hands the chart back to the nurse and inclines his head at us. "I'll be back to see you tomorrow, Mr. Anderson."

Gabe grumbles a response and winces before his eyes fall on me momentarily. The same dark uncertainty lingers there before he closes them. The tension in his jaw and neck relax slowly as the morphine they gave him finally takes effect.

Thank God for narcotics.

I can't stand to see him suffer. Not just because I love him so much, but because this is far too reminiscent of what I went through with Savage after the accident. I couldn't even fully grieve for Star because I was so worried we were going to lose Savage too. Gabe's strength held me and the rest of the family together.

Now, I need to be the one who's strong, for both of us. Savage may have pushed Gabe away but I'm not going anywhere. And I know Mom, Storm, and Stone would never let what's going on between me and Gabe get in the way of how they feel about him. He's a Hawke, even if he wasn't born that way.

34

SKYE

*G*abe isn't even awake for half a day before the police show up, again.

"Miss Hawke? Can I speak to you out in the hall, please?"

The same detective who met with me when I first got to the hospital waits for me in the hall just outside the door. As I exit Gabe's room, another detective moves in and shuts the door behind him, but not before Gabe offers me a less than reassuring smile.

I know he's been dreading this just as much as I have.

"Can't you wait to interview him until he's stronger? He's still in a lot of pain and on some pretty heavy medications."

Detective Morris shakes his head and leans against the wall. "Unfortunately, no. But I wouldn't be too concerned. At this point, it's just a formality. I don't anticipate any charges being issued against him."

"What? But what about my landlord, and what he did to Lucas' place?"

His eyes narrow on me. "Well, it would seem that neither landlord wants to press any charges given the circumstances. They indicated you have already paid for the damages."

What? How is that possible?

I haven't left Gabe's side or spoken to anyone about what he did except the police and the family.

Suspicion builds in the back of my mind.

"What about the hospital?" I need to play dumb on this part. The hospital has been trying to keep a tight lid on the whole situation. The hospital CEO, the compliance officer, and the head of the legal department paid me a visit in Gabe's room two days after I brought him in. I thought they were there to notify us that they were pressing charges against Gabe for breaking into the human resources department. Instead, they shocked the shit out of me by asking me not to mention the incident to anyone other than the police.

The fear of the breach becoming public knowledge, coupled with the fact that they were employing someone who turned out to be a psychotic stalker, made the hospital very amenable to sweeping it under the rug and agreeing not to press charges against Gabe.

That was a huge weight off my shoulders, but the lingering issue of the property damage, plus the breaking and entering at my apartment and Lucas' has been a black cloud over the joy of Gabe's recovery.

"Well, luckily for Mr. Anderson, the hospital has also decided not to pursue charges against him. The district attorney's office isn't going to waste its time pursuing charges with uncooperative victims." His tone makes it clear he thinks something is going on behind the scenes, but he doesn't press it any further.

Time to play dumb.

"Oh, really? That's great news."

"Now, with regard to your actions..."

My stomach knots. I know I killed Lucas to save Gabe's life, but there is a very real possibility that any evidence of what Lucas did to him was washed away by the flooding. I know Lucas doesn't have any family, so I doubt there is anyone harping on the district attorney's office to pursue charges, but that doesn't ease the feeling of dread.

"As you know, we were able to recover the body. And the cabin remained largely intact despite the flooding. We located several items that corroborated your story. My partner is taking Mr. Anderson's statement for our reports, but I can tell you, we plan on recommending no charges be issued against you either."

It feels like I take my first deep breath in days.

Gabe and I are free from the weight of the potential charges hanging over our heads. He can concentrate on his recovery, and I can concentrate on helping him.

"Thank you, Detective Morris."

He nods and gives me a half smile. "You two are very lucky things worked out this way. The situation could have gone very differently."

No shit.

The thought of Gabe going from hospital bed to jail cell has been eating away at me. And now, I can't help but wonder who had a hand in keeping him in the free and clear.

"Do you need anything else from me, Detective?"

He shakes his head. "No. I'll call if I do, and my partner should be finished with Mr. Anderson soon."

I brush past him and pull my cell phone from my back pocket, immediately dialing Stone.

"Skye, what's wrong? Is Gabe okay?" His voice is laced with panic, and I realize what me calling him out of the blue must have made him think.

"He's fine. More than fine, actually. The police were just here and told me there aren't going to be any charges against me or him."

Stone releases a rush of air into the phone. "Thank God. Like I told you the other day, given everything you explained to me, I wouldn't have anticipated them charging you, but what Gabe did is a whole other story. I know you told me about the hospital, but why aren't they issuing any other charges against him?"

"That's why I'm calling. The detective said I already paid the landlords for the damage Gabe did to the buildings, but I definitely didn't do that. Did you have something to do with this?"

He may have only graduated from law school a year ago, but Stone was already making decent money at the firm he worked for. It made sense that he would have stepped in once I explained our predicament.

"I wish I could say it was me, sis. But I had nothing to do with it. I know things are weird between you right now, but if I had to take a guess, I would say Savage is probably the one throwing money at your problems."

Well, shit.

Savage has been such a raging asshole about this entire thing, if he really did step up and help Gabe like this, I'm not exactly sure what that means.

I sigh and dig my fingers into my eyes. "Yeah, that was my next guess."

"Why do you sound so upset? Isn't this a good thing? Maybe it's an olive branch?"

I wish I could believe that to be the case, but the fact that I haven't heard anything from Savage leads me to think it's more likely he still doesn't want to speak to me or Gabe.

There's one way to find out without having to put myself in yet another tense standoff with him.

"Maybe. I gotta go. I'll talk to you later."

I hang up with Stone and shoot a text to the one person who may actually know what's going on.

GABE

By the time Detective Landry finishes taking my statement and leaves the room, I'm so exhausted, I can barely keep my eyes open. The only thing that keeps me awake is wondering what Skye is doing out in the hall with the other detective.

She could be in serious trouble over what happened. Regardless of how justified we know her actions were, the legal system isn't always so cut and dried.

Skye slips back into the room shortly after he leaves. The furrow in her brow makes my body tense, which in turn sends spikes of pain radiating everywhere.

Fuck.

I bite back the curse that wants to rip from my throat so I can avoid another apology from Skye. It's less painful to suffer through the agony in silence than it is to hear her begging for my forgiveness for the hundredth time since I woke up. No matter how many times I told her to stop, it seems any time I give any indication of my physical pain, she's incapable of stopping the "I'm sorry" from pouring out.

"What did that detective tell you?" Her question isn't unexpected, but the way she asks it makes me think she probably already knows the answer. She drops down into the chair next to my bed and waits for my answer.

"He took my statement about what happened and then told me I must have a fairy godmother looking out for me because no one wanted to press any charges."

She snorts out a laugh and stares down at her phone. "More like a bipolar best friend."

Savage?

"What do you mean?"

A sardonic laugh slips from her upturned lips. "Detective Morris told me the landlords didn't want to press charges because I had already paid for the damage you caused."

"What?" I sit up and immediately regret the movement. "Fuck!" My abdomen burns like someone is shoving a red-hot poker into it. I press my hand over the pain and squeeze my eyes shut.

"Gabe..."

Her hand lands on my bicep but I brush her off. "I'm fine."

I open my eyes and meet hers. The apology is on the tip of her tongue but I hold up my hand to silence her.

"Did you pay them off so they wouldn't prosecute me?"

"No, I was just as surprised by the detective saying that as you are. My first thought was Stone, but I just called him and he said he had nothing to do with it. The only other person with that kind of money readily available and aware of the situation is Savage."

As much as I'd love to believe Savage stepped up and helped out, the way he acted when he was here doesn't give me much hope that it was him.

"Are you sure? Maybe it was Storm or your mom?"

She shakes her head, her messy black hair falling around her face. "No, it wasn't them. I sent Dani a text and asked. She confirmed it was Savage. I'm not really sure how to feel about that."

Me either.

Part of me wants to see it as a crack in his defensive stand against us, but the Savage who was here wasn't the one who has always been my brother. This could very well have just been done out of a sense of loyalty to Skye, knowing what me going to jail would do to her.

"What did Dani say?"

Skye hands me her phone, already open to her conversation with Dani.

< Did Savage have anything to do with the landlord at my place and Lucas' getting paid? >

> Yes. I heard him on the phone with his lawyer yesterday morning, and then he disappeared for a while. I think he may have hand delivered the payments. <

< Did he say anything to you about it? Or about Gabe? >

> :(No. He hasn't mentioned him or you since we came back from the hospital visit. <

< So he's still pissed. >

> That's a pretty fair assumption. I'm sorry I can't do more to get through to him. I've tried talking to him a hundred times, but he doesn't want to hear it. <

< I appreciate you trying. >

I let the phone fall onto my lap and drop my head back against the pillow. Dani has always helped calm Savage's sometimes hot temper. If she can't get through to him, I doubt any of us can.

"Should I call him?"

It's a fair question and, when I turn to look at her, Skye's face is marred by the uncertainty of what to do. The fact that she has to even ask if she should contact her own brother makes my chest tighten.

"That's your call, Skye. I'm not ever going to try to stand in the way of your relationship with him. Anything you can think of to do to fix things, you should at least try."

A single tear rolls down her cheek. She swipes it away and blows out a breath. "I'm just so mad at him, Gabe. The things he said..."

She shakes her head and balls her hands into fists. "You didn't hear everything. This isn't just about him forgiving us. There shouldn't *be* anything to forgive. He owes both of us, but especially you, a huge apology. We don't owe him anything."

This is where Skye and I will always disagree.

She can't see why us going behind his back and hiding our relationship is such a betrayal to him. I've struggled for a way to explain it to her so she'll understand. "Skye, if Star had hidden something like this from you, how would you have felt?"

Her eyes narrow on me. "Star would never have done that."

"And I'm sure Savage never thought I would either. That's what you don't get, and you never have...my friendship with him is more like your relationship with Star than you could ever know. We spend basically all our time together. We know each other better than anyone. Wouldn't you have felt betrayed if Star had lied to you and gone behind your back?"

Her hands shove her hair back from her face and she examines the ceiling for a minute before returning her eyes to mine. "I would have been pissed. I probably would have said some really awful things that I didn't mean and would have acted like a dick."

"Exactly."

I pray that, given time, Savage will realize we never intended to hurt him with our actions. The fact that we won't be together anymore will hopefully help ease some of the sting of betrayal. I've managed to put off any discussion of "us" since I woke. I was too worried about the legal situation, and I think Skye is too concerned about my medical condition to press the issue.

When we finally do have that talk, things will never be the same.

35

GABE

*S*kye holds the door open for me, and I shuffle through it. My entire body aches, and my shoulder throbs. But at least the never-ending headache hasn't reached its normal midday crescendo of pain yet.

Thank fuck I'm finally home.

Everyone says they hate hospitals, but I really, *really* hate them. Between the time I spent in one after the RPG in Iraq and with Savage after his accident, I could have easily avoided one altogether for the rest of my life. If it wasn't for that little gunshot wound. And the dislocated shoulder. And the concussion. And the hypothermia. And being struck by lightning.

I manage to make it to the couch before dizziness makes the room tilt, and I'm forced to lower myself onto the cushion before I face-plant onto the hardwood.

"You okay?"

She's kneeling in front of me in a second. I cast a fleeting glance her way before I close my eyes and drop my head back against the cushion.

Breathe.

Breathe, and tell her you're fine. If you don't, she's going to dote and she'll never leave.

If she doesn't leave, she'll keep assessing you and stripping you bare with that look, and you'll start reconsidering the very wise decision you made to stick to your guns and keep things strictly platonic.

Why does she have to be so fucking beautiful, though?

I swallow and open my eyes to make sure the room has stopped spinning before I move my head up and meet her eyes again. "I'm fine. Just tired. I'm going to head to bed."

She eyes me suspiciously and purses her lips. "I'll make you something to eat first. You look pale."

Having never had a mother, aside from Mrs. Hawke, I'm not a hundred percent sure what being babied feels like, but I'm pretty sure this is it. And I don't like it.

"Skye, go home. I'm fine. I'll eat later."

The scowl on her face is so damn cute, I want to kiss it away, no matter how annoyed with her I am. But I can't.

Have some balls, Anderson.

"Gabe, you need help. Let me take care of you. It's the least I can do considering—"

I hold up my hand. "Stop. We are not doing that again. I can't hear you apologize one more time. Please, just leave. Go sleep in your own bed. I really am perfectly capable of taking care of myself. I'm just going to sleep anyway."

She doesn't bother to hide her hurt or anger at my words. The daggers she shoots at me could cut fucking diamonds. With an annoyed sigh, she climbs to her feet and turns to reach into the purse she dropped on the coffee table.

The bottles with my prescriptions and a few other personal

items are unceremoniously dropped onto the table before she zips her bag, drapes it over her shoulder, and turns back to me.

"You are due to take your Percocet and Cipro in four hours. Make sure you set an alarm so you don't miss any doses. I'll be back to check your surgical site tomorrow morning."

Stubborn girl.

With some difficulty, I use my good arm to push myself up off the couch. I waver slightly before I catch my balance. Skye steps forward to help me, but I put a hand up, stopping her in her tracks. That adorable scowl returns.

"I've taken pain medication before, Skye. I'm also capable of putting on my own fucking Band-Aids." It's far more than a Band-Aid, and we both know it, but I'm not going to let her go all "nurse" on me and treat me like an invalid.

She growls and stomps to the front door like a petulant child. "Fine, suit yourself, but don't come crying to me when you forget to take your meds, you're writhing in pain, and you can't move your fucking arm enough to actually *reach* the wound you need to clean."

The front door slams before I can reply.

Not that I know what I would even say to that. I stare down at my slinged arm.

Fuck. She does have a point.

I'll cross that bridge when I come to it. Right now, the only thing I can think about is climbing into my own bed and passing the fuck out.

I don't remember my hallway being this long, though. The throbbing starts, splitting my skull just as I finally make it to the open bedroom door. I pause, leaning against the doorjamb, to catch my breath and get my bearings.

When my eyes finally land on my bed, it's Heaven and Hell all rolled into one. The sheets are still rumpled from my last sleepless night here, and while the thought of climbing in is inviting as fuck, I know as soon as I fall into it, the memories of being here with Skye will flood me.

No choice though.

I'm about to fall over. I stumble the last couple steps to the bed and drop down, then lay back.

The heady aroma of sex envelops me.

"Fucking eh."

Like I need another reminder of Skye or what happened here that night. Since I woke up in the hospital and saw Skye, it's all I've been able to think about. She sat by my side for twelve fucking days, while my best friend only came once and only when he thought I was unconscious. This is precisely what I was trying to avoid the last time she was here by letting her go.

Now, the reminder of making love to Skye permeates the air around me, the pillow, and sheets beneath me so heavily, I can almost feel what it's like to be inside her again.

If I weren't so fucking exhausted, and in so much pain, I might be tempted to rub one out.

SKYE

"He's an idiot." I slam my martini glass down on the bar top and crumple a napkin in my hand, just to destroy something.

Storm's eyes widen, and she holds her hands up in surrender. "I didn't disagree with you."

Byron approaches us and quirks an eyebrow at me. "Problem with your drink?"

I glower at my half-empty glass. "No. In fact, bring me another." Bryon tosses a look at Storm, and I glare at them both. He shrugs and backs away slowly, as if any sudden movements might result in loss of limbs.

Judgmental assholes.

I might as well get drunk tonight. It's the first time I've left the hospital in twelve days. The only reason I even let Storm convince me to come to the club is because I drink for free, and she assured me Savage wouldn't be here.

After the way Gabe acted today, I deserve some liquid refreshment. It may be the only way to calm me down after that stunt he pulled.

"Skye, I'm sure Gabe is fine." Storm's words do nothing to placate me. Quite the opposite. They incite me more.

"Where the hell does he get off treating me like that? After everything I did for him. I was just trying to help. Why is that a bad thing?"

Byron sets down my drink and chuckles. "Oh, honey, you can't be serious."

"Of course I'm serious!"

He leans against his side of the bar and gives Storm a knowing look. "Gabe is a soldier. Always will be. And do you know what big, macho soldiers hate? Little girls like you babying them and treating them like invalids."

My jaw drops and my blood pressure skyrockets. "Fuck you, Byron. That's not what I was doing."

Storm pulls the plastic stick from her drink and bites off the olive. "He has a point, Skye."

"What is this, dump on Skye day?"

Byron laughs and pushes off the counter to his full height. "Cut the woe-is-me persecution complex shit. You can't see the situation clearly because you love the man. Take a step back and pretend it was anyone other than Gabe and tell me you weren't being a little, well, hovery."

Hovery?

Is that even a word?

Thinking back over the last twelve days, I see myself checking his IV, reading his chart, talking with his doctors and nurses, *instructing* his nurses when they did something wrong, feeding him, fluffing his pillows...

Holy shit!

"Aww, fuck." I drop my head into my hands and squeeze my eyes shut.

I had been the hovering, controlling, bossy, *annoying* girlfriend, and I'm not even his fucking girlfriend. Never was, really. I had been the person all nurses and doctors hate and patients complain about as soon as they leave the room. No wonder Gabe wanted me out of his place so badly.

He had barely been freed from the hospital prison for half an hour before I was creating a new harpy one in his own home.

Storm's arm wraps around my shoulder, and she nudges me with her hip. "Don't stress about it, Skye. When he's feeling better, he'll appreciate what you did for him. Just give him some space."

Space. Pfft.

Isn't him putting space between us what caused this entire clusterfuck in the first place? If he hadn't pushed me away, we would have been together, and none of this would have happened.

It's not my fault. Never was, despite what my own misplaced guilt led me to believe.

It was his, for not having the fucking balls to just say what he fucking wants and to take it.

Storm pulls her arm away when I don't respond. "Speaking of space...have you spoken with Savage since he came to the hospital?"

I pull my head up long enough to down half of the second martini Byron made me before I answer. "No. And, frankly, I don't want to right now. Even though he made things right for Gabe legally, I told you the things he said to me, about me, and about Gabe. That was some messed up shit right there. I don't know if I'll ever forgive him for what he said."

"You don't mean that."

"Yeah, I do."

She shakes her head and pushes away her empty glass. "Maybe you think you do. But remember what it was like when we thought we might lose him? We already lost Star, are you really going to push Savage away over this? I already said basically the same thing to Savage, hoping it would help pull his head out of his ass."

My stomach clenches and the martini and a half start to rise up my throat.

Gabe was right.

This is exactly what he had warned me about, what he had feared more than anything. He and I both lost Savage.

And to make things worse, we lost him and have nothing to gain from it. We're both still alone, and while I'm not sure about him, I know I'm fucking miserable. But it doesn't have to stay that way.

36

GABE

Searing pain stabs my abdomen and radiates throughout my body. Every single inch of me is a giant, raw nerve.

"Fuck…"

I try to roll onto my side to tuck myself into a ball, but the motion just sends new arrows of agony shooting everywhere. A gasping breath is all I can manage as I try to breathe through it and the nausea now rolling through my stomach.

"Motherfucking fuck…"

Even opening my eyes hurts.

The clock next to my bed reads 2:00.

Well, shit.

I missed the pain med dose I was supposed to take at noon. That would explain the utter misery I'm in right now.

A vivid image of the medication bottles on the coffee table jumps into my head, and I groan. How the hell am I supposed to get all the way out there to get them. I can't even roll over without the pain making me want to puke.

Admitting Skye was right is like taking a swift kick to the junk. I would prefer a kick to the junk over the agony I'm in right now.

But, the truth is, I fucking need someone to get my meds for me.

Dani.

She's right across the hall—hopefully. And I sure as fuck hope she won't freeze me out the way Savage has.

I just need to call her.

But where the hell is my phone? Another glance at the nightstand tells me I'm shit out of luck. No phone. When was the last time I even had it?

It's not like anyone was calling to check on me while I was in the hospital. The only people who have ever given a shit about me are the Hawkes, and I fucking blew that now too. I will never be able to be a part of the family again. Savage won't even talk to me, and chances are, it's only a matter of time before Skye stops wanting to speak to me too.

She's still holding out hope I'll change my mind. And maybe I would have, if I hadn't seen the way Savage reacted in my room.

He will never forgive me. But he will forgive her, because she's blood. After losing Star, he will eventually get over his feeling of betrayal and forgive Skye rather than lose her too. Things between them will probably never be the same, but at least there's hope there.

If I'm selfish and tell her how I really feel—that I want nothing more than to be with her, that I can barely take a breath without thinking about her, and that I have no fucking clue how I'm supposed to go on every day without her in my life—she'll be here in an a millisecond and Savage will be gone not only from my life, but hers as well.

Fuck.

As if the anguish of losing her isn't bad enough, I need to get those fucking meds before the agony makes me pass out again.

Phone.

Need to find my phone.

I grit my teeth and fight through the searing pain to pull myself into a sitting position against the headboard.

A cold sweat covers my skin and the trembling of my body brings back very unwelcome memories from the cabin.

Breathe.

In.

Out.

Repeat.

I force my legs over the side of the bed and pause again to work through the pain before I even make an attempt to stand. My hand grasps the night stand, and I push myself up.

Sweet motherfucking Christ...

Agony rips the air from my lungs and I sway, the only thing keeping me upright is my death-grip on the table.

Instead of cursing Lucas for my current state, I can only blame myself. I probably deserve this. Karma can be a real fucking bitch, and I pissed her the fuck off.

Fucking your best friend's little sister is pretty high on the bro code violation list. I never should have gone to her apartment that night. What the fuck did I think I was going to accomplish? How could I have really thought I had the willpower to be alone with her like that and not act on what I knew we were both feeling?

Shit.

Phone. Find it.

I push up off the table. The room spins, and I wobble but manage to keep myself upright.

Living room. Just make it to the living room.

Each step is a test of not only my physical will but also my mental fortitude. With my hand on the doorjamb, I pause momentarily before venturing into the hallway.

Deep breath.

Step forward.

I place my right palm flat against the wall and inch my way toward the living room.

The agonizingly long hallway stretches out in front of me.

My vision blurs at the edges, and I pause again. This was a bad idea. I'm not going to make it. I'm going to collapse on the damn hardwood floor and probably die here, alone and hated by the only family I've ever known.

SKYE

The elevator dings when it reaches the top floor, and I wonder for the thousandth time if I'm making a mistake coming here again.

He doesn't want you here.

I step out into the hallway, and my eyes automatically go to the left, to Savage and Dani's door. He still hasn't spoken with me, or anyone else in the family for that matter, and I'm beginning to think it will take an act of God for him to come out of his Fortress of Solitude and Assholeness.

Ignoring the burning desire to knock on their door, I turn to the one on the right and pause to collect myself.

Don't mother him. Don't ask him to make decisions about the future while he's high on pain meds and recovering from the ordeal. Don't say something smart assy that you'll regret later. Don't be *you*.

The knob turns easily in my hand. It still blows my mind that Gabe and Savage never lock their doors. I mean, I get it.

The elevator is secured with a passcode to reach their floor, but considering how anal Gabe is about security, I would have expected him to have ten locks, not zero.

Not wanting to wake him if he's asleep, I inch the door open quietly and slip inside. The living room lights are off but the midafternoon light streams in the floor-to-ceiling windows.

My eyes immediately go to the coffee table where I left Gabe's medications and cell phone before I stormed out.

Shit.

The bottles lay in the same haphazard positions, and his phone sits unmoved.

He didn't take his meds.

Fuck.

I drop my purse onto the couch and practically race to where the hallway leading to his bedroom branches off from the living room.

"Gabe!"

He's little more than a huddled mass on the floor halfway down the hall. The only response I receive to calling his name is a muffled groan. I fall to my knees in front of him and pull his head up from where it's buried against his arm.

His eyes flutter open and he grimaces. "Skye?"

"Jesus, Gabe. What the hell are you doing?"

With what looks like great effort, he sucks in a breath and brushes my hand away from his face. "I was going to get the meds...or my phone...something? Fuck..."

I knew I shouldn't have left him.

Internal bleeding or return of the infection are my biggest concerns. I grab his wrist and check his pulse. Some of the tension in my chest releases when it's 110. His pain must be off the charts right now, but his pulse isn't high enough to overly concern me.

"Okay, big guy, let's get you back in bed. I'll bring you every-thing you need."

His eyes narrow, and for a brief moment, I think he's going to be stupid enough to fight me on this. Then the fight leaves his glassy gaze, and his head drops again. "All right."

Admitting he needs my help was probably a giant knock to Gabe's ego, but it seems like a step in the right direction.

I pull his arm up over my shoulders and he curses with even that little movement. Getting up is really not going to feel good.

"Here we go. On three. One, two, three." I push up and drag as much of his weight as I can while he tries to help me get him on his feet. His head falls forward, and I'm surprised his jaw doesn't break with how hard he's grinding it together.

His room is only ten steps away, but with all two hundred and twenty pounds of him leaning against me, it seems like much farther. I can only imagine what it feels like to him. Probably ten miles.

"Let's get this done one step at a time." He nods, and we shift forward slowly—inch by agonizing inch.

I fight back the tears burning in my eyes.

Don't cry. He's going to be fine.

It doesn't matter that the nurse in me knows he'll recover from his injuries or that this pain is only temporary; the hormonal, overly-emotional, stereotypical girl in me wants to sob at seeing him suffer.

But crying will do neither of us any good.

Suck it up, Skye.

I push through my swelling emotions and concentrate on getting him horizontal. By the time we finally reach his room and stand next to his bed, a cold sheen of sweat covers his face and he's shaking against me.

There's no way he could have made it back here by himself, or to the living room to reach his meds for that matter. He was here all alone, and if I hadn't come by...

No. Stop. That didn't happen.

I shake my head and help lower him down to the bed. The strangled groan emanating out from between his clenched teeth makes me wince. He takes several ragged, uneven breaths before grimacing.

He doesn't say anything, but it's clear he's not making it the rest of the way on by himself. I reach down and help lift his legs up onto the bed. When he's finally lying down, the number one priority becomes getting his medication into him so he can rest.

"Don't move. I'll be right back."

"As if I could...even if I wanted to..."

I dash back to the living room, scoop up the medication bottles and his phone. There's no way in hell I'm going to leave him without a way to communicate again. It was so fucking stupid not to make sure he got to bed okay. Even though he would have fought me with whatever energy he had left, I should have known he was too out of it to do it himself.

After a quick stop to the kitchen for a bottle of water, I bolt back to him. He hasn't moved an inch. If it weren't for the way his face is scrunched up in pain, I would think he's asleep.

"Here, take these." I dump two Percocet into my hand and open the bottle of water for him. His eyes flutter open and lock with mine. "You're going to need to sit up a little bit."

"You say that like it's easy." He groans and pushes himself up on his good arm until he's semi-reclining.

I hold the pills up to his mouth and his lips brush my fingers when he takes them. That fleeting touch against my skin sends a shiver down my spine. Vivid memories of those lips devouring my mouth and pussy heat my body.

His eyes study me as I hold the water up for him. Why does he have to look at me like that? He's in agony but his gaze still sets me on fire. And why does it have to be so fucking sexy to watch the muscles of his neck flex when he swallows?

Only Gabe could turn taking medication into fucking foreplay.

37

GABE

*T*he familiar smell of homemade sauce tickles my nose and drags me from sleep. I don't even want to open my eyes. Last time I did that, bad, *bad* things happened.

So, I lie still, taking stock of my body.

No searing pain in my side and only a dull throb in my head and shoulder.

Thank fucking Christ.

A muffled bang from the kitchen finally compels me to force my eyes open. The pitch black of the room surrounds me, and I'm tempted to close my eyes and let sleep pull me back under. I'm fucking exhausted.

But the scent coming through the crack in the bedroom door calls to me. My stomach rumbles.

Shit.

I'm not sure what time Skye got me back into bed, but the clock tells me it's almost 8:00 and I haven't eaten since 8:00 this morning—shitty hospital food at that.

I push myself up with my right arm and swing my legs over the side of the bed. The room only slightly spins this time and it quickly rights itself. With some concerted effort, I get myself on my feet and shuffle to the door.

The moment I open it fully, the aroma of familiar spices and tomato makes my mouth water.

By the time I make it down the hallway to the kitchen, I'm completely convinced Mrs. Hawke must be here cooking for me. Talk about awkward. Savage won't even talk to me but his own mother is taking care of me. This is precisely what I'd been trying to avoid when I ended things with Skye.

But the dark-haired woman at the stove isn't Mrs. Hawke. It's Skye, and my heart constricts watching her stir the large pot. Who would have thought seeing her cooking in my kitchen would be so Goddamn sexy and feel so fucking right?

God, I'm so fucked when it comes to this woman.

She pulls the spoon from the pot and brings it to her mouth. When she slips it between her lips and moans, my cock twitches to life. I must make a noise without even realizing it because her head whips around and her surprised eyes meet mine.

"Oh, you're awake." She drops the spoon back into the pot and approaches me where I lean against the wall. "How are you feeling?"

"Better." *Thanks to you* goes unsaid. She knows as well as I do that if she hadn't shown up, I may have spent an inordinate amount of time in agony on the fucking hallway floor before anyone found me.

A bright smile spreads across her face. "Good." She glances at the clock. "It's almost time for your next dose. I was going to wake you up soon anyway. I'll go grab the meds."

While she wanders down the hallway toward my bedroom, I slowly lumber over to the island and slide onto a stool facing the stove.

It feels so fucking good to sit down.

Despite my pain being manageable now, the effort it took to get all the way here after this morning's ordeal has utterly exhausted me.

She returns and places the bottles and water on the island in front of me. "Take them in ten minutes."

"Yes, ma'am." I would salute her, but expending energy on unnecessary movement right now sounds like a horrible idea.

When she returns her attention to the stove, I take stock of my kitchen. Cutting boards, half-chopped herbs, and other items are strewn across the island and counter next to the stove.

"I didn't know you could cook."

Skye barks out a laugh and grins at me over her shoulder. "I can bake, too. Pretty well, when I'm not being distracted in the kitchen." And just like that, the feeling of her hot, wet core wrapped around my dick while I pumped into her on her fucking counter sends my cock into full, raging hard-on mode.

A beautiful pink blush spreads up the back of her neck. Even with her back to me, I'm confident it's overtaken her cheeks. She's remembering that night too. I bet she's wet as fuck just thinking about it.

No, stop.

I shake my head to break the spell she put on me with one simple reminder. "What are you making? It smells like your mother's sauce."

She clears her throat and stirs the pot again. "It is. And I have the water going for pasta. You need to eat something."

"Where did you get all the groceries?" I know I didn't have anything she needed in my fridge or pantry. I don't exactly keep either stocked. "Did you leave and come back?"

"No." She turns around to face me and steps up to the other side of the island. "Actually, Dani brought everything over for me."

I scoff. "Does Savage know she's aiding and abetting the

enemy?"

The corner of Skye's mouth twitches up. "I doubt it. She said he was at the club tonight for something for a while, so she ran to the store, picked me up what I needed, and then went home."

"So does this mean she's staying neutral in all this? 'Cause I have a hard time believing she would do anything to upset Savage."

She shrugs. "I don't know. I didn't ask, but she did refer to herself as Switzerland at one point, so maybe she's withholding judgment."

Maybe.

But I'm pretty confident when it comes down to it, she will do what is best for her relationship with Savage over her friendship with me. And I can't say I blame her for that. He's her husband and the father of her child. I'm just the guy who tore her husband's heart out and created a rift in his family.

SKYE

Gabe's eyes darken with sadness. What's he thinking about? I probably shouldn't ask. Chances are I won't like his answer.

"You okay?"

He nods slowly. "Yeah, just wondering if all this was really worth it for you?"

My breath catches in my throat. I certainly wasn't expecting that question. "What do you mean?"

A sad smile turns his lips up. "I mean, would all this be worth it if we were together? Losing your relationship with Savage. Putting Dani in the middle. This break in your family. Would you be able to accept losing all that if we were together?"

Wow.

In a million years, I never would have anticipated Gabe initiating this conversation. I guess we aren't waiting until he's recovered.

I swallow and scrutinize my hands spread out on the granite countertop to avoid meeting his eyes. "Well, you know how much Savage means to me, so I'd be lying if I said it didn't break my fucking heart to know he's mad at me, and you, and that neither of us may ever get back what we had with him. But, the rest of the family? I don't think they would really care one way or the other what we did if it didn't upset Savage so much. And I think they'll get over that. So, worth it?" I force myself to meet his gaze. "Yes. A thousand percent yes, it's worth it."

He seems surprised. "But why? Why are you willing to lose all of that?"

"Because I love you and want nothing more than to spend the rest of my life with you."

His expression doesn't change.

He doesn't respond.

He doesn't move.

He simply sits there and stares at me unwaveringly.

Fuck. That hurts.

Maybe laying it all out like that was an incredibly awful idea. My stomach roils as I continue to wait for him to have some reaction, *anything* to tell me what he's thinking.

His lips press together in a firm line and his knuckles whiten on his fisted hands.

When he finally speaks, his voice comes out soft and demanding. "Come over here."

On shaking legs, I make my way around the island. He turns on his stool so by the time I make it to him, he's facing me.

I step forward until the front of my thighs meet his knees and study him. He reaches up with his good arm and places his large, warm palm against my cheek. His simple touch combined with the trepidation over what he's going to say make my legs weak. My body shakes, and I have to steady myself with my hands on his knees.

He lets out a small sigh and brushes his thumb across the line of my jaw. "Do you have any idea how hard this has been for me?"

Unshed tears burn my eyes. I reach up and wipe them away. "I know. You lost Savage...I'm so sorry."

"Yes, I did lose Savage. But that's not what I meant."

Oh God, this doesn't sound good.

My stomach churns and my heartbeat whooshes in my ears. "Then what did you mean?"

The corner of his mouth ticks up into that lopsided smirk that is so damn sexy. "I was referring to how it's been tearing me fucking apart having to pretend I'm not in love with you."

I can actually feel my heart stop. Everything freezes. It's one of those crazy time-stop things people describe that I always thought were total bullshit.

Did Gabe just tell me he loves me?

"Skye?"

I'm pretty sure he's saying my name. His lips are moving. The hand that was cupping my face moves under my chin and directs my eyes up until they meet his.

"Skye? Say something."

"I—"

I've been waiting for this moment for over a decade, and yet, when it happens, I completely forget what words are.

String letters together to make words.

String words together to make sentences.

Concern fills his eyes. "Skye, you're starting to freak me out. Say something."

A few deep breaths allow me to find my voice. "What does that mean?"

38

GABE

ear and confusion swirl in her eyes, and I can't say I blame her. I've been jerking her around since the night of the wedding—hot and cold, on and off, asshole and lover. Of course she would be unsure right now.

"It means I've been thinking...a lot. There's not much else I could do since I woke up in the hospital. When you brought me home this morning, I had one hundred percent convinced myself that ending things was the right thing to do. I saw it as the only potential way you could save your relationship with Savage. I was prepared to bow out and take a step back from the family so you could all try to mend the damage done. I thought it was the only reasonable choice to make..."

Tears well in her eyes again, and I pause, struggling to find the right words.

"I was willing to sacrifice my own happiness to ensure you could have Savage back. But now..."

A single tear rolls down her cheek, and I brush it away with my thumb.

Her lip quivers. "Now what, Gabe?"

I take a deep breath. "Now, I can't imagine my life without you, and I am so fucking sick of always doing what's right for everyone else and never what's right for me. You're right for me. You're fucking everything."

Fuck, I never thought I'd get that out.

The small gush of air rushing from her mouth tells me she's been holding her breath. The tears fall steadily now. "Do you really mean that?"

"Jesus, Skye, you've known me practically your entire life, when have I ever said something I didn't mean?"

A genuine smile appears for the first time, and she shakes her head. "Never."

"Exactly, so tell me what you want."

Her brow furrows and her eyes narrow. "What I want?"

A growl rumbles low in my chest. "Yes, woman, tell me what the fuck you want."

She moves her hands up from my knees to cup my face and tilts my head back as she steps between my legs. "I want what I've always wanted, what I've craved since I was sixteen. I want you, Gabe. Just you."

In a millisecond, her lips are on mine, and the familiar taste of her luscious mouth makes my cock swell again. She directs the kiss, pushing against my mouth with uncontrolled hunger and probing with her tongue. I relent to her control and let her take what she needs from me; it's the least I can do after all the bullshit I've put her through.

If I were physically capable, I would push up off this stool and pin her to the ground so I could fuck the ever-loving shit out of her. The animal instinct to claim her and somehow mark her as mine drives me forward, and I reach down and grasp her ass, pulling her in tight against my hard cock.

Moaning into my mouth, she nips at my bottom lip before drawing it in between her teeth and biting down.

Fucking fuck fuck.

For the second time, Skye almost makes me come in my fucking pants.

I drag my mouth away from hers. "Fuck, Skye...you need to stop or I'm going to go off like a fucking hair trigger"

She grins and leans in to press her lips against mine again. "What's wrong with that?"

"I just had a fucking organ removed, for one thing."

Her lips find that spot behind my ear, and I dig my fingers into her ass. "I'll be gentle." The warmth of her breath and the uttered words almost cause me to make a fool of myself, again.

The smell of something burning hits my nose just before the fire alarm starts blaring.

Again?

"Shit!" She yelps and pulls away from me, darting around the island to the stove where I turn to see the pot of sauce boiling over and into the flame under the burner. "Shit. Shit! *Shit!*"

The piercing wail of the fire alarm continues. My eyes travel all the way to the fourteen-foot ceiling where the red light is flashing.

Fuck.

How the hell am I supposed to get that turned off? A loud bang has me jerking my head back toward Skye, and she's emerging from the pantry with the broom in hand.

She grins at me. "Old trick."

With little more than a quick tap of the end of the handle against the alarm, the deafening noise ceases just as the apartment door flies open.

Dani stands in the jamb with Savage immediately behind her. "Is everything okay?" True concern darkens her eyes, but for the first time in over two decades, I can't read Savage.

Skye rests the broom against the island and takes a step toward the door. Dani holds it for Savage to enter.

Well, this isn't awkward at all.

SKYE

The look that passes between Savage and Gabe is indescribable —a combination of anger, hurt, relief, and something else.

I offer Dani a reassuring smile. "Everything's fine, the sauce pot just overflowed."

"Oh, is that what smells so good?" She brushes past me and waddles over to the stove, leaving me standing at one point of a triangle with Savage to my left and Gabe to my right.

I'll take uncomfortable family situations for a thousand, Alex.

"Mmm, Savage, you should come try this. It might be better than your mom's, but I'll never admit to saying that if you tell her."

I know Dani is just trying to break the ice and warm the chill between Gabe and Savage, but it doesn't look like either of them is going to make any move toward peace.

Men can be so fucking juvenile. Savage is acting like a caveman, and Gabe is just, well, silent.

A quick glance at the clock over the microwave tells me it's past time for his next medication dose. "Gabe."

His eyes move from Savage to me, and he quirks an eyebrow.

"Take your meds." He nods and turns his back on me and Savage, before opening the bottles and downing his pills.

Savage turns his attention to me. "What are you doing here?"

"Seriously?"

His eyes narrow. "Yes, seriously."

"What the fuck does it look like I'm doing? I'm cooking dinner for Gabe and helping him. He just had major surgery, Savage. I would think you'd be a little more empathetic given the circumstances. I seem to remember him dropping everything to fly to Germany to be with you after the accident and being here to help you when you returned."

Savage purses his lips together but doesn't respond. That's because he knows there isn't any response except "you're right, I'm sorry," that won't make him sound like a fucking hypocrite and a huge asshole.

Dani and Gabe's murmured words reach me but I can't tell what they're saying, and I refuse to be the one to back off from the stare-down Savage is giving me right now. He may be able to intimidate other people, but he doesn't scare me.

"Well." Dani returns to Savage's side and out of my peripheral vision, I see her rub her belly with one hand while placing the other on his shoulder. "Since things appear to be all right here, we'll just head home."

Without breaking my eye contact with Savage, I nod. "Thanks for stopping by."

I don't mention anything about her getting me the groceries. There's no point in starting another war with Savage right now or dragging Dani any more into our family soap opera.

If that's even possible.

When the door finally clicks shut behind them, I turn back to Gabe. He's watching me intently, a slight frown on his face.

I move over to him and resume my spot between his legs. "What's this frown for?" I brush my finger across his lips.

He puckers his lips and kisses my finger. "I just don't like seeing a standoff like that between you and Savage. It actually kind of breaks my fucking heart."

Mine too.

But Savage is the one being ridiculous and irrational about

the situation. Until he can realize how utterly ludicrous his reaction is, I refuse to feel guilty about my role in our rift. I've done nothing wrong. Gabe has done nothing wrong. Savage needs to learn to deal.

"It won't always be like this, Gabe."

"You seem pretty confident of that."

I sigh and run my hand back through his hair. He leans into my touch. "That's because I know my brother. This just rattles his control-freak tendencies. That, coupled with the storm and Dani's pregnancy, I think he's just at the end of his rope when it comes to things he doesn't have power over."

Gabe eyes me skeptically. "You really think it's that simple? Because I think he feels betrayed, and betrayal is not something you just get over and forget about."

As much as I wish he were wrong, Gabe may have a point. My only hope is that Dani can work her magic on him and convince him he's doing no one any good by holding onto his anger over this.

"It'll all work out."

The look Gabe gives me tells me he isn't convinced, but he still pulls my face down and kisses me like he believes everything will actually work out. His stomach growls, and I break away.

"You need to eat. Those drugs are going to kick in soon, and I don't need you passing out on an empty stomach."

Finding him on the floor like that scared the crap out of me. It's one thing when it's some random patient, but when it's someone you love, all the sterility of medical training goes out the door.

"Yeah, I'd rather avoid another couple hours on the hallway floor if I can. Although, at least I could rest my head on your lap this time."

39

GABE

Skye's gone for work by the time I finally open my eyes. She insisted on spending the night even though she would have to run home in the morning to change. I know she was probably worried I'd forget to take my meds again, and I promised her I'd set alarms on my phone. But that did nothing to dissuade her from staying.

It's not that I didn't want her here. I wanted nothing more than to wrap her in my arms and sink my dick deep inside her. It was the fact she insisted on sleeping in the guest room that annoyed me.

Nothing would have happened. There's no way in hell I would physically be able to have sex with her, not with the drugs muting my senses and my injuries still throbbing despite the narcotics. But she was worried she might roll over and hurt me, or that I might instinctively move toward her and do the same.

So, I slept alone, with the woman I love, who I just fucking *told* I love, asleep in the guest bedroom down the hall instead of next to me.

Which really fucking sucked.

The note on the counter in the bathroom tells me I'm not to attempt taking a shower until she gets back.

Shit.

All I want to do is stand under scalding hot water for hours. No matter how many sponge baths they give you in the hospital, there is nothing even close to resembling the feeling of being clean after a long, hot shower. I must smell like shit; I certainly look it.

The swelling on my face is gone, but the bruises have reached that lovely yellow and brown phase, making it appear like I went ten rounds with Tyson. I'm not even going to attempt getting my shirt off by myself, so examining the clusterfuck of my torso will have to wait.

My phone alarm goes off on the nightstand, and I move from the bathroom to grab it, silencing it as quickly as I can before I slide it into the pocket of my shorts. Loud, high pitched noises are not good when you're recovering from a severe concussion. I take my pills and slowly make my way out to the couch. I could have stayed in bed all day watching TV, but sitting on the couch doing it makes me feel a lot less like an invalid.

Sweet.

A Naked and Afraid marathon is on. My chest tightens remembering the last time I watched it with Savage. We always get off on making fun of the idiots on this show who think they are tough as nails but are crying like little fucking babies by day two. They think this shit is hard? Try having the hose turned on you while naked in the middle of October, or being forced to stay awake for thirty-six hours straight while under interrogation from a three-hundred-pound man who's repeatedly decking you. They wouldn't last five minutes in the SERE training I went through.

I'm just settling in for the episode when there's a knock at the door. That's odd. No one can get up here without the code or the doorman calling up. And anyone who has the code would just walk in like they always do.

Getting up to open the door sounds like climbing Everest right now.

"Who is it?"

A long silence greets me, and I start to get the prickly uneasy feeling that always came before an ambush.

"It's me."

Savage.

What the fuck is he doing here?

"Come in." I feel like maybe I should be concerned for my own safety given his anger and my weakened state, but I'm too tired. If he wants to add to the contusions and broken shit on my body, I'll let him. Maybe it would end this bullshit.

The door opens and he enters without a word. He sits there staring at me from across the room, and I'm not sure if I'm supposed to be saying something. So, I wait. And wait. The air in the room thickens uncomfortably with the tension between us.

Finally, he moves over to the windows and focuses out at the water. "I saw Skye leaving early this morning when I was on my way to the gym."

Oh, shit.

It's not like we can hide it from him, nor do we want to, but from his perspective, that was probably a slap in the face.

"Uh, yeah, she had to go to work."

Even from across the room, I see his shoulders tense. I brace myself for his next question. "So, are you two officially together now?"

I should have seen it coming. He was bound to come

confront me about it sooner or later. When I first told him, there had been the worry about Skye to distract him. In the hospital, I was near death, so he wasn't going to do it there. Still, his question throws me a little.

How the hell do I answer him without making this worse?

Just tell the truth.

"Yeah, we are. You may not believe me, Savage, but I love her."

Savage pushes his hands back through his hair and tugs. I know him well enough to know he's stressing—big time. It's only a matter of time before he blows, and I don't want to get hit with the shrapnel.

"I'm not going to hurt her, Savage."

The sigh he releases doesn't sound like resignation. It sounds more like he's gearing up to go twelve rounds. He frees his hands from his hair and turns his chair to face me again.

"You've already hurt her."

Bam. Right hook.

He's not wrong though. I've done nothing but hurt her since the night of the wedding. And yet, she keeps coming back and won't accept my attempts to push her away.

Savage scowls. "You know what she means to me."

It isn't a question; it's a statement—one that I absolutely understand. Even though there's only three years between them, the twins were so young when their father died, Savage has always felt more like a father than an older brother to them. When Star died, Savage fought hard to keep Skye on track, but she pushed everyone away then veered into the land of smartass remarks and hostile attitude.

We all knew what she was doing and were helpless to stop it. And being powerless is the one thing Savage cannot handle.

"I do know, Savage. That's why I fought my feelings for her for so long. I'm not good enough for her. You think I don't know that?"

That fucking hurt.

Saying the words out loud is so much worse than just thinking them. But it's time to lay it all out on the line. One hundred percent honesty is the only hope I have of making him understand.

Savage quirks an eyebrow at me. "Is that what you really think?"

"It's true, isn't it? That's why you hate the idea of me being with her so damn much."

He has the audacity to look offended. "*No one* is good enough for Skye, Gabe. And yes, if she has to choose someone to be with, I would much prefer it wasn't someone who goes through women like Kleenex..."

Bam. Left jab.

I think I actually recoiled from that one, but he just keeps going.

"...but..."

Wait, there's a but?

I hold my breath and wait for him to continue.

"...you are the most loyal, responsible, dedicated, honorable person I know. I never would have made it through the accident and recovery with my sanity without you, let alone kept the business afloat. We wouldn't have new locations going up if it wasn't for you. You've been behind me through the worst shit of my life, on more than one occasion. Hell, you're the only reason Dani is even here. I'm going to be a father and that never would have happened if you hadn't killed Abello's men..."

He trails off again, but this time, he doesn't continue. He just stares at me.

In the twenty plus years I've known Savage and called him my best friend, he has never left me speechless. But in this moment, I have no fucking clue what I'm supposed to say, or if I'm even supposed to say anything.

I don't understand what he's trying to tell me, and I'm not

going to risk reading into it too much. If I do that and I'm wrong, I could dig a deeper hole than I'm already in.

His clenched jaw ticks, and I can practically see the cogs spinning in his head.

He finally releases a pent-up breath and runs a hand back through his hair with a chuckle. "I can't fucking believe I'm going to say this, but if Skye has to be with anyone, I'm glad it's you."

Holy. Fucking. Shit.

Did he actually say those words?

Is this a dream?

Am I high from the Percocet and imagining this whole conversation?

There's no fucking way Savage Hawke just gave me his blessing to be with his baby sister.

"Seriously?" It's the only thing I can think to ask. He's just done a complete one-eighty in front of me, and I have no fucking clue why or what happened to bring this on.

He nods and a small smile tilts his lips up. "I can't believe it either."

"What made you change your mind? I mean, you were so fucking pissed when I told you and then at the hospital..." I let my words trail off because I don't even know how to describe what went down there. I only caught bits and pieces of his conversation with Skye, but I heard enough to know he thought I was taking advantage of her and also believed I fucked anything with a hole indiscriminately.

He shrugs and lets out another sigh. "Honestly? Dani set me straight."

That doesn't surprise me in the least. That woman is the best thing that ever happened to Savage. She tames the wild beast within him.

"The fact you were willing to be with Skye even though it meant losing your friendship with me showed me you really loved her. If the positions had been reversed, and it had meant choosing between you and Dani, I would have chosen her without question. So, I get it. You have no control over who you fall in love with. Do I wish it wasn't my baby sister? I'd be lying if I said I didn't have any reservations, but ultimately, it means my best friend, who has always been a member of the Hawke family as far as I'm concerned, and who I've always thought of as a brother, might actually be one legally speaking someday."

Shit. Brother?

The room spins and I have to drop my head into my hands to stop myself from puking.

Does he actually expect me to propose to Skye?

~

SKYE

I hated leaving him this morning. I know he's a big boy and can take care of himself—when he's not forgetting to take his medication and passing out in hallways—but I would have loved to stay with him for another day or two to help him get settled.

That was out of the question, though. I've already used any vacation time I had left to stay with him at the hospital, and I need to get paid.

Returning to work has been brutal in more ways than I can count. Not only am I worrying about Gabe, I'm also having to dodge answering the same questions over and over again about what went down with Lucas.

Why can't they just leave it alone?

The dirty looks cast my way and whispered words whenever I pass are really getting on my frayed nerves.

Maybe I shouldn't blame them for being curious. It isn't exactly common-place for someone to kill a coworker. I guess we never technically *worked* together, but we were members of the same small community.

And despite being completely cleared legally, some people are angry, refusing to believe Lucas could have done anything violent enough to warrant me taking his life. I don't need to explain myself to them. I protected Gabe, and I don't want to have to look into the teary eyes of one more coworker who is mourning the loss of that psychopath.

So, I've spent most of my day hiding in the back office when I'm not seeing patients.

I peer up from the tedious charting I've been doing for over an hour at the clock; it's almost 2:30. I can get away with leaving at 3:00 if nothing urgent comes up.

Gabe's text from earlier saying we needed to talk about something has left me uneasy. The vagueness of the message isn't like him and it worries the part of me that still can't believe he's a hundred percent on board with us right now. I just want to get out of here.

Please, no more patients.

I scribble a few notes in the chart and toss it on the top of the pile before grabbing another from the next stack.

"Skye?"

Damnit.

Leave it to my boss to thwart my escape plans. "Yes, Dr. Bradley?"

He closes the door behind him and leans against the filing cabinet. His kind eyes narrow on me with concern. "Are you okay? I know today can't have been very easy for you."

I don't know whether to be relieved he isn't asking me to see another patient or annoyed he's bringing up the one thing I don't want to discuss. He's a great boss: easy-going, understanding, and generous. His question isn't meant to pry. The concern is genuine, and he doesn't deserve the attitude I was just about to throw at him.

With a forced smile, I turn fully to face him. "I'm all right."

There's no need to offer additional information to my boss if he's not asking.

He frowns and pushes his hands into the pockets of his lab coat. "I just want you to know that if you need some additional time off or if you need me to prescribe something for you, all you have to do is ask."

Some people might find it odd to have their boss offering them drugs, but given everything that happened, he's probably wondering if I need something to help me sleep or for anxiety.

Surprisingly though, I haven't had any problems with either since I was confident Gabe was going to recover. Even the uncertainness of the situation with Savage isn't causing me the distress I had imagined it would.

Maybe that's because I don't believe it will last, or maybe it's just because I don't have the patience to deal with petty shit anymore. Either way, I feel good for the first time in a really fucking long time, and while I appreciate Dr. Bradley's offer, I don't need or want to numb my senses now that I'm finally with Gabe.

"I appreciate the offer, but really, I'm good."

Pushing himself upright, he offers me a half smile and then looks up at the clock. "Feel free to take off when you're done charting. I'm sure you're anxious to get back to your boyfriend."

Boyfriend.

Holy shit!

Gabe Anderson is my boyfriend.

I've been so busy worrying about everything that I haven't taken a moment to appreciate that fact. The man I've loved since I was a teenager is officially my boyfriend instead of just the object of my obsession. And fuck, does that feel good.

40

SKYE

"Gabe?" The dark silence of the condo sends a shiver of dread down my spine. I haven't heard from Gabe in a couple hours, and his message was less than detailed.

I drop my purse on the end table and make my way back to the bedroom. "Gabe?" Voices from the TV echo in the hallway, and I step into his room.

Damn.

How can he be so fucking sexy passed out?

I check my watch. He must have just taken his meds about an hour ago. He'll probably sleep for a while. And a nap sounds fucking awesome.

My scrubs hit the floor as I make my way around to the other side of the bed. Slipping under the covers and lying down in a bed that smells like Gabe is absolute heaven. He stirs next to me and rolls toward me slightly. I freeze. The last thing I want to do is wake him.

It was torture sleeping in the guest room last night, but there was no way I was going to risk potentially hurting him more just so I could fulfill my need to have his body close to mine.

But I just couldn't resist today. I've missed him. I've missed this.

Instead of closing my eyes and resting, I watch him sleep. The healing bruises on his face are a constant reminder of what he went through trying to protect me. How can Savage not see what an amazing man Gabe is? Why can't he understand how perfect we are for each other?

He curbs my snark and tames my self-reproach. I understand what he needs and won't let him dwell on his pain and guilt.

Christ, I really love this man.

I would give anything to be able to talk to Star right now and share my joy with her. Although, chances are I wouldn't even have to tell her how things have played out, she would feel my euphoria and know, inherently, how happy I was and that the only person who could do that is Gabe.

Even when we were teenagers, and fawning over my brother's friend was pointless and juvenile, Star never teased me about it. She was a realist with respect to the fact that it would probably never happen, but she understood why I felt the way I did about him and kept my secret when she could have easily said something to him that would have made things very awkward.

It's hard for me to believe this is real. I'm actually here with Gabe, we're actually together, but Star is gone.

His eyes flutter open and the corner of his mouth tilts up. "Are you just going to lie there staring at me? Because it's kind of creepy."

I giggle and reach out to touch his lips. He kisses my fingers and grins at me. "Did you just get home?"

Home?

Did he just refer to his place as *my* home?

It's probably just the drugs talking.

"Uh, yeah. Just a minute ago. I thought you'd be asleep longer so I was going to join you for a nap. I hope I didn't wake you."

"No, I've been nodding in and out, just waiting for you to come home."

There it is again—home.

I'm sure he doesn't even realize he's saying it, but every time he does, my heart gives a little wild flutter. I would love nothing more than to wake up with Gabe every morning and fall asleep in his arms every night. But that can't happen. Not with Savage living across the hall, not to mention the fact we've been technically back together for what? Twenty-four hours?

Or maybe not even back together, because were we even technically together before?

Who the fuck knows?

As much as I'm thrilled Gabe finally came to his senses, things are far from settled.

He reaches out and brushes my hair back behind my ear, settling his palm against my cheek. "What's wrong? You look upset."

"No, just thinking."

He chuckles. "Well, that never leads anywhere good."

I swat his hand away playfully. "Ass."

"You love my ass."

Not going to lie, I really, *really* do love his ass, and it has been far too long since I've gotten to see it. I slide my hand around him and give it a good squeeze. "Speaking of your ass, you ready to take a shower?"

He groans and gives me a relieved smile. "Fuck yes."

I grin at him and shift off the bed. "Okay, then let's get you naked."

"My thoughts exactly."

GABE

There is no hiding my reaction to her as she helps me undress. My raging erection is right in her face when she slides off my boxers.

She smiles up at me. "I'm glad you're so excited for this. Let me check your surgery and drain sites before we get in the water."

My dick jumps. "Did you just say *we*?"

Her hand slides across my abdomen softly and she examines the puffy train track scars bisecting my body vertically, being held together with steri-strips, and over to the left side where the surgical drain had been. "Everything looks good." She straightens fully and cups my dick in her hand as she leans in next to my ear. "Especially this."

Jesus.

"No way you can wash everything properly with that shoulder. You're going to need my help."

Normally, I would bristle at the word *help* and the suggestion I need it, but after what happened yesterday, I'd be stupid to protest. And frankly, having her naked in the shower with me can only be a win-win situation.

She leans into the shower stall and tests the water. "Perfect. Get in, I'll be right behind you."

I'd much rather have her in front of me so I can stick my cock between her ass cheeks, but I comply and step in under the stream of hot water.

Fucking heaven...

I turn my face up into the flow and let the heat warm my skin and wash away the grime of the last two weeks. The glass door opens and clicks shut, and then her arms are around me. Pressing her lips to my spine, she then buries her face between my shoulder blades.

Despite the warmth of the shower, a shiver rolls through my body, and I bite back a groan. I've missed her touch more than I thought was even possible.

Note to self: don't get shot again, it will really eat into your sex life. So will pushing away the woman you love.

I won't make that mistake again.

"Turn around." She murmurs the words against my skin and the vibration of her lips against my spine makes my entire body tingle.

Without hesitation, I comply, turning to face her and letting the water beat down on my shoulders and back. She reaches out, grabs the soap, and works up a good lather. The anticipation of having her hands all over me has my body shaking and my cock jumping in the space between us.

My eyes drop to her breasts, and I don't bother to try to stop the appreciative groan. "Christ, Skye, you're so fucking beautiful."

She grins at me and runs her slippery palm over my cock. "You aren't so bad yourself."

I grab her face with my good hand and claim her mouth with a searing kiss. Words cannot describe what it feels like to have her in my arms again; it's like that first breath of air after being held under water. Like your lungs crave oxygen, I crave her. I drag her to me to deepen the kiss.

Fuck.

Pulling back reluctantly, I grit my teeth against the pain in my shoulder. I hadn't even realized I had used my left arm to pull her closer.

"Shit, Gabe, I'm sorry. I wasn't thinking."

I shake my head and breathe through the pain until it dissipates. "It's not your fault, I just got a little overzealous." She squeezes my cock, and I hiss in a breath. "Because you keep doing that."

She grins, releases my dick, and drops to her knees. Water flows over my shoulders, down my stomach, and streams off my erection toward her face. Her wide eyes lock with mine with clear intent. She leans forward and slides her tongue along the underside of my cock from root to tip.

"Fucking Christ, Skye."

Heat flames across my skin, and she licks around the head of my cock, over my piercing, and back again, teasing me mercilessly. I want nothing more than to thrust forward and bury myself down her throat, but I manage to find a modicum of restraint. It has been way too fucking long since something felt this good, and I'm not going to ruin it by taking charge when she's so obviously enjoying working me over at this torturously slow pace.

With a fucking adorable little hum, she sucks the head into her mouth. Just. The. Fucking. Head. Then she does some sort of rollercoaster tongue roll maneuver along the bottom edge, right along that spot that drives me insane.

My hands tighten in her hair, and I can't stop the strangled groan or desperate plea from leaving my mouth. "Please... Skye...fuck...just..."

Her eyes dance with amusement and lust. She has never been sexier or more beautiful.

"Christ, I love you."

That must have been the right thing to say, because, without any warning, she sucks my cock into her hot mouth and so far down her throat, I swear to God, the head practically reaches her stomach. She hums and moans around my hard flesh, sending vibrations shooting along my shaft and up my spine.

I'm going to come.

It's only been a fucking minute and I'm already ready to blow.

If I wasn't so lost to the bliss of her mouth sucking and sliding along my cock, I might be embarrassed by the fact that I'm going to bust a nut quicker than a high school freshman. Although right now, I wouldn't give a flying fuck if the world was crumbling down around us as long as she keeps doing what she's doing.

When she wraps her hand around the base of my shaft and begins twisting up on every withdrawal of her mouth, I know it's a fucking lost cause to hold back any longer.

The telltale tingle of my impending orgasm starts at the base of my spine, and I tug on her hair to get her to look up at me. I want her eyes locked with mine when I come down her fucking throat.

41

SKYE

That animal heat is back in Gabe's eyes. He holds me captive with his gaze, and his hands, as his orgasm nears.

Having his hard cock in my mouth is better than any wine or booze I've ever tasted. I crave his release as much as he does, because knowing I'm the one who does this to him is the greatest compliment he could ever give me.

His breathing speeds up, his body tenses, and his dick bulges against my tongue. I suck harder and swirl my tongue along the underside, concentrating on the back of the head in that spot that makes him a fucking madman.

He pulls my head toward him, forcing his cock further down my throat while still maintaining his controlling gaze and then roars as he empties himself. I swallow every spurt of hot cum and hum, knowing the vibrations will only drag his orgasm out further. He comes longer and harder than even I thought possible, his eyes eventually rolling back in his head and closing in bliss.

When his body finally stops spasming, he releases his grip on my hair, clutches his abdomen, and wobbles slightly. He slams his palm flat against the tile wall to steady himself while the other continues to hold his center. He opens his eyes and finds mine.

Damn. That look.

If I were wearing any panties, they would have melted off the moment his eyes locked with mine again.

Instead of looking satisfied, his stare screams that he's about to do something really, *really* stupid considering he just got out of the hospital a day ago.

"Gabe…" I rise to my feet and move toward him. His chest and abdomen heave, and my eyes fall on the angry, red puffy skin there, reminding me of his weakened state. I know he's in pain. He didn't come that hard without the muscles in his abdomen contracting. Maybe I shouldn't have blown him like that, but I've missed him so much, and I just wanted him to feel good after all the anguish he's been in for the past two weeks.

I press my hand to the center of his chest, over his heart and just above the surgical site. "No, Gabe. Whatever you're thinking, just no. It's a bad, *bad* idea."

He growls and tugs my face to his, stopping my mouth a mere hairsbreadth from his. "I don't care how much it hurts, I need to do for you what you just did for me. I need to be inside you." His mouth descends on mine before I can reply, and his cock presses into my stomach, already hard again.

Well, shit.

His words cause my already wet core to clench. Having his cock in my mouth has my body primed and ready to go. But there's no way in fucking hell I'm going to let him risk his health just so I can get off. Even the sensuous assault on my mouth won't convince me to set aside the very real danger to him.

I break away from his mouth. "No, you *cannot* and *will not* try to fuck me right now, Gabe."

Humor glints in his eyes and he grins. "You're right, I'm not going to *try*, I'm going to *actually* fuck you."

With a scowl, I push away and step back, out of his immediate reach.

Fuck, it's cold over here out of the water.

I shake my head. "No."

His eyebrow quirks up. "Are you seriously saying no right now? Don't try to deny you want me."

"Jesus, Gabe, that isn't the issue. Of course I want you to fuck me. I want you to shove me against the tile and pound into me from behind until I fucking scream and beg you to stop, but it's *not* going to happen. Not today, and not anytime soon. Did you forget you just got shot and had major surgery to remove a fucking organ? You need to get better, and sex is not in the cards."

He growls deep and low, like a wild animal giving off a warning. "Do you really expect me to be okay with not getting you off after you just made me come harder than a freight train?

Saying this is going to fucking kill me.

"Yes. And if you can't keep your hands to yourself, I'm getting out."

The anger boiling inside him reflects in his hard eyes. He's pissed. It's probably a huge slap in the face for me to deny him sex, but it's for his own good.

"Well? Are you going to behave, or do I need to leave?"

Ha! Behave is not a word I would normally associate with Gabe.

I have little confidence in his willpower right now.

He closes his eyes and takes a breath. I'm sure he tries to hide it, but I catch the slight wince and crinkling around his eyes. Deep breaths don't exactly feel good after having your abdomen sliced open.

When he opens them again, he gives me a small, tight smile. "Fine. I'll behave."

I step forward, returning to the hot spray and Gabe. The sadness and longing in his loving gaze actually makes my heart ache. "I'm sorry."

"I told you to stop apologizing."

To avoid the pain in his eyes, I turn my attention to lathering up the soap in my hands. "I know. Now, turn around so I can wash your back."

He hesitates briefly before turning and letting the water hit his face and chest, giving me access to his strong, muscular back. I rub my palms across the taut flesh, working my way down to his tight ass then his long, powerful legs.

Gabe really is beautiful—a true work of art. The myriad of tattoos on his tan skin only add to the splendor of his form and accent every dip and valley of his toned muscles.

My pussy clenches again. I want his cock more than I want air right now, but I need to keep it together and be strong for both of us, 'cause Lord knows, if I even hint at a crack in the armor, he will take advantage of my weakness.

The next few weeks are going to be a real struggle for both of us.

GABE

Skye is trying to kill me. I'm one hundred percent confident of that now. There's no other explanation for why she tortured me with her mouth and hands in the shower and wouldn't let me even touch her.

I contemplate the situation as she towels me off. Her breasts sway, and I bite back a growl. My cock starts to harden again. How that's even possible after she sucked me off and then jerked me off is beyond my comprehension.

She glances at my semi and then up at my face. "Damn baby, keep that thing in control."

I bend down and nip at her collarbone, and she laughs and pulls away, moving behind me to dry off my back.

"What was it you wanted to talk to me about?" The towel moves across my skin in slow circular motions, and fuck, it feels incredible.

Shit.

I totally forgot to tell her about my conversation with Savage. She distracted me with the promise of finally being clean and with orgasms.

"Savage came to see me today."

Her hand stops midstroke, and she steps around in front of me again. Trepidation mars her beautiful face. "What did he say?"

"That he thinks I'm a manwhore—"

She growls. "Fucking asshole!"

"And that I am not good enough for you—"

Her lip curls and she clenches her fists. "Fucking *prick!*"

"But that he thinks we are perfect together."

It takes a couple seconds, but her eyes eventually snap up to meet mine. "Wait, what?"

I grin at her and pull her into me for a short, sweet kiss. "He is okay with us being together."

The confusion she's no doubt experiencing is understandable. Savage made his feelings about us very clear from the moment he found out. Considering his temper and the way he tends to hold on to grudges, I hadn't expected this change of heart either.

Maybe it's Dani and the fact he's going to be a father soon that ultimately led him to accept our relationship. Whatever it was, I don't care. I'm not stupid enough to think our friendship will remain unaffected by this. We still lied to him and went behind his back. The sting of betrayal will linger there for a while, maybe forever. But, this is a huge step toward mending what was broken by our actions.

I just hope Skye can forgive Savage for his knee-jerk reaction and the things he said when he wasn't thinking clearly or considering the repercussions.

"But why? What happened that he all of a sudden decided he no longer wanted to strangle you with his bare hands?"

Good question.

I chuckle and pull her to me. "To be honest, I'm not completely sure. He still seemed pissed when he got here, and I thought for sure he was going to tell me he wanted me out of the business. He said he had seen you leave this morning and asked if we were together now. I told him yes, and I was pretty confident there would be physical violence." Skye chuckles and buries her face in my chest, wrapping her arms around me.

"Then he insulted me a few times, and I was ready to kick him out. But then it was like a switch flipped or something. He started telling me what a great friend I'd always been to him and how he trusted me with his life and Dani's." She squeezes me gently and places a kiss over my heart.

"And then he said if you had to be with someone, he was glad it was me."

Skye pulls back and her brow wrinkles. "That's it? That's all he said?"

I shrug and then wince when pain shoots through my shoulder. She watches me intently. I know she saw that, but I'm not going to let her dwell on every time something hurts me by giving it voice. "Basically, yeah. He said that, then left."

Her brow furrows. "Huh...well, it doesn't sound like he's thrilled. It sounds more like he's resigned to the idea."

"I'll take that over fury or a freeze-out any day."

It will take time to rebuild the friendship and trust I had with Savage, but at least the door is open now.

She sighs. "I guess. Do you think I should go talk to him?"

I shake my head and tilt her chin up so I can press my lips to hers. "Give him some time. He'll talk to you when he's ready."

Instead of answering me, Skye responds by smashing her lips against mine fiercely.

I guess she's happy about this turn of events.

My cock twitches between us, and she moans into my mouth before she pulls away and looks down at it.

"You are killing me slowly, you know." Her eyes move up to meet mine, and I smirk. "How long do I have to wait until I can be inside you?"

42

GABE

*T*wo fucking weeks.

It has been fourteen agonizing days since I asked Skye when I could fuck her again, and it will be another fourteen before we hit the four week timeline she'd laid out.

Epic. Fucking. Torture.

While I've passed the time recovering and trying to figure out ways to rebuild my shaky friendship with Savage, Skye has spent it tormenting me with her sweet ass, hot mouth, and stunning tits.

I haven't officially asked her to move in with me yet, but it's only a formality at this point. She hasn't wanted to leave me after the whole hallway incident, even though I've quickly regained my strength and my pain level has dropped off drastically. I know she's just being overly cautious and protective of me, but Christ, I just need to fuck her already.

My aching cock can't take it anymore and neither can my pride. The woman won't even let me get her off like I want to, as if going down on her is going to somehow impede my recovery. At least I've gotten to feel her wet cunt squeeze and clasp my fingers when she comes on my hand. If she wouldn't have let me do that, I think I would have gone insane and just pinned her down by now.

And that's exactly what I plan on doing the moment she walks through that fucking door. I'm done waiting to be with her. The doctor told me four to six weeks after surgery and we are at almost four. I'm not one hundred percent yet, but a seventy-five percent fuck is better than a zero fuck.

The door opens, and she yelps when she finds me sitting in the chair facing the door, waiting for her. "Fuck, Gabe, you scared the crap out of me! What are you doing here? I thought you were going into the office today?"

I rise from the chair and approach her slowly. "I did, but Savage is still kind of avoiding me and only speaking to me when it's absolutely essential, so it makes being there a little awkward. Plus, every time I sit in my office chair, all I can see is you touching your wet cunt on the couch while I jerked off. I swear my office still smells like your fucking orgasm."

A red flush creeps up her neck and spreads across her cheeks just as I finally stop mere inches from her. "Jesus—"

The word tumbles from her lips but I don't give her time to finish the thought. I tug her against me and crush my mouth to hers, pushing everything into the kiss I've been wanting for the last month.

Her lips move against mine, pushing, biting, nipping.

Fuck yes.

My hands tighten on her ass and yank her against my throbbing cock. I slide my tongue along her lips, begging for entrance and praying she won't stop this.

She jerks away and holds a hand up. "Wait!"

Oh, come the fuck on.

"No, Skye. No more waiting. It's been almost a month. I feel fine—better than fine. But if I don't bury myself in you right now, I'm not going to be fine much longer."

Her blue eyes are a turbulent mix of desire and concern. She wants this just as much as I do, and if she says she doesn't, she's a fucking liar.

"Stop treating me like I'm glass and I'm going to fucking break. You have made me come more times than I can count the last two weeks, let me do the same for you, with my *cock*, not my fucking hand."

She shudders at my words, and I can almost physically see the moment she lets go of her worry and starts thinking as my girlfriend and not my fucking nurse.

Shit, she is my girlfriend, isn't she?

I haven't called anyone my girlfriend since high school. Instead of making me feel queasy, and like I want to take the next plane out of here, it actually feels right and makes me want to fuck her even more.

Without hesitation, I close the distance between us and wrap my arms around her, hauling her up my body until she wraps her legs around my waist. Momentary fear clouds her eyes, but before she can ask if she hurt me, I slam my lips to hers in a commanding kiss meant to tell her that her reservations are completely unwarranted.

Every step I take toward my bedroom causes my cock to rub against her pussy and clit. The wet heat seeps through her scrubs and my sweatpants. I groan against her mouth and lower her to the bed, trying to hide the slight discomfort it causes in both my shoulder and abdomen.

Either I hide it well or she doesn't care at this point, because she clasps the back of my head, dragging my mouth back down to hers while her feet, still hooked around my back, yank my cock back against her core. I pull back from her kiss because there's something I need to say before I lose myself in her.

"Fuck, Skye, I need you so fucking much. I'm so stupid for

not seeing it sooner. I know I've told you a hundred times in the last two weeks, but it should have been a million. I love you, more than is probably healthy, and I need you with me, always."

She laughs and tilts her head to the side with a smug smirk. "I know, you're completely helpless without me."

I chuckle and bury my face into her neck. She's joking, but she doesn't know how right she is. Before Skye, I was drifting aimlessly, I just didn't realize it. Booze and women helped me through each day, and the drugs prescribed by Doc Cochran eased me through the nights, but I was never really whole until I admitted my feelings for Skye and let her into my heart fully.

And now, it's time to show her how I really feel. I reach back and grasp my shirt before yanking it off over my head. My shoulder twinges with the movement, but it doesn't stop me from my mission—getting Skye naked and my dick inside her. She must have the same idea, because by the time my sweatpants hit the floor, she's already managed to strip.

Skye's legs are spread, exposing her pussy, already wet with her arousal. Her skin glows in the midafternoon sun streaming in from the windows, and I want to kiss and lick every single inch of it.

But not now. "Baby, we can do the long, slow love making shit later. Right now, I need to fuck you—hard and fast."

Her feet hook around my lower back, and she pulls me down to her. "Yes, fuck yes."

I kiss her and reach between us, aligning my cock, and dragging it through her wetness. Then I shove into her with one thrust, every fucking inch of my cock being cocooned in her heat.

Fucking heaven.

∾

SKYE

Gabe's cock stretching and filling me is the greatest feeling in the world—hands down. It's better than any booze or drug I've ever tried, or any combination of the two. He thrusts into me over and over, setting a punishing rhythm designed to push us over the edge quickly.

His hips drive against mine while his tongue swirls and glides along my lips, seeking entrance. I gasp when he changes the angle of his dick slightly, and he takes the opportunity to slip his tongue into my mouth and tangle it with mine.

That goddamn piercing drags against my G-spot with every plunge and withdrawal, sending pulses of pleasure shooting through my body.

Holy fucking shit.

I break away from his kiss to suck in air. He drops his mouth to my neck and sucks behind my ear. My hips bow off the bed and meet his snapping pelvis even harder.

"Fuck...Gabe...I've fucking missed you."

He groans and pulls back to look in my eyes. "Not as much as I've missed you. I fucking love you." His hands slide under my ass, and he raises me, tilting my hips up to give him deeper penetration.

I push my concern over him overexerting himself to the back of my mind. Then, he rolls his hips and drives into my body like a fucking madman, grinding his pelvis against my clit.

Stars dot the edges of my vision, forming a halo around Gabe as he beams down at me with lust and love in his eyes. I cling to the sheets and squeeze my pussy around his cock with every retreat.

His head drops back.

Fuck.

He's so damn beautiful with his neck muscles straining and sweat glistening across his skin.

And he's mine.

I will cut any bitch who's dumb enough to try to come between us.

This cock is meant for me. *Mine.*

Heat spreads across my skin, and I know I'm going to come soon. I need him to go over the edge with me. I need to watch his face when my pussy milks his cock. "Gabe...look at me."

He moans and drops his head down so his eyes meet mine. The muscle along the side of his clenched jaw twitches. The pistoning of his hips continues at the relentless pace. He's close too.

"I'm gonna come. You're gonna come with me."

"Fuck yes," he growls, sliding his hand over where our bodies meet. His thumb finds my clit and he swirls it hard and fast while he continues to plunge into me.

The combination of the attention to my clit and the drag of his flesh and damn piercing inside me crescendo until I shatter beneath him. White light flashes against my lids and fire rushes throughout my body.

He roars and slams into me with erratic strokes before he collapses. Our hearts race against each other. His ragged breath flutters over my ear. I can't remember ever being this happy, not even when Star was alive.

I shouldn't feel guilty about that. She would want me to be happy.

Gabe pushes himself up on his right forearm and looks down at me with a satisfied, cocky grin on his face. "Two things. First, never question my ability to fuck you senseless again."

I chuckle, any momentary feeling of guilt forgotten, and he leans in to kiss me gently.

"Second, I need to be able to do this every single day, as many times as I want and wherever I want. I need to fuck you on every surface in this place, a dozen times each, and that still won't be enough. And the only way it's going to happen when and how I want it is if you move in with me."

Well fuck me stupid.

I'm hearing things again.

"Seriously?"

He has the balls to look surprised and hurt by my question. "Yes, seriously. Why is that so hard to believe?"

I chuckle and cup his face in my shaking hands. "Because we haven't been together very long, living together is a huge step, and you live across the hall from my fucking brother."

With a satisfied groan, he leans into my touch. "Skye, we have known each other for over twenty years. I don't think it's possible for anyone to know me better than you do, or for me to know anyone as well as I know you. We've been through way too much to put off taking and having what we want. I don't want to wait anymore. And as far as Savage goes..."

He leans in and presses a kiss to my lips before pulling away with a grin. "He'll just have to grow the fuck up."

EPILOGUE

SKYE

*M*aybe I'm biased, but I'm pretty confident this is the most beautiful baby in the world. Smiling down at my niece, and her perfect, tiny fingers and toes, I can't help but feel that pang in my ovaries telling me to get to the baby making.

Whoa! Slow down there, ladies.

No matter how adorable little Kennedy is, Gabe and I are nowhere near thinking about having babies. We've only been living together for a little less than two months, the last thing we need to do is toss a baby into the mix.

I'm perfectly content to snuggle with my niece to get my baby fix.

Her dark hair and blue eyes are all Savage. Even though I know all babies have blue eyes when they are first born, I'm fairly confident hers will stay that way, given the vivid blue of both Savage's and Dani's.

She's going to be a little heartbreaker when she grows up.

And it's going to drive Savage fucking crazy.

I just hope she learns from her daddy, and not uncle Stone, how she should be treated by a man—with respect, the way Savage treats Dani. My baby brother is barely visible out on the back patio. He paces back and forth, in and out of my line of vision, his cell phone glued to his ear.

There's no way to hear what he's saying, and I'm a shitty lip-reader, but he's angry.

Leave it to Stone to come for a visit but spend the entire time working. And manwhoring it up. I swear, in the week he's been here, I've seen him with no fewer than three different women. And those are just the ones he's brought out in public. Who the hell knows how many he brought back to his hotel room that I know nothing about.

I love the kid, but he's a fucking mess sometimes.

He's certainly not the type of influence Savage is going to want for Kennedy. But Uncle Gabe has been reformed by yours truly, and I'm confident he will always keep a watchful eye on her to make sure she's treated well by any poor sucker who tries to date her.

A snicker works its way up my throat envisioning Savage and Gabe answering the door for her first date with fully-loaded weapons strapped on and threatening looks in their eyes.

It's definitely going to happen.

Gazing at Kennedy, it still blows my mind how much every-thing has changed so rapidly.

Just two years ago, Savage was alone and thought he would be forever. Now, he has a beautiful wife who puts up with all his demanding bullshit and a new daughter.

Back then, I was a miserable pain in the ass who did everything I could to make everyone else just as miserable as I was. I was a flat-out bitch to Dani when she started dating Savage, even though I only had his best interests at heart, and I pushed everyone away so I would never have to experience losing someone who meant as much to me as Star had.

If no one ever got close, I could never suffer again. And it worked, for over four years, it worked beautifully.

But Gabe changed all that.

Thank God I let him.

I could have turned my anger at his rejection into a full-on vendetta. But who the fuck am I kidding? I was lost to him the moment he showed up at my apartment that night. There was no way I could have pushed him away in the long run.

That man is everything and always will be.

I let my eyes wander over to where he stands chatting with Savage and Ben near the archway leading into the dining room. He laughs at something Savage says and tosses his head back. Seeing them talking and joking around together again is such a weight off my shoulders.

The rift between them has been the one lingering blemish marring my happiness with Gabe.

Deep down, I knew they couldn't keep up the animosity and tension between them. They're the epitome of bromance and have been friends too long, been through too much together to let anything, even me, push them apart for long.

I'm frankly surprised it lasted as long as it did. Gabe went into work like nothing had changed between them, and Savage continued to be cold and standoffish, only speaking with him about business decisions, even after he told Gabe he was okay with us being together. He just couldn't let go of it fully.

The breaking point finally came when Dani went into labor, two weeks early.

Savage had a total fucking meltdown of epic proportions and was too panicked to drive her to the hospital. Leave it to

Mr. Control freak to completely lose his shit when something doesn't go as planned.

Gabe called to tell me he was bringing them in, and I went to make sure the birthing center was ready for her then waited for them at the hospital entrance. Savage looked more concerned than Dani. His face was pinched as if he were the one in pain. She just gave me a knowing smile and whispered, "Keep an eye on him so he doesn't pass out," as I helped her lower herself into the wheelchair.

I pushed her into the birthing center while Gabe tried to keep Savage from either hyperventilating or telling off some poor staff member while getting them checked in.

The way Gabe took care of Savage that day must have reminded Savage of the time he was in the hospital in Germany after the accident. Gabe had spent months traveling back and forth between there and New Orleans. He took care of the business alone so it didn't crumble in Savage's absence and stood by him through every painful surgery.

Savage remembering that is the only thing that would explain the one-eighty he pulled with his attitude.

Although, having a baby may have helped tame him somewhat too.

Whatever it was, I'm just happy it's over.

Seeing Gabe this happy and content warms my black heart.

And he's become even more amorous since his reconciliation with Savage and has more than kept his promise to fuck me on every surface of the condo, multiple times.

This morning, it was bent over the counter in the guest bathroom. He drilled his cock into me from behind and angled us so we could both see the mirror and watch his hard flesh sliding in and out of me. Seeing my wetness coat his dick every time he pulled out had to be about the sexiest thing I've ever seen.

Fuck, that was hot.

Gabe turns and his eyes meet mine just as a shudder runs through me, and I clench my thighs together at the memory.

He saunters over to me and leans down, brushing my hair back away from my ear. "You really need to stop eye-fucking me, or we're going to end up doing it on your childhood bed again, and we both know how weird that was the last time we were here." He eases away and the fire in his eyes causes a rush of heat and moisture between my legs.

I try to remain unaffected. "I wasn't eye-fucking you."

His lips curl into a sexy smirk. "Sure you weren't."

I glance down at the baby to avoid making eye contact with Gabe. He will see right through my pathetic attempt at lying. "I was not eye-fucking you. I do not eye-fuck when I'm holding my innocent little niece."

He chuckles and brushes his finger down Kennedy's cheek. "I hope you don't want one of these anytime soon."

GABE

Skye appears momentarily pained at my statement.

Shit. Real smooth, Gabe. Real smooth.

I meant it as a joke. There is no way she wanted kids, especially now. But that look she's trying to hide has me wondering if I've read her wrong. We haven't exactly discussed it. I assumed we were both on the same page, just enjoying being together.

Like this morning in the bathroom.

Sweet fuck!

That was so damn hot, I almost came with three pumps into her.

But maybe I misread her about the whole baby thing.

She smiles and squeezes Kennedy against her. "Of course

not. I'm not ready to be a mom...yet. I'm content with being the cool aunt who teaches Kennedy how to use *fuck* like a comma."

I burst out laughing, and Kennedy stirs in her arms. Skye glares and shushes me.

"Shit, sorry." I'm clearly not cut out to be a father. With conscious effort, I lower my voice. "Sorry, I had to laugh, because I'm pretty sure Savage and Dani both say fuck enough that the baby would learn it whether you're around or not."

Skye cracks a smile, but there's still something lingering underneath the humor there.

She said *yet.*

What if Skye wants a baby...eventually?

Images of a little boy with Skye's eyes and my coloring darting around the condo flash through my head. A giggle echoes in my ears. The little guy throws himself into my arms and wraps his tiny arms around my neck. He leans in and blows a raspberry on my cheek.

My stomach roils a little.

I have no fucking clue how to be a dad. I barely had one and the one I did have was a no-good, dirty, lying criminal. Sam Hawke was the only father figure in my life, and he was only around a few years before he died. The thought of being responsible for a tiny life like that scares the fuck out of me.

But what terrifies me more is the way my heart sped up and joy flooded me when that little boy ran at me.

Someone slaps me on the back. "Hey guys, I'm sorry, but I have to take off."

I turn to Stone and frown. The bags under his eyes and pallor of his skin tells me he hasn't been sleeping and makes me wonder what he's been up to the last several days.

Stone has always been the risk-taker of the Hawkes. And not always in the good sense. He tends to jump off a cliff and then check to see if he has a parachute.

We all know he's fucking brilliant, but he can never seem to get his shit together. I actually thought this visit was a good sign. He seemed more with it and grounded when he arrived a week ago than I've seen him in years. But as the week progressed, he's become less and less focused, and it's clear something is going on with him.

The mysterious phone calls he's been taking always have him returning rattled. He said this trip was to spend time with the family and to meet Kennedy. After his cancelled trip during the hurricane, he's only come out once, and that was only for two days to see me and Skye at the hospital and to have Sunday dinner with everyone else.

I can't help but wonder what he has himself involved in this time. "Where are you going?"

His phone dings. He types something in reply and doesn't look up at me. "I need to go meet a friend."

Skye's exasperated sigh is loud enough to draw Stone's eyes up to her. "Seriously? We haven't even eaten yet."

Stone is bailing on the Hawke family Sunday dinner. He knows how important this is to his mother, but he's still going to leave. It must be something really important for him to be willing to face Savage's wrath for skipping out.

His hard eyes soften as they meet Skye's and brush over Kennedy. "I know, but I have to go. I'll try to make it back later, but if it's too late, I'll try to see everyone tomorrow before my flight leaves."

"What time is your flight?"

"Three, so I have time to stop and say goodbye to everyone before I have to be at the airport."

She's still pissed, but her shoulders relax somewhat with his promise to see her one more time before he heads back to California. I'm not so easily appeased. I want to confront him about what's been going on since he got here, but I'm not going to do it in front of Skye or the rest of the family. There's already been enough drama. I don't need to start more.

I place my hand on his shoulder and lean in so Skye won't hear me. "We are going to have a conversation about what the hell you've been up to. Make sure you tell your mom goodbye before you leave."

When I pull away, he narrows his eyes at me. The look is so reminiscent of the one I get from Savage, there's no mistaking its meaning—stay the fuck out of it.

No fucking way.

The Hawkes are my family and always will be. I will do whatever it takes to make sure all the members of my family are safe and well, even if they don't want me involved. Stone is just going to have to fucking deal with it.

Dani bustles out of the kitchen and beelines for us. "She's probably going to wake up screaming for my tits anytime, so I'll take her."

Skye and I chuckle, and she reluctantly relinquishes the sleeping baby before she stands and steps into me. I wrap my arms around her as she presses her face into the crook of my neck. "Don't look so worried, if we decide to have kids it'll be a long way down the road. But that doesn't mean we can't practice making one. I'll meet you in my room in five."

My cock hardens, and I press it into her. She peers up at me with a sexy grin then saunters away from me, swaying that sinful ass as she goes.

That woman is going to be the death of me.

I hope you enjoyed *Tortured Skye*! Click here to get an exclusive BONUS SCENE with Gabe and Skye on Christmas!
https://BookHip.com/JKDGQBC

ABOUT THE AUTHOR

Gwyn McNamee is an attorney, writer, wife, and mother (to one human baby and two fur babies). Originally from the Midwest, Gwyn relocated to her husband's home town of Las Vegas in 2015 and is enjoying her respite from the cold and snow. Gwyn has been writing down her crazy stories and ideas for years and finally decided to share them with the world. She loves to write stories with a bit of suspense and action mingled with romance and heat.

When she isn't either writing or voraciously devouring any books she can get her hands on, Gwyn is busy adding to her tattoo collection, golfing, and stirring up trouble with her perfect mix of sweetness and sarcasm (usually while wearing heels). Gwyn loves to hear from her readers. Here is where you can find her:

Website: http://www.gwynmcnamee.com/

Facebook: https://www.facebook.com/AuthorGwynMcNamee/

FB Reader Group: https://www.facebook.com/groups/1667380963540655/

Newsletter: www.gwynmcnamee.com/newsletter

Twitter: https://twitter.com/GwynMcNamee

Instagram: https://www.instagram.com/gwynmcnamee

Bookbub: https://www.bookbub.com/authors/gwynmcnamee

OTHER WORKS BY GWYN MCNAMEE

Billionaires of New Orleans:

The Hawke Family Series

Savage Collision (The Hawke Family - Book One)

He's everything she didn't know she wanted. She's everything he thought he could never have.

The last thing I expect when I walk into The Hawkeye Club is to fall head over heels in lust. It's supposed to be a rescue mission. I have to get my baby sister off the pole, into some clothes, and out of the grasp of the pussy peddler who somehow manipulated her into stripping. But the moment I see Savage Hawke and verbally spar with him, my ability to remain rational flies out the window and my libido takes center stage. I've never wanted a relationship—my time is better spent focusing on taking down the scum running this city—but what I want and what I need are apparently two different things.

Danika Eriksson storms into my office in her high heels and on her high horse. Her holier-than-thou attitude and accusations should offend me, but instead, I can't get her out of my head or my heart. Her incomparable drive, take-no prisoners attitude, and blatant honesty captivate me and hold me prisoner. I should steer clear, but my self-preservation instinct is apparently dead—which is exactly what our relationship will be once she knows everything. It's only a matter of time.

The truth doesn't always set you free. Sometimes, it just royally screws you.

AVAILABLE AT ALL RETAILERS:

books2read.com/SavageCollision

Tortured Skye (The Hawke Family - Book Two)

She's always been off-limits. He's always just out of reach.

Falling in love with Gabe Anderson was as easy as breathing. Fighting my feelings for my brother's best friend was agonizingly hard. I never imagined giving in to my desire for him would cause such a destructive ripple effect. That kiss was my grasp at a lifeline—something, anything to hold me steady in my crumbling life. Now, I have to suffer with the fallout while trying to convince him it's all worth the consequences.

Guilt overwhelms me—over what I've done, the lives I've taken, and more than anything, over my feelings for Skye Hawke. Craving my best friend's little sister is insanely self-destructive. It never should have happened, but since the moment she kissed me, I haven't been able to get her out of my mind. If I take what I want, I risk losing everything. If I don't, I'll lose her and a piece of myself. The raging storm threatening to rain down on the city is nothing compared to the one that will come from my decision.

Love can be torture, but sometimes, love is the only thing that can save you.

AVAILABLE AT ALL RETAILERS:

Books2read.com/Tortured-Skye

Stone Sober (The Hawke Family - Book Three)

She's innocent and sweet. He's dark and depraved.

Stone Hawke is precisely the kind of man women are warned about—handsome, intelligent, arrogant, and intricately entangled with some dangerous people. I should stay away, but he manages to strip my soul bare with just a look and dominates my thoughts. Bad decisions are in my past. My life is (mostly) on track, even if it is no longer the one to medical school. I can't allow myself to cave to the fierce pull and ardent attraction I feel toward the youngest Hawke.

Nora Eriksson is off-limits, and not just because she's my brother's employee and sister-in-law. Despite the fact she's stripping at The Hawkeye Club, she has an innocent and pure heart. Normally, the only thing that appeals to me about innocence is the opportunity to taint it. But not when it comes to Nora. I can't expose her to the filth permeating my life. There are too many things I can't control, things completely out of my hands. She doesn't deserve any of it, but the power she holds over me is stronger than any addiction.

The hardest battles we fight are often with ourselves, but only through defeating our own demons can we find true peace.

AVAILABLE AT ALL RETAILERS:

books2read.com/StoneSober

Building Storm (The Hawke Family - Book Four)

She hasn't been living. He's looking for a way to forget it all.

My life went up in flames. All I'm left with is my daughter and ashes. The simple act of breathing is so excruciating, there are days I wish I could stop altogether. So I have no business being at the party, and I definitely shouldn't be in the arms of the handsome stranger. When his lips meet mine, he breathes life into me for the first time since the day the inferno disintegrated my world. But loving again isn't in the cards, and there are even greater dangers to face than trying to keep Landon McCabe out of my heart.

Running is my only option. I have to get away from Chicago and the betrayal that shattered my world. I need a new life-one without attachments. The vibrancy of New Orleans convinces me it's possible to start over. Yet in all the excitement of a new city, it's Storm Hawke's dark, sad beauty that draws me in. She isn't looking for love, and we both need a hot, sweaty release without feelings getting involved. But even the best laid plans fail, and life can leave you burned.

Love can build, and love can destroy. But in the end, love is what raises you from the ashes.

AVAILABLE AT ALL RETAILERS:

books2read.com/BuildingStorm

Tainted Saint (The Hawke Family - Book Five)

He's searching for absolution. She wants her happily ever after.

Solomon Clarke goes by Saint, though he's anything but. After lusting for him from afar, the masquerade party affords me the anonymity to pursue that attraction without worrying about the fall-out of hooking-up with the bouncer from the Hawkeye Club. From the second he lays his eyes and hands on me, I'm helpless to resist him. Even burying myself in a dangerous investigation can't erase the memory of our combustible connection and one night together. The only problem... he has no idea who I am.

Caroline Brooks thinks I don't see her watching me, the way her eyes rake over me with appreciation. But I've noticed, and the party is the perfect opportunity to unleash the desire I've kept reined in for so damn long. It also sets off a series of events no one sees coming. Events that leave those I love hurting because of my failures. While the guilt eats away at my soul, Caroline continues to weigh on my heart. That woman may be the death of me, but oh, what a way to go.

Life isn't always clean, and sometimes, it takes a saint to do the dirty work.

AVAILABLE AT ALL RETAILERS:

books2read.com/TaintedSaint

Steele Resolve (The Hawke Family - Book Six)

For one man, power is king. For the other, loyalty reigns.

Mob boss Luca "Steele" Abello isn't just dangerous—he's lethal. A master manipulator, liar, and user, no one should trust a word that comes out of his mouth. Yet, I can't get him out of my head. The time we spent together before I knew his true identity is seared into my brain. His touch. His voice. They haunt my every waking hour and occupy my dreams. So does my guilt. I'm literally sleeping with the enemy and betraying the only family I've ever had. When I come clean, it will be the end of me.

Byron Harris is a distraction I can't afford. I never should have let it go beyond that first night, but I couldn't stay away. Even when I learned who he was, when the *only* option was to end things, I kept going back, risking his life and mine to continue our indiscretion. The truth of what I am could get us both killed, but being with the man who's such an integral part of the Hawke family is even more terrifying. The only people I've ever cared about are on opposing sides, and I'm the rift that could end their friendship forever.

Love is a battlefield isn't just a saying. For some, it's a reality.

AVAILABLE AT ALL RETAILERS:

books2read.com/SteeleResolve

Then check out the Billionaires of New Orleans: The Hawke Family Second Generation Series to meet the children of the original characters!

www.ingramcontent.com/pod-product-compliance
Lightning Source LLC
Chambersburg PA
CBHW061513020726
47502CB00006B/2056